Russian

Commanding princes unlace the ladies of London!

Princes Nikolay, Illarion, Ruslan and Stepan were once the toasted royalty of Kuban, renowned for their daring exploits. Now, banished and distanced from their titles, they've arrived in London—where balls and carriage rides take precedence over swordsmanship, revolution and battle...

But in this new and unknown city, they're about to encounter women the likes of whom they've never encountered before. These ladies have resisted the rakes of London—but these princes are about to embark on the most alluring of seductions...

Read Nikolay and Klara's story in

Compromised by the Prince's Touch

and Illarion and Dove's story in

Innocent in the Prince's Bed

All available now!

And look out for Ruslan's and Stepan's stories—coming soon!

Author Note

Welcome to the Russian Royals of Kuban! This is a series about journeys—both the literal, physical sort and the internal journey of the mind. Prince Illarion Kutejnikov, once the royal poet laureate of Kuban, and Lady Dove Sanford-Wallis are on their own internal journeys to find their "voice"—Illarion as poet exiled from his country for inciting protest and Dove as debutante facing an unwanted marriage to please her family.

I think there is a timelessness to Dove and Illarion's story. Unlike Nikolay and Klara's story, which is told inside real historical happenings, this story could happen at any time and is still happening today. The external issues might be different, but not the struggle. The struggle to express ourselves, to claim our dreams and to discover who we are remains a vital part of the human experience.

Through Dove and Illarion, I hope readers will appreciate the courage it takes to claim one's voice in a world that promotes conformity (regardless of time period) over being oneself. I also hope the story highlights the difficulties of acting on that courage. One of my favorite sayings is "In a world where you can be anything, be yourself," but that is far easier said than done. As Dove's and Illarion's journeys highlight, it's not always realistic or fair to put oneself ahead of others. Sometimes it is selfish. Dove's and Illarion's journeys explore the balance between being true to oneself and being true to those you love.

BRONWYN SCOTT

---

*Innocent in the
Prince's Bed*

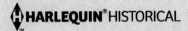

Recycling programs
for this product may
not exist in your area.

ISBN-13: 978-1-335-05165-3

Innocent in the Prince's Bed

Printed in U.S.A.

Bronwyn Scott is a communications instructor at Pierce College in the United States and is the proud mother of three wonderful children—one boy and two girls. When she's not teaching or writing, she enjoys playing the piano, traveling—especially to Florence, Italy—and studying history and foreign languages. Readers can stay in touch on Bronwyn's website, bronwynscott.com, or at her blog, bronwynswriting.blogspot.com. She loves to hear from readers.

Books by Bronwyn Scott

Harlequin Historical

Scandal at the Midsummer Ball
"The Debutante's Awakening"
Scandal at the Christmas Ball
"Dancing with the Duke's Heir"

Russian Royals of Kuban

Compromised by the Prince's Touch
Innocent in the Prince's Bed

Wallflowers to Wives

Unbuttoning the Innocent Miss
Awakening the Shy Miss
Claiming His Defiant Miss
Marrying the Rebellious Miss

Rakes on Tour

Rake Most Likely to Rebel
Rake Most Likely to Thrill
Rake Most Likely to Seduce
Rake Most Likely to Sin

Visit the Author Profile page
at Harlequin.com for more titles.

For Sophie W. Congrats on graduation, best of luck in college. You've always been a girl who's been true to herself. Continue to find your true north.

Chapter One

London—May 1823

So this was how dreams died—ignobly. Expeditiously dispatched to the hereafter in a mere two hours after eighteen years in the making, bludgeoned to death in Lady Burton's ballroom by what passed for Strom Percivale's, the very eligible future Duke of Ormond, wit. Lady Dove Sanford-Wallis watched her court of gentlemen nod sagely as Percivale expounded on fire-building techniques he'd seen demonstrated on his latest diplomatic excursion: 'It takes two sticks and a beastly amount of rubbing to get a spark.' The group laughed, a poignant reminder that it was unfair to place all the blame on Percivale. Like Brutus stabbing Caesar, he had help.

Dove leaned forward, one white-gloved hand gently resting on Percivale's dark sleeve to forestall any further comment. She smiled at the circle of gentlemen. 'It's probably easier when one of the sticks is a match.'

On her right, young Lord Fredericks's fair brow knit in confusion, not grasping her remark, and her long-nurtured dream of a London debut breathed its last.

'A match would allow you to light the other one,' she explained patiently.

'Oh, I *do* see! A *match*.' He chortled, overloud and over-exuberant. 'Quite so, quite so.' Lord Fredericks's brow relaxed. 'You're a wit, you are, Lady Dove.'

She was also quite disgusted and it was only her first formal outing of the Season. Disgusted. Disappointed. Devastated even. Her dream had betrayed her. Neither her debut nor London were remotely like she thought they would be and yet the source of that betrayal was hard to pinpoint.

Dove surveyed her godmother's famed ballroom, searching for the cause of her antipathy amid the surreal swirl of pale silks and dark evening clothes, finding it everywhere and nowhere. She was surrounded by bland perfection on all sides, which made it that much harder to fault the evening, and to explain her sense of dissatisfaction.

The ballroom itself was architectural excellence with its twin colonnades parading down the left and right sides of the dance floor, columns draped in expensive but simple swathes of oyster satin bunting and ivory roses bred in her godmother's private

Richmond hothouses, brought to town especially for the ball. Pairs of imported chandeliers crafted from Austrian crystal glittered overhead, a gift from Metternich himself to her godfather. Every inch of the room was decorated to emphasise the three essential 'E's' of *ton*nish entertainment: elegance, excellence and expense.

There was no doubting the elegance of the decoration, just the creativity of it. Beneath it there was a strong note of uniformity—or was that conformity? Minus the Metternich chandeliers, Dove suspected other ballrooms in London looked *exactly* the same as this one—virginal and uninspired, a setting worthy, unfortunately, of the guest list. Where was the colour she'd dreamed of? Where was the life? How could the 'happy ever after' she'd spent her girlhood imagining occur in such a sterile environment?

Several girls had made their official curtsy at the royal drawing room today, but only the crème de la crème was present with her at her debut, and none of them was as highly anticipated as she. It was not arrogance that drove her to that conclusion. Lady Dove Sanford-Wallis knew her own worth. She was the pampered, well-loved only child of the Duke of Redruth. She came with a dowry valued at fifteen thousand pounds annually, plus an initial bridal portion of twenty thousand and three coal-producing properties in the West Country. She would have been the most anticipated debutante of the Season even if she'd had the face of a horse. That she didn't was a pleasant bonus for this year's crop of marrying gentlemen.

And yet, knowing this had not made her a cynic; not before tonight anyway. She'd approached the year leading up to her Season with excitement. Excitement over leaving the isolated West—she'd never left the environs of Cornwall in eighteen years—excitement over the prospect of planning her wardrobe in London with the finest drapers in the business—up until now she had worn only proper muslins and gabardines in the spring, dark wools in the winter, as befitted a young girl—and excitement over visiting London with its entertainments.

She could hardly wait to ride in the park, to see Astley's, to tour the Tower, to eat Gunter's sweet ices, to receive flowers and chocolates from well-heeled gentlemen, to shop and to dance late into the night and drive home sleepy in her father's carriage. All of which would lead to the discovery of her very own Prince Charming. He would sweep her off her feet and happy ever after would begin, if not this Season, then most certainly the next. Not even her mother's endless admonitions during the journey from Cornwall about the expectations for a good match had dimmed her enthusiasm for fabled London.

It was the fairy tale she'd been raised on. Her mother, her maid, her aunts, all had exclaimed over the magic of a Season in London. Not once had they mentioned that somewhere between the journey from Cornwall to the altar of happy ever after there was *this*: listening to men like Strom Percivale prose on about primitive fire-making techniques, spending her evenings explaining simple jokes to the handsome, empty-headed Lord Fredericks of the *ton* and dancing with men who were trying to peek down her bodice while calculating the prospect of what they could do with her fifteen thousand a year. *This* was definitely not the dream, not her idea of happy ever after. Was this the best London could do? She'd been raised to expect better. Therein lay her disgust. What did one do when a dream died? Find another one, she supposed. But at this late date, what would that be? A most disquieting thought indeed, one that left her feeling empty, hollow.

A loud burst of energy at the ballroom's entrance snared her attention and her gaze went past Percivale's shoulder to where people gathered about the doors in excitement. Perhaps it might be someone interesting? Hope surged as a broad pair of shoulders parted the crowd. She caught sight of champagne-blond hair, a square-jawed face sporting a broad smile and penetrating blue eyes. Excited whispers ran through the ballroom, announcing that this wonder of a man was the royal poet laureate of Kuban, Illarion Kutejnikov, not just a real-life prince, but a larger-than-life one who was nothing like the fairy-tale charmer of her childhood stories.

Unlike every other man in the room, this Prince made no attempt to fit in. From head to toe, he was *different*. His champagne-blond hair was worn long

and thick, caught back with a black silk bow. Instead
of dark evening attire, he wore a thigh-length tunic of
brilliant royal-blue silk with a heavily embroidered
placket of dark blues and teals at the collar, sashed
at the waist with a swathe of black silk, emphasis-
ing the trimness of his physique and the long legs
that supported it. Long legs that were no more tra-
ditionally clothed than the rest of him. He wore *tight*
dark trousers that left no room for discreet padding
or doubt that his legs were all muscle.

He was without question the most attractive man
she'd ever seen, the most exotic, the most sensual,
the most vibrant. He was simply *more* than any man
in the room, a peacock in a ballroom full of black
wools and white silks. His presence excited her and
discomfited her. She wanted him to look in her direction and yet there was a flutter of panic, too, at
such a notion. What would she do if he *did* glance
her way? A Russian Byron, the women called him,
only much more hale, the audacious would titter behind their fans; a man with a poet's soul and a warrior's body. The gossips had got the warrior's body
part right. Already, within moments of him enter-
ing the ballroom, women flocked to him, forming
an entourage of fawning females as if he were the
pied piper. He stopped his progression to bow over
Lady Burton's hand, who was all smiles. Even her
redoubtable godmother, it seemed, wasn't immune
to the man's notorious charm.

Her godmother lifted a hand and gestured towards

her, directing the Prince's gaze. Dove froze, a hasty litany forming in her mind. *No, no, do not bring him over here.* She knew instinctively she should not want his attention. She was not meant for a man like the poet-Prince. She was meant for a man like Percivale, perhaps even Percivale himself. The realisation blossomed heavy and dark in her chest. That was the source of her dissatisfaction. She didn't want the Strom Percivales of the *ton*. She wanted *more* and *more* was looking right at her.

The Prince's champagne head followed her godmother's gesture, his eyes locking on her, his smile acknowledging her. To the great regret of every other woman in the ballroom, he and her godmother began to move towards her, his intentions clear to her and to everyone else present. Good manners required there could be no escape now, not with her godmother doing the introductions. 'My darling, here's someone I want you to meet,' her godmother began. At her words, part of Dove wanted to run. There was nothing but trouble here if she tempted herself with a sweet she couldn't have. She should settle for Strom Percivale's dukedom and be done with it. But the girl from Cornwall who wanted *more* stood her ground and let *more* bend over her hand with a kiss. Heaven help her, she would need all her wits now.

London in Season did not disappoint. This was heaven on earth: twelve weeks of exquisite entertainments, a never-ending flow of champagne, of dancing, of beautiful women, Lady Burton's goddaughter included. Twelve weeks of drinking from life's cup, a most heady elixir, heady enough to forget what he'd left behind in Kuban, heady enough to bring him to life once more, if only for a short while. Illarion Kutejnikov took a deep breath and bowed confidently towards the pretty chit in an exquisitely made white creation with her hair done up in seed pearls. Not a bad way to start the night—his favourite time of day.

The night meant freedom, each glittering ball-room offering release from the restlessness that plagued his mornings. He did his best work at night these days, when the scent of a woman still hovered on his skin, lingered in his sheets, the feel of her touch still fresh on his body, the champagne still thrilling through his blood, freeing his mind to wander the paths where emotion and philosophy conjoined into words and phrases.

Illarion let his eyes rest meaningfully on the girl as if she was the only woman in the ballroom. In truth, he didn't have to try too hard to convey that sense. It was difficult to look away from the silver-grey depths of her eyes. A man could lose himself there. If the eyes didn't do a man in, there was the perfection of her skin, all pearly translucence, the heart-shaped face with its pert, snub nose and delicately pointed chin resting atop the slim column of her neck in sculpted perfection. And that hair; that glorious hair! A crown to her beauty. He would write an ode to it; it was the colour of snow, a veritable avalanche of platinum silver waiting to be set free from its pins. To be the man to do so would be a pleasure indeed, *and*, he was quite sure, a privilege that came only through marriage. She had all the hallmarks of a girl who'd been raised swaddled in the cotton wool of her parents' protection. He took her hand and bent over it with a kiss at her knuckles. 'Prince Illarion Kutejnikov, at your service.'

Those quicksilver eyes looked him over with a hint of challenge, an air of arrogance as if his adoration was her due. Perhaps it was. She was a duke's daughter, after all. She was not the sort just any man could entertain thoughts of loosening hair about, yet Illarion could not look away. The orchestra struck up a waltz and he slipped her hand through his arm. 'Shall we?' He meant the question rhetorically. Women didn't protest the opportunity to waltz with Prince Illarion Kutejnikov, dance cards be damned.

For a moment, he thought she might break with that precedent. He wasn't used to being refused. That would be theoretically interesting up to a point, a point he had no intention of testing tonight. Illarion showed her no quarter. He swept her out on to the floor, his hand at her waist, matching his body to hers as he moved them into the waltz.

She danced exquisitely, her body never closer than the proper distance required between them, her eyes never lingering too long on his to imply undue interest, but remaining correctly fixed on a spot just over his shoulder. Her smile never wavered. Her conversa-

tion was neutrally polite; Yes, the weather was fine
for May, was it not? Yes, she was enjoying the evening. He'd wager that was a lie. She didn't act like
someone enjoying the ball. There was no spark in
her eyes as they turned at the top of the floor. By the
time he asked her if she'd been to London before, he
was heartily tired of the bland neutrality that came
with her unwavering smile—a pasted-on smile, a
doll's smile, not a real one. So when she said, no,
she'd never been to town, this was her first time,
Illarion could not resist.

He seized her attention on one of the rare moments she wasn't looking over his shoulder, his gaze
becoming a smoulder as he drawled, 'It's my first
time, too. We're no longer virgins, you and I.' He'd
meant to shock her out of her neutrality. Women
were never ambivalent about him and yet *she* was.
He was ready for one of two reactions: a laugh because he'd finally melted her cold resistance with
an audacious remark, or a stunned silence because
she was far too innocent to marshal an adequate response. He got neither.

Dove Sanford-Wallis gave him a steady gaze. 'I
am neither shocked nor impressed by what passes
as your attempt at wit. I am sure there are some
women who find your bon mots appealing, but I am
not one of them.' She nodded her head to the corner
of the ballroom where his coterie of pretty women
sat eyeing them and waiting for his return. 'I am sure
they'll forgive your momentary desertion,' she hinted

broadly. Good lord, Lady Dove Sanford-Wallis was pure as the driven snow and as frigid, too. Or was it something more? For a horrible moment, an idea flickered. Was it possible she didn't like him?

Illarion bent close to her ear. 'Do you know why you can't tell a joke while standing on ice?' he murmured. 'Because it might crack. But I see there's no risk of that here.'

'Am I supposed to be the ice in your juvenile metaphor?' The music was winding down. This had turned out to be a most intriguing waltz. He'd not anticipated such an outcome. He had anticipated something very different; taking his hostess's goddaughter out to the garden, for politeness's sake, spending a little time with her, giving her a few moments of his attentions and then politely disengaging her. But not this.

'If the shoe fits, Princess.' He bowed as the dance ended.

'Thank you for the dance, Prince Kutejnikov.' She dipped a small curtsy, turned her back on him and did the unthinkable. She fled the floor. It took him a moment to realise what had happened. He'd been glass-slippered. It was not only intriguing, but inspiring. Word pictures rose in his mind, his hand itched to write and a spark of hope sputtered to life; perhaps she was the one to break the curse that had plagued him since he'd left Kuban. She had only disappeared a moment ago and he already wanted her back.

Chapter Two

She wanted to see the Prince again. It was probably not a unique thought. Dove supposed that was how most women felt after meeting him. It was, however, an exceedingly incongruous thought to entertain over breakfast, especially when she'd made every effort last night to *not* see him again. She'd all but left him on the dance floor and her conversation had been designed to be off-putting. Apparently, her behaviour had been to no avail. He'd managed to spend the night in her mind and he was still there this morning. Not even her mother's marital-expectations lecture had managed to drive him out of her head.

At the moment, those expectations were being drilled into her yet again over shirred eggs and kippers. 'Drilled' might be too harsh. 'Politely laid out' would be more apt. Her mother did not shout or raise her voice. Ever. Her mother did, however, tend to elucidate in the extreme. This must be the twentieth time since leaving Cornwall those expectations had been gone over.

Redruth's daughter must comport herself with the utmost dignity, polite to all but never falsely encouraging those who are beneath her. Only marriage to another duke will do, that is how grand families are perpetuated. You, my dear, are from a grand family...

Dove was starting to feel less charitable towards those discussions. Fortunately, she had them down by memory so she could let her thoughts wander.

'It will be interesting to see who comes to the at-home this afternoon.' Her mother moved on to her second-favourite topic with a knowing smile. 'Percivale will come, certainly, although I dare say if he's smart, he'll come late. I imagine Alfred-Ashby and Lord Fredericks will be here early. Lord Fredericks is a handsome fellow. It's always nice to have a handsome man in one's court even if he's not a duke.'

Fredericks? Handsome? Perhaps if one liked a blank mind along with the golden hair. The combination wasn't particularly to her taste. Dove's own thoughts went straight to a man with a head less golden than Fredericks', but with rather more going on inside. 'What do we make of Prince Kutejnikov?' Dove ventured with assumed nonchalance.

Her mother hesitated. 'Well, now there's a handsome man, to be sure.' She cast an enquiring look at Dove's father, who had managed to glance up from his newspapers. 'He's popular and on everyone's guest list this Season. He's the new novelty.'

'No one knows much about his antecedents,' her father said calmly, reaching for another slice of toast. 'Olivia dear, I hear the Constable picture at the Academy art show this year is most impressive.'

Her mother smiled at her father, the Prince forgotten between them. 'I am looking forward to it. I am told he's made remarkable use of the light in how he depicts the weather.' The Duke and Duchess of Redruth dismissed the Prince somewhere between the newspaper and the marmalade. It was so subtly done, one could not truly be offended. Indeed, Dove thought, if one didn't know her parents well, one would hardly notice what had happened. But *she* did. The brevity of her father's comment said it all. The Prince was not to be considered. By any of them. He was beneath them, an outsider and certainly not a contender for her hand.

Illarion Kutejnikov had just become forbidden fruit. Dove had heard her mother's lectures about expectations often enough to know the words by heart. But she had not fully understood their import until now. Some people mattered. Some people didn't. *Couldn't.* Because they'd not been born to the right family, at the right time, in the right place, or the right country even. Such a judgement seemed uncharacteristically harsh.

Dove quietly studied her parents as they talked about art, the one appreciation all three of them shared. She'd always seen her parents as kind, conscientious people, who took their roles as community providers responsibly. Her father didn't drink or gamble excessively, like other men of the *ton*. Her mother was always dressed in the height of fashion, but not extravagantly so; she did charity work, she took care of the sick and infirm in their village. They'd raised her in love. Dove had never doubted their affection for her. And yet, those same people who loved her and whom she loved in return had just set aside an individual as if he was no more than an ant on the floor to be crushed beneath an arbitrary boot heel.

Something rebellious stirred inside Dove, perhaps flickering to life for the first time, stoked by the questions blooming in her mind, or perhaps it had already existed, ignited by her dissatisfaction with London and her first brush with the reality of the Season and all that entailed. She was meant for the likes of Percivale or someone of his calibre. Even Alfred-Ashby and Lord Fredericks had been relegated to the hangers-on, those who were merely window dressing for the main pursuit of catching a duke. But knowing that didn't make her like Percivale any better.

What would happen if she didn't comply? Would she, too, lose her value? This was new ground. It had never occurred to her to *not* comply. Her parents had always wanted what was best for her and she'd been raised to obey those decisions. She'd never thought to question those decisions. She'd never had a reason to. Until now. These were heady thoughts, indeed, as if she'd seen light for the first time.

A blazing glare of white light attacked Illarion's eyelids in one sweeping, orchestrated assault. He groaned and flung an arm over his face in a belated attempt to ward off the morning. Who the hell had let the sun in? To answer that question he'd have to open an eye, or wait until the intruder spoke. He didn't have to wait long.

There was a growl of disgust from the window, which meant the intruder was Stepan, his friend and occasional *adhop.* When the four princes had fled Kuban, they'd needed a leader and Stepan had effortlessly stepped into the role, giving them direction and making decisions. Now that they'd arrived in London, they seemed to need him even more as they adjusted to their new lives, whatever those might be. 'What happened in here? The place looks like a storm passed through.'

'Inspiration struck,' Illarion ground out. His tongue felt thick. It was hard to find the motivation to make the words.

'Looks more like lightning.'

Illarion could hear Stepan moving about the room, clearing a path as he came. There was the sound of books being stacked, papers being shuffled in to order. 'Don't touch anything!' he managed a hoarse warning.

'I don't know how you can find anything in here. I should send a maid up to clean.' *That* galvanised Illarion into action. He pushed himself up, remembering just in time how narrow the sofa was that he'd fallen asleep on, and how uncomfortable. His neck hurt, his back was stiff, his legs cramped. Inspiration was deuced difficult on a body.

'I don't want a maid, Step. I have everything just the way I like it.' Illarion pushed his hands through his hair and tied the tangles back with last night's ribbon.

'Half-empty sheets with words scrawled on them randomly strewn across any available space? You *like* it that way? It's impossible to find anything.'

Illarion gave an exasperated sigh. Stepan didn't always grasp the nuances that went with having an artistic temperament. That Stepan tolerated such nuances was a sign of the tenacity of his friendship. 'I write poetry, not novels. I don't need to fill up pages.'

Stepan waved a crumpled sheet. 'When I said half-sheets, I was being generous. There's five words on this page. "A bird in my hand…" That's not even a complete sentence.' Or a terribly original one when it came down to it.

Illarion grimaced and lurched forward, grabbing for the paper despite the pounding in his head. 'Give me that! Of course it's not complete, it's not done.' He hated people reading what he wrote before he was ready, especially people who didn't understand the artistic process, people like Stepan who understood numbers and balance sheets. Protectively, he smoothed the sheet and set it down beside him. 'You should know better than to disturb a writer at work.' In Kuban, he'd been a royal poet, the Tsar's own laureate. But his latest efforts were an embarrassment.

Stepan gave a harsh laugh. 'At work? I would hardly call the state I found you in work, or the schedule you've been keeping, up all hours of the night, asleep all hours of the day.' Stepan made an up and down gesture indicating the length of him. 'Look at you. You're as dishevelled as the room. Your hair's a wreck, your clothes are wrinkled from sleeping in them, I might add, and they're starting to *hang*. You're losing weight, you need a shave and this place is a shambles: half-empty decanters, dirty glasses and not a plate in sight. When's the last time you *ate* something?' Sometimes having a friend like Stepan was a pain in the backside. He saw too much.

Illarion stumbled to the basin and poured water. Cold. Good. It would wake him up faster. 'You know how it is when I'm trying to write.' He braced his hands on either side of the bowl and caught sight of himself in the little mirror above it. Good lord, Stepan was right. He did look a bit rough, but nothing a razor and a hot meal couldn't fix. He just wished his stomach didn't rebel at the thought of the latter.

A knock at the door brought the servants and the threat of Stepan's hot meal materialised. Illarion gave a tentative sniff: sausage, toast, coffee. Ah, coffee. That would help immensely. He took his time washing while a space was cleared and food laid out, giving his stomach a chance to ready itself. Breakfast was starting to smell delicious, a good sign he'd get through the meal and pacify Stepan, whose residence in a newly excavated chair made it clear he wasn't leaving until he was satisfied his friend had eaten.

It was time to get a place of his own, Illarion thought, like Nikolay had done. Stepan was worse than having a father sometimes. Of course, Nikolay had married first. One couldn't very well be living with three bachelors when one had a new wife. Illarion had no such intentions of marrying. There were far too many women in the world for sampling to limit himself to just one. Besides, the institution of marriage Kubanian style hadn't exactly recommended itself to him, with all its rules and expectations. Love was not one of those expectations. He'd seen too many people—close friends—forced into marriages not of their choosing. And then he'd seen them wither away; strong people, vibrant people like Katya, becoming husks of their former selves.

Illarion dried his face and took a chair across from Stepan, letting Stepan pour him a cup of coffee. 'How's the writing going?' Stepan passed him the cup, his tone less surly.

'Better.' If one called five cliché words strung together in a phrase 'better'. He'd hurried home from the Burton ball last night, scribbling madly in the carriage, racing to his room to pull out paper and pen in an attempt to capture the emotions brought on by the haughty Lady Dove Sanford-Wallis. The flurry of images, however, had flown, his pen unable to capture the feelings in words, his mind unable to focus, preferring instead to follow the questions she'd prompted. Why hadn't she *liked* him? He'd done everything right; he'd allowed the hostess to introduce him, he'd made the guest of honour the centre of his immediate attentions. He'd waltzed with her, made conversation with her. He'd been the ideal gentleman. No woman in Kuban could have faulted his manners or his deportment. But *she'd* found fault aplenty and, truly, he didn't understand why.

'I met a woman who inspired me last night,' Illarion began, sipping at the hot coffee. 'The first in a long while, to tell the truth. She was like...sin in satin.' He had been stirred not just by her beauty, but also her spirit, buried deep behind those eyes, a rebel in white, the outer purity of a debutante juxtaposed against the inner shadow on her soul, the shades of rebellion hidden within. He found it intriguing even if that rebellion had been aimed at him. He wondered now in the clarity of daylight if her dislike had been of him or of the occasion? Was it possible she hadn't enjoyed the ball? He'd thought she was lying earlier when he'd asked.

'That sounds promising,' Stepan encouraged.

'It was!' Illarion replied passionately. 'Right up until I got home and nothing would come. My head was so full I couldn't get the words out and then the images were gone, just like her.'

'Ah, hence the bird in the hand,' Stepan murmured. 'I like sin in satin better.'

Illarion gave a wry smile and reached for a pen. 'That is pretty good, isn't it?' He'd been disappointed in himself last night. He'd tried everything, even brandy, to get the creative juices to flow, but nothing had worked. Candles had burnt down and eventually he'd thrown himself on the mercy of sleep just before the sun had come up, another night that had begun with promise, wasted. He couldn't afford many more nights like that. 'She inspires me, Stepan, and I have to write something. I have the reading in three weeks and nothing to perform. An original work is expected.'

It was to be a grand affair, attended by the *ton*'s best. He'd been invited to do a reading from some of the poems that had got him exiled from Kuban. People had been clamouring for months now. He'd wisely kept them under wraps until the time was right to make the most of them. But there was also an expectation he'd have something new as well, perhaps something that celebrated his new life in London. To capture that celebration, to seek inspiration from the subject, he'd immersed himself in the *ton*, with all its beauty and entertainment, its lavishness and grandiosity, and he'd come up empty night after night. Until last night when a woman who disdained him had lit a spark. 'There's nothing for it, Stepan, I have to have her.' He pushed a hand through his hair and went to his wardrobe. He had an introduction and her name. It shouldn't be too hard to find her.

Stepan, however, was more cynical. 'You have to *have* her? How, precisely, do you mean that? Surely you don't mean to bed her. Is she even beddable?' Meaning, was she of the merry-widow variety and eminently available, or was she a virginal debutante, and as such, untouchable? It was a highly salient question indeed, although one Illarion had no intention of answering. For one, it gave away who the muse was and he wanted to savour the thrill of the secret. For another, he simply didn't have an answer.

Illarion turned from the wardrobe. He hated when Stepan was a step or two ahead of him. The truth was, he didn't know exactly what 'having' Lady Dove Sanford-Wallis entailed at this point. He was only interested in feeding his muse, but Stepan, as usual, had a point. He couldn't bed her, not without marriage first and that seemed a bit extreme to contemplate at this point. He just wanted to write poetry the way he used to—poetry, by the way, that focused on *avoiding* marriage, not engaging in it.

'Well?' Stepan pressed. 'This is important, Illarion. You can't seduce every Englishwoman you meet.'

Illarion thought back to the night before and all the men gathered around her. 'I will be part of her court, nothing more. A few dances, a few social calls, a bouquet of flowers now and then.' It would probably take more than that for what he had planned, but the answer would pacify Stepan and it actually seemed a good place to start when he thought about it. He would play the potential suitor well enough to get her alone, long enough to be inspired. His mind hummed with a plan.

'You, the swain? It's hard to imagine,' Stepan teased.

'Well, desperate times call for desperate measures.' Illarion didn't laugh. He was deadly serious about finding his muse. 'I have to do something or I will show up to my own reading empty-handed.' He dived back into his wardrobe, rummaging for a waistcoat.

'I am sure it's not as dire as all that. Something will come to you, it always does. In the meantime, I'll send someone to clean up,' Stepan offered the reassuring platitudes nonwriters gave their literary friends.

'Time?' Illarion said distractedly, hauling out two waistcoats, one blue, one a rich cream. 'What time is it?'

'Two o'clock. I'm afraid you slept away most of the day.'

'Perfect.' Illarion was undaunted by his friend's scold. Stepan believed every day began at sunrise. He pulled out a dark blue coat and reached for the bell pull. He needed his valet and a shave. At-homes began at three. He had just enough time to make himself presentable and stop for flowers on the way.

'What are you doing?' Stepan asked, undoubtedly perplexed by the burst of energy.

'I am going calling.' Illarion rifled through a bureau drawer. 'Where did I put my cards?'

Stepan rose, rescuing a chased silver case from being drowned in paper on the desk. 'They're here. Who may I ask are you calling upon?'

Illarion turned from the wardrobe with a grin. Stepan was like a dog with a bone, but Illarion would not give up her name. 'My muse. Who else?' This time he'd be prepared for her. He was already planning how he might separate her from the herd. He had no illusions about finding his muse alone. She'd been vastly popular last night. Gentlemen would be sure to flock to her at-home today to extend their interest. He'd have to charm her into a walk in the gardens, or a tour of the family portrait gallery. Thankfully, charm was his speciality. His haughty inspiration in white satin would not give him the slip again.

'You are quite determined—' Stepan began and Illarion sensed a lecture coming on. He cut in swiftly.

'Don't you see, Step, she might be the one, the one to break the curse.'

'You're not cursed.' Stepan shook his head in tired disbelief. 'I can't belief you're still carrying that nonsense around with you. It's been a year and you've been able to write. You did an ode last week to the Countess of Somersby. The ladies were wild for it. The society pages even reprinted it.' Stepan was as practical as they came. On the other hand, Illarion had a healthy respect for the supernatural.

'That was drivel. It wasn't a real poem. The Countess is easily impressed,' Illarion argued. He'd produced nothing but soppy, superficial lines on tired themes for the past year. But that was hopefully about to change. With luck, he'd be able to write tonight.

Chapter Three

Dove glanced at the clock on the mantel and double-checked her mathematics. With luck, no one else would arrive and these gentlemen would leave when their half-hour was up. Then, she'd have the rest of the afternoon to draw. Freedom was only a few minutes away. It *was* possible. It could happen. After all, so many of the expected gentlemen had arrived as soon as it was decent to do so at quarter past three and they'd kept arriving in wave after wave. The footmen had been kept running for vases under the onslaught of bouquets. Too bad the gentlemen hadn't brought new personalities instead. If she'd hoped they might shine better by daylight than they had by the light of her godmother's chandeliers, that notion had been quickly dispelled. The only bright spot was that Percivale hadn't arrived yet.

Her mother beamed with pride each time a new gentleman had been announced, keeping up a quiet running commentary at her ear, 'Lord Rupert has four estates and stands to inherit an earldom from his uncle. Lord Alfred-Ashby has a stable to rival Chatsworth in the north. Of course, all that pales compared to Percivale. He is the real catch. He'll inherit his uncle's dukedom.' On the prattle went, each gentleman assessed and categorised as he entered, smiled and bowed, as if he were oblivious to what was really happening, as if he thought he might truly be valued for himself. Dove wondered: Did they know who had already been discarded? In counter to that, who was here simply for politeness' sake? Who in this room had already discounted *her*?

Dove was not naïve enough to think her mother was the only one doing any assessing. Each of the gentlemen were appraising her in turn. It was why her hair had taken her maid an hour to style so that it softened the sharp jut of her chin. It was why she'd worn the pale ice-pink afternoon gown to bring out the platinum of her hair. Heaven forbid she be seen in any colour with yellow undertones that clashed with her skin. Even with that effort, there would be those who decided they would do better to marry elsewhere. The idea that she'd been dismissed carried a surprising sting. She wasn't used to rejection, implied or otherwise.

Dove scanned the room, wondering. To whom in this room had she become only a trinket to be added to their social cache? It was a bitter pill to think that some of the gentlemen were only here because she was the Season's Diamond of the First Water and they would benefit from association with her. They had no intentions of getting to know her. Just of using her.

Such assessment had never been part of the fairy tale she'd grown up on. How splendidly everyone filling her drawing room pretended to be themselves and how disgusting it was. Her newly awakened sense of injustice rose again. People were basing life-long decisions on these façades. Coupled with the ridiculous rules of courtships and calls it was downright farcical; a gentleman might stay no longer than a half-hour, preferably somewhat less, and he might certainly not be alone with the subject of his affections.

How did one get to know anyone in the confines of a large group and conversation limited to the weather and the previous night's entertainment? Lord Fredericks laughed at something said in his small group by the window and she heard his standard reply: 'Quite so, quite so.' Perhaps the rules weren't so limiting after all. She already knew she couldn't spend a lifetime with him, or any of the gentlemen present for that matter. It had only taken one ball and one at-home to make that clear. Maybe the rules had done her a favour, after all, by sparing her any more of Lord Fredericks' company.

At the stroke of half past four, the last group of gentlemen dutifully began to take their leave and

Dove began to hope. She crossed her fingers for good luck in the folds of her skirt as she smiled politely and accepted goodbyes. She could almost feel the charcoal in her hand, she was that close to freedom. She was working on a drawing of a mare in the mews, bought for her riding pleasure. The mare had a soulful face and she was eager to capture it on paper. She'd already done several sketches in the attempt. But something was missing. Perhaps if she took the mare outside where the light was better?

The last two gentlemen had just left, the door barely shut behind them, when disaster arrived.

'His Royal Highness, Prince Illarion Kutejnikov,' the butler intoned.

He was dressed in dark blue superfine and buff breeches and cream waistcoat, far more English today than he'd been last night, but no less tempting. Dove's pulse sped up in a turmoil of anxious excitement. Just this morning she'd wanted to see him again and now he was here. Lesson learned. One needed to be careful with what one wished for, because wishes could end up in one's drawing room.

'Prince Kutejnikov.' Dove nodded politely as he presented her with a pretty bouquet of lilies of the valley. 'How kind of you to call and what a surprise.' What sort of man called on a girl who'd left him on the dance floor? Two options came to mind: obtuse or arrogant. Perhaps the Prince was one of those men who thought every woman was dying of love for him. Only in this case, he might be right.

'These reminded me of you,' he murmured with a smile. She waited for the usual accolades to follow— 'you are like springtime in bloom, you are fresh, innocent'. She'd heard them all today. But none of the usual came. Instead, he leaned close and whispered, 'Beautiful on the outside, poisonous on the inside.'

'What a lovely concept.' She forced a smile to match his, but hers was nowhere near as convincing. What did a girl say to a man she'd rejected the night before? He knew he had her cornered. He was laughing at her. She could see it in his eyes—cobalt and merry. The chandeliers last night had not done them justice. 'I'll find a vase. I know just the one I want.' *Any vase that took a half-hour to find.* The search would let her escape the drawing room for a little while. Perhaps he'd made his point and he'd be gone by the time she returned.

In the hallway, she drew a calming breath. The Prince was outrageous. Another gentleman would have taken her rather broad hint last night and not bothered to call. *At least he's not boring*, a small, perverse part of her mind whispered for the sake of argument. True, but what he was might be worse: a temptation, handsome, different, a diversion from the disappointments of the Season. He lit up a room with his presence, where the other gentlemen merely filled up a room with theirs. A footman hurried up to her, a vase in hand, cutting short her search. Her parents' servants were too well trained. Dove took her time walking back to the drawing room, only to make two discoveries. First, that leaving had been her first mistake. Second, not even her mother was insusceptible. The Prince, it seemed, was not as easily dismissed in person as he had been over breakfast.

Prince Kutejnikov sat beside her mother, smiling, leaning forward, eyes riveted on the Duchess as if the conversation was the most interesting he'd ever had. He rose when she entered, flashing that smile in her direction. Her mother rose, too. 'There you are, dear. I was just saying to the Prince that it's too lovely a day to stay inside. He suggested you might enjoy a drive in the park. I've sent your maid for your bonnet and gloves.'

'I have my curricle waiting at the kerb,' the Prince added, mischief sparking in his eyes as if he knew the very protests running through her head. There'd be no relief for her. She was trapped. With him; a man she'd deserted on the dance floor last night, and he'd given every indication with his lilies of the valley he meant to claim retribution for it. This was his revenge: a drive in the park where they would have to make conversation with each other, where he could say more audacious things and talk about debauching London's virgins. She didn't deserve it. She'd been acting out of self-protection.

Her maid arrived with her things and he took the light shawl, settling it about her shoulders, his touch sending sparks of awareness through her. The question of going was settled, too. It did not escape

Dove's notice that she'd not actually accepted the invitation. Now it was too late to turn it down.

The Prince offered her his arm and her awareness of him piqued. She was cognisant of his height, of the breadth of his shoulders, the sheer muscled bulk of him. It was hard to believe he was a poet with a body like that. Poets were wan, pale, intellectuals. 'Time is of the essence, Lady Dove. Let's be off before you are beset with more callers.' To her mother he nodded courteously and said, 'We won't be overlong. Thank you for the conversation. I haven't enjoyed such a talk in a while. I look forward to another one soon.' Was her mother blushing? It made Dove curious. What *had* they'd talked about?

She was still pondering the transition as the Prince helped her up to the bench of his curricle. Her mother, a stickler for propriety where her daughter was concerned, had proved not the least bit resistant to her driving in the park with a foreign prince the Duchess of Redruth barely knew. What had happened to rule number two: being polite to all but never falsely encouraging those who are beneath her? There was only one explanation for it. 'You manipulated my mother,' Dove said, partly in accusation, and partly in admiration. The Duchess was not easily swayed.

He winked, all easy confidence. 'Most women like my persuasion. Besides, it's not every day one's daughter goes driving with a prince.' He laughed, settling beside her, his long legs stretched out. He flashed her a smile. 'What good is it to be a prince if one can't throw one's title around?' But Dove thought it wasn't entirely the title that had done the trick. She *knew* what her parents thought of him—that he was not worthy of the Redruth attentions. It made his feat all that more impressive. She was coming to believe that Illarion Kutejnikov usually got what he wanted, prince or not.

'I did not think I would find you alone, today,' he began, pulling out into the traffic. 'I had elaborate plans for stealing you away from your crowd of adoring suitors. A drive is so much better.'

'They were here earlier. You just missed them.' She kept her answers cool and short. It was all the defence she had. Perhaps if she did not encourage him a second time, he would leave her alone. *What a pity that would be.* Her thoughts had grown a mind of their own. She was supposed to be resisting him, dissuading him. And yet, there was no denying he was the most intriguing person she'd met in London.

'Then I am the lull before the second wave. I've saved you. Perhaps you should be thanking me.' He chuckled conspiratorially, his laugh warm and congenial as he nudged her with his elbow. 'You are disappointed? I wonder, Lady Dove, if it's me that disappoints you or that you'll miss the other suitors? Was there someone you were hoping to see?' That was the problem. The only one she'd been hoping to see was him. Now that he was here, she had no idea what to do with him. She couldn't encourage him and she didn't want to turn him away even though she should.

'I am disappointed by neither,' Dove protested.

He fixed her with a sideways slide of his blue stare. 'Don't lie to me. That's the second time in two days, Lady Dove. It's why I am here. I want the truth about last night. Why were you dismayed to dance with me? Was it me or the occasion? I was lying in bed… Well actually, I was lying on a sofa—very narrow by the way—thinking of you and our dance and it occurred to me that perhaps your reaction was not to me specifically.'

Dove felt herself blush at the image of him lying in any sort of bed. 'That is a most improper reference, your Highness. In England, unmarried men and women don't discuss their nightly, um, rituals with one another.'

'From what I've seen, I don't think married men and women do either,' he answered boldly. 'Perhaps they should.' Dear heavens, his conversation was positively rash! This was not how gentlemen talked.

'Perhaps it is your use of innuendo I object to,' Dove replied. 'This is the second time in two days *you've* couched our conversation in rather intimate terms.'

'Couched. I like that,' Illarion said wryly, his blue eyes merry. 'Now who's being audacious, Lady Dove?'

Her cheeks heated. The schoolroom had not prepared her for matching wits with a man like this.

She was out of her depth, but not outdone. If she couldn't match wits, she would do her best to end the interaction. 'If I were truly bold, your Highness, I wouldn't be here at all, toeing society's line like a good daughter.'

He ignored the finality in her tone and pursued the conversation. 'Where *would* you be?' The breeze changed. She caught the scent of him: lemon and bergamot mixed with basil and the exoticism of patchouli. He smelled better than any man had smelled today with their heavy colognes. If she closed her eyes, Dove could imagine herself in Tuscany, or perhaps even further east in Aladdin's Arabia or far-off India, pencils and charcoal in hand, drawing everything she saw. 'Not London. Not now that I've seen it.' She prevaricated, unwilling to let him into her thoughts. He'd divined enough as it was. Did he also see that she was not nearly as opposed to him as she let on?

'Ah ha! It *is* the occasion you are opposed to, not the man.' He grinned, teasing her. 'I am relieved. I thought I was losing my charm.'

'You are arrogant in the extreme. I think it's important you know I don't care for conceited men,' Dove cautioned. She was glad his arrogance was back. It gave her something to be annoyed at. For a moment, he'd been far too likeable.

'And I don't like liars,' he cautioned, his eyes on her again. 'Be honest, Lady Dove—the truth is you wanted to escape this afternoon. So badly, in fact, you made quite the deal with the devil, didn't you? You had to choose to go with the arrogant prince and claim an afternoon of freedom, or stay behind in the drawing room to entertain whatever boring gentlemen walk through that door until six o'clock.'

Dove did not reply. What would her response be? That he was right? It occurred to her, however, that she was not the only one who'd made a bargain. The Prince had, too. After all, what could he possibly want badly enough to take a girl driving who had made no secret of her dislike for him?

Chapter Four

In the end, they went to Kensington Gardens instead, a less-populated alternative to crowded Hyde Park. 'I think it's quieter here. I come when I want to think or talk. There's less chance of being interrupted,' the Prince explained, coming around to help her alight. Dove was suddenly self-conscious of her hands on his broad shoulders, of his strong hands at her waist, blue eyes laughing up at her. Were those eyes *always* laughing? Her reaction was silly. She'd touched him before. She had danced with him last night and they were in public with his tiger and her maid just a few feet away, to say nothing of the other carriages and couples nearby. This was hardly an intimate moment or an intimate setting, yet she was acutely aware of him.

He reached past her for something under the seat, a canvas bag he slung across his chest, then offered her his arm, taking them down to the Long Water, where the lake joined Hyde Park's Serpentine on the park's western edge. Her maid trailed discreetly behind them.

The light breeze off the water was refreshing and the lake was quiet. Not many were out today. An empty bench beneath a tree at the shoreline beckoned invitingly. 'This would be the perfect place to draw.' Dove sighed wistfully, the words slipping out. She had not drawn or painted nearly as much as she'd hoped since she'd come to London and she missed it sorely.

'What would you draw?' He dusted off the bench with his hand, ridding it of random tree debris.

'The ducks and the trees with their low-hanging branches skimming the water's surface. If I had my pencils, I could practise with the light, like Constable does.'

'Then we should come again some time and bring your things. Today we can sit and enjoy the lake,' he offered, 'and you can tell me why you found your coming-out ball so distasteful last night.' Another trade. He was constantly bartering with her, giving her what she wanted in exchange for her secrets.

'Is everything a negotiation with you?' Dove said amiably, settling her skirts as she sat. He'd traded her a chance at escape in exchange for his company in the drawing room and now this; the peace of the lake.

'Is everything always defence with you? You are a suspicious soul, Lady Dove.' Prince Kutejnikov laughed, undaunted by her boldness. He was probably used to bold women. 'Now, tell me what had you so prickly last night. Your secrets are safe with me.' In that moment, she wanted to believe him. Maybe it was the eyes, the smile, the pleasantness of the afternoon, the freedom of being out of doors that she found so intoxicating. Or maybe it was simply that someone had asked her what she wanted. Whatever the reason, the dam of her polite reserve broke. Her newly formed truth came out haltingly as she searched for words to express it.

'I think I am a bit disappointed in London. It had been built up for me as a shining city of fairy tales, a metropolis beyond belief. For years, I had this image of London—women in silks and jewels, beautiful ballrooms filled with music, gallant men full of honour waiting on them.' Dove shook her head. 'But London wasn't like that.'

The Prince nodded, his gaze contemplative. 'Were there no silks last night? No jewels? No ballrooms? No gallant men?'

Dove argued. 'Of course there were, except perhaps the gallant men, but it wasn't enough.' She paused, letting out a sigh. 'You're making me sound ungrateful.'

'Not ungrateful. Honest, perhaps, even if that honesty is based on some rather naïve assumptions.' The Prince crossed a long leg over a knee. 'Are you comfortable with that?'

Dove shook her head. 'It's a rather unflattering depiction.'

'Innocence is unflattering? I thought it was valued—virginity, innocence, purity, all one and the same,' he prompted obliquely.

'Last night you said London had taken our virginity.'

He chuckled. 'So I did. The city has deflowered you if you have become a cynic. How does that feel? To have the proverbial scales lifted from your eyes? London is a lover who demands to be accepted on its own terms.' His allusion was wicked and highly inappropriate. Not unlike the man himself. He was being audacious on purpose. Perhaps part of her had waited all day to hear such things, to be secretly thrilled by a man who dared to speak his mind instead of posturing. And yet, she was required to scold him for it, lest he think her too easy.

'Does everything come back to...?' Dove groped for a decent word, one she could say out loud and still convey what she meant, which was a scold for his boldness.

'Sex?' he filled in coolly. 'Definitely. Most things in this world come down to sex. If you haven't figured that out yet, you are still in possession of your innocence.'

'I thought most things came down to money,' she retorted sharply, to be perverse. It was too easy to call to mind the calculating gentlemen from the ball.

'That is also true,' the Prince acceded, leaning towards her conspiratorially. 'But I think *more* things come down to sex.' He laughed at her reaction. The more she scolded the more audacious he became. 'Does the truth scandalise you, Lady Dove?' It was easy to see him as a poet today, the way he played with words to derive certain responses. 'Do I make you uncomfortable?'

Uncomfortable seemed a mild adjective for what he did to her. He set her skin to tingling, her thoughts to jangling, the order of her world to spinning. 'No one has ever talked to me in such a way.'

'Honestly? No one has ever talked to you *honestly*? Would you prefer I be like everyone else and continue to tell you sugar-coated versions of reality? You've seen how well that's worked out.'

That might have been the hardest truth yet. Maybe she *had* wanted that, *expected* that at least; that he would argue against her version of the ball, that London was indeed the fairy tale she'd dreamed of. He'd made none of those arguments. Instead, he'd held up a mirror to her own flaws. In his mind, the problem wasn't London, the problem was *her*; her naïvety in *not* questioning the assumptions her mother and aunts had fed her; *her* arrogance in assuming such a fairy tale was her due as the daughter of a duke. 'Life was simpler in Cornwall. I spent years yearning to get away from there and now I find I wax nostalgic for it.'

'Are you homesick? I know something about that. London takes getting used to.'

Dove gave a little laugh. 'I don't believe that. London suits you perfectly.' With the exception of his clothing last night, she couldn't imagine a man better adapted. His manners, his athletic grace on the dance floor. He had every nuance London valued in a gentleman and he was entirely at ease with himself. That was where his confidence came from, his boldness.

'Is that your way of telling me you find me superficial, empty and disappointing?' His words were sharp.

'That is not fair!' Dove snapped. He was putting words in her mouth and twisting them to be unflattering.

'Is it honest, though?' he pushed with a wry smile.

'I don't know you well enough to make such a verdict.' The line was a flimsy refuge and he charged straight through it with all the bluntness of a raging bull.

'And yet, you have. I saw it in your eyes last night. I saw it again this afternoon. You wanted to refuse. It was quite the sacrifice you made for your freedom back there in your drawing room. You don't know what to make of me. It's easier to push me away than it is to figure me out. You're not sure you like me, but you want to.'

She blushed hotly and rose from the bench, 'You are the most infuriating man! Is this what you wanted? To take me out so you could insult me at every turn? You've managed to malign innocence as a virtue and you've equated naïvety with stupidity. Is that what you see when you look at me? An empty-

headed debutante, a spoiled princess?' Her temper
was running far ahead of her words. She was embarrassed to have been caught out, embarrassed to be
seen as a hypocrite, a woman condemning the shal-
lowness of others while being thought shallow in her
judgements as well. Her mother would have a fit if
she'd witnessed her daughter's outburst. Dove had
managed to break at least two of the rules.

'Forgive me if truth and honesty are offensive to
you, Lady Dove.' His tone was cool. He didn't want
the forgiveness he alluded to. He was not sorry. She
could see that in his eyes.

Dove huffed in frustration. 'Being truthful and
being honest are not permissions to be rude and in-
sensitive. If you'll excuse me, I'd like a moment to
collect myself.'

Dove wandered to the shoreline, wanting space
between her and the Prince. What sort of gentleman
said such things to a lady? An honest one, apparently,
to resort to his overused word of the afternoon. But
such honesty created awkwardness. It was one thing
to think such things privately, it was another to say
them. Sharing such thoughts made interacting more
difficult. How did one manage to communicate with
someone who had announced your flaws out loud?
Without the necessary screen of a façade, there was
no protection. Perhaps she was a hypocrite after all.
She was starting to understand the callers in her
drawing room with their posturing and façades, but
that didn't make her like them any better.

Prince Kutejnikov was a paradox of a gentleman. For all of his royalty, he was ill bred, if this conversation was anything to go on. Actually, she had two conversations to go on and both had been highly unacceptable. The schoolroom had not taught her to converse on such subjects or in such a manner. Now they were stuck in Kensington Gardens, with awkward truths and behaviours between them. It was like being caught out of doors in an unexpected spring deluge and no refuge in sight. Unless the Prince apologised. That might be enough repair for them to survive the carriage drive home in decency.

Yes, an apology would be just the thing. She needed to prepare herself for that. Dove ran through the scenario in her mind. He would come down to the shoreline and make reparations for his boldness. In return, she would do her part and murmur regret over her own reaction. She'd better start thinking of the words she wanted to use.

But after five minutes, five very *long* minutes, he hadn't come. After ten minutes, she began to fear he had left her. How would she explain *that* to her mother? How would she explain that the Prince had merely been exacting retribution for her having left him on the dance floor? Or that they'd quarrelled over her perceptions of him? Any one of those explanations would horrify her mother. For two more minutes, she fought the urge to look over her shoulder and see if he was still on the bench.

The curiosity was killing her. Dove bent down, feigning a check of her shoe for a non-existent pebble and shot a hasty glance at the bench. She felt some relief. He was still there and he was writing. *Writing?* A small travelling desk was open on his lap, a quill in hand, and he was utterly engrossed in whatever he was doing. At least that explained why he hadn't come to her and what had been in his bag. But it was still odd. She'd been down here, worrying over an apology, *expecting* an apology, and he had so obviously moved past the quarrel. Blown right by it, in fact. It had not even been a ripple on his pond. Unless that was an apology he was penning?

She was watching him with those silver eyes that hid and revealed her by turn. He could feel the intensity of her gaze on him. That gaze would expose her if he looked up. But he didn't need to. He knew what she wanted. 'I will not give you a lie, Lady Dove.' Illarion concentrated on the paper before him, on the words flowing out of his pen. He almost had it. He wouldn't look up until he was done. 'I cannot give you what I don't possess.'

'And what is that?' She was cross with him anew, no doubt for giving her riddles when she wanted a very certain speech from him.

'Remorse.' He did look up then, setting aside his pen. 'You want an apology from me. I cannot give it since I possess none over our last exchange. In short, I am not sorry for a single word I said.' He watched her gaze move from him to the paper on the writing desk. He blew on the sheet once more to ensure the ink was dry and tucked the sheet inside the case. 'Did you think I was *writing* you an apology?' Lady Dove had confidence in spades to make such assumptions, to think that every man she met was dying of need to make himself presentable to her.

'I *did* think it was a possibility given the nature of our conversation.' The straightforward expectation of her due was fast becoming part of her appeal. Illarion studied her carefully, seeing beyond the outer shell of loveliness. There was a beautiful boldness to such naïve belief that she would never be denied. It was that which he had tried to capture on paper today, not an apology. That boldness could not last. It was like a bloom of spring, a bright splash of colour for a season, but ultimately destined to fade after heat and weather had its way. He had seen it happen to too many women. He didn't want to see it happen to Dove.

He rose, tucking his writing case back into the canvas bag. 'Since I cannot offer you an apology, I shall make a peace offering. Before we go, I would like to show you one of my favourite places, if you'll permit?' He placed a hand lightly at her back, guiding her towards the path, the gesture giving her permission to stay a while longer. He had decided for them. He guided her down the Lancaster Walk towards the Queen's Temple, keeping up easy conversation as the building came into view through the trees. 'It was built for Queen Caroline in 1734. It was meant to be a summer house.' How odd to be the guide and not the tourist. Perhaps London truly was becoming his home now.

He paused long enough to let her study the classical parchment-coloured architecture of the last century before leading her inside where it was dim and cool and empty. Whatever treasures the Queen had once kept in here for her comfort had long been removed. Illarion let Dove wander through the three chambers ahead of him, taking in the grace of her movements, the way her hand trailed against a wall, tracing the etched initials irreverently marking the presence of guests before them. 'That's a shame,' she murmured. 'To deface a thing of beauty by marking it.'

Illarion stopped behind her, close enough to catch the light spring lilac of her perfume. 'This is naught but an empty building to the public.'

She shook her head. 'But once it was someone's refuge, a place they went for privacy, where the world could not touch them for a brief while.'

There was such longing in her voice and knowledge, too, about the value of such a place. Illarion could not help but ask, 'Did you have refuge like this in Cornwall?'

She did not look at him. Her gaze remained riveted on the ignoble etching on the wall, but a smile quirked at her lips. 'I did. We had an orangery. It was always warm, even in the winter. I would go there and draw. In the summers, I would open the doors and sit outside.'

'Had?' Illarion gave a laugh. She talked as if she'd never go back. 'London isn't the end of the world.'

Her grey gaze swivelled to him, her voice quiet in the empty space. 'It may not be the end of *the* world, Prince Kutejnikov, but it is the end of the world as I know it. Lady Dove Sanford-Wallis will not go back there. When I return, it will be as someone's Duchess if my father has his way. I will only return to visit, never to live, never to stay. My place will be with my husband. There is no question of *if* I will "take" this Season, or *if* I will wed. The only thing left to be decided is to whom.'

She moved away from him, her back to him as she spoke as the enormity of her realisation swamped her anew. 'The stories, the fairy tales I'd been raised on about the Season, all grew my hopes. I was so excited to come and it distracted me from what coming here really meant.'

'And what is that?' Illarion asked carefully. He could feel the old anger begin to stir in him, the anger that had seen him exiled from Kuban, the anger that had earned the Kubanian Tsar's displeasure.

'That I have a duty to my family in marrying well, and that marrying "well" is not defined by finding someone with whom one shares a mutual affection, but by finding someone who's bloodline and title and wealth are worthy of your own. My duty is to show up at the church, a beautiful symbol of my family's part of the alliance. A *symbol*!' she spat. 'Not a person with any free will of her own.' Her resentment was raw, palpably new and she was grappling with what it all meant.

Illarion was struck by the irony beneath her struggle. For all the liberalism of London, for all the modernity of England, some things had not changed. Even among the glittering ballrooms of the *ton* with its silks and jewels, women were still slaves. The hatred of such a system flooded back to him, a reminder of how dormant his passions had been in the year since he'd left Kuban, of how he'd tried to bury them, forget them. Life was easier when one did not trouble oneself with issues of social justice. It had also proven to be emptier.

Here, in the dimness of the Queen's Temple, he felt himself coming to life. The poet-warrior in him waking after hibernation, old habits, old emotions surfacing. He closed the distance between them, wanting to touch her, wanting to give her reassurance, protection against the reality she'd glimpsed, the anger she felt over the betrayal and her own impotence, he wanted to remind her that she was a person, with free will and real feelings. 'Perhaps it doesn't have to be that way for you.' He let his voice linger at her ear, let his hands rest at her shoulders as he whispered his temptation.

'Of course it does. I cannot shame my family.' He heard the resignation in her tone. Despite her anger, she was a loyal daughter. Did she even think of fighting it? Or like Katya, did she feel forced to accept her fate?

'At the expense of your own happiness?' he said softly, urging her to think about the cost of her acquiescence. He turned her then, moving her to face him, his hand tipping her chin up, forcing her eyes to meet his. 'It's easy to give up that which you don't understand. You don't fully know what you'd be missing.' He wanted to awaken her, wanted to give her a reason to fight. He could show her and, if she drew certain conclusions from the demonstration, then so be it. He dropped his eyes to her lips in the briefest of warnings before he claimed them.

He teased her lips apart, his mouth patient in its instruction as she opened to him, her body answering him along with her lips and he knew then he was her first kiss, her first taste of desire, first taste of a little wickedness, too. He deepened the kiss, slowly, expertly, so as not to rush her or pressure her, but to answer her, to lead her at her pace where he wanted her to go. She was delicious in her inexperience, eager and hesitant by turns. He would ensure she didn't regret this…until she did. Without warning, she was out of his arms and *thwack*!

Her palm struck his cheek, her eyes ablaze. 'What the hell was that for?' He was too stunned to correct his language. It wasn't the first time curiosity over a kiss had sparked a rebellion, but it was the first time he'd been slapped for it.

Chapter Five

Sweet heavens, her hand hurt! She hadn't bargained on that. And, oh, dear Lord, she'd marked him! Dove stared at Prince Kutejnikov in stunned disbelief. She'd never struck anyone, or anything, in her life and now the palm of her hand was a glaring red mark on the Prince's cheek. This was insanity! She'd only wanted to scold him for his impertinent boldness and now they were both smarting. The Prince rubbed his jaw, glaring his surprise and his disapproval. He probably wasn't used to being slapped. Women probably liked his kisses. She certainly had, although she wouldn't dare admit it to him, not now that she'd put her handprint on his face. What she hadn't liked was the indiscretion of the act. In no way did it embody any aspect of her mother's rules.

'Have you no thought for our reputations?' Dove gathered her thoughts long enough to answer his question. 'We are in a public place where anyone could come strolling through and my maid is just in the other room. She could have walked in at any time! Do you know what could have happened if we'd been caught?' *That* lesson had been drummed into her quite thoroughly: kisses of any nature were compromising. They led straight to the altar, the very thing the Prince seemed intent on counselling her against. 'Perhaps the better question is not what was *I* thinking, but what were *you* thinking?'

The Prince's blue eyes were hot flames fixed on her, his voice low. He might have been stunned for a moment by her act, but he was not angry. He was… amused? But his words were serious. 'I thought you should know what you're sacrificing, what your parents and society are asking you to give up in order to make *their* alliance.'

Something inside Dove shrivelled and she realised she'd been hoping for a different answer, something along the lines that she'd been irresistible, or that he'd been overcome. The Prince gave a wry smile. 'You are disappointed. Still clinging to the fairy tale, are we?'

Dove flushed. Perhaps she was. Perhaps it took more than two hours to kill a dream after all. 'Prince Kutejnikov, I think we should return home.' There was no reparation that could call back the peace of the day now.

'*I* think after this afternoon you should call me Illarion.' He offered her his arm, negotiating again: the use of his name in exchange for escorting her home. 'And I shall call you Dove.'

'First names are shockingly informal. It is impossible. It cannot be done.' If she allowed such a liberty, she'd be admitting to their intimacy. Admittance meant acceptance. Acknowledgement. At the moment, she would rather not acknowledge what had passed between them, the press of his mouth on hers, the way her body had responded. She'd been all too aware of the need to lean into him, the shocking thrill to feel the hard, muscled planes of a man's body up close for the first time. Even through layers of clothes, there'd been an intoxicating intimacy in that physical connection. Her reaction had surprised her, confused her.

Illarion gave a wicked chuckle. He was laughing at her again. This time at her expense. He thought her a prude. 'We'll use those names only in private then.' He winked, assuming her consent.

They stepped out into the lingering sunshine. Late afternoon shadows had begun to fall, hinting at the onset of a spring evening. Illarion leaned close to her ear as they walked. 'A piece of advice for you, my dear. *I* don't let the title wear me.' He fell silent, letting her absorb the words as they walked to the curricle. He handed her up as if there'd been no break in the conversation. 'Of course, it's dangerous. They want you to wear the title. It's easier for them if you're not a person. It's easier for you, too; you forget to think about what *you* want, until you realise it's too late.'

He moved around the horses' heads and sprang up to his seat, his body taking up space beside her.

His thigh rested against hers unapologetically as he gathered the reins, making her even more aware of him now than she had been on the drive out.

He clucked to the horses. 'Is it me or my ideas that make you uncomfortable?' He slid her a sideways glance. 'Perhaps it is my kisses? You may have stopped the kiss, but that doesn't mean you didn't like it.'

She was seized with the urge to put her hands over her ears, to shout at him to stop! It was too much to take in for one day, his radical ideas, his kisses. Her mind was swimming in the newness of her thoughts and the confusion they brought, panicking even. Like a drowning victim who would drown her rescuer along with her in her confusion, she lashed out. 'I'm beginning to think you didn't leave Kuban. They most likely kicked you out if this is how you behave.' She'd meant the words to be scolding, the kind of set down a lady might offer a forward gentleman who'd crossed the line of politeness. She had not expected her words to hit a target.

The line of Illarion's jaw went hard, the features of his face going tight, his words terse. 'You know nothing about me.' He didn't like the quizzing glass turned his way, although he hadn't minded probing her psyche.

'And *you* know nothing about *me*.' Dove straightened her shoulders and fixed her gaze on the road. Another lesson learned today: this was what happened when one confided in someone one didn't know well. 'I was wrong to have burdened you with my confidences. I was unforgivably impetuous. I would appreciate it if you would forget my disclosures.'

A proper gentlemen would accept her apology and would understand what it meant: that they should limit their association. She was counting on Illarion to know that and to act accordingly. But he did not. 'What about the kiss? Should I forget about that, too?' His tone was hard with cynicism as if he knew she could not forget that as easily. Indeed, she suspected she might think about that kiss far longer than was prudent.

The town house came into sight and she was saved from answering as Illarion pulled the carriage to the kerb. The street was quiet and for a moment they were nearly alone except for the servants sitting on the back. She slid him a questioning look when he didn't immediately come around. 'Give me your hand, Lady Dove.' The hardness had left his face and he was charming once more, his voice low. 'I want to give you a talisman. If you would forget the first kiss, perhaps you would do better to remember the second.' He took her hand and raised it to his lips, pressing a kiss to her open palm. It was nothing like the first kiss, but gentle as the gesture was, she could feel the fire start to burn once more. Would it be like this now every time he touched her? The question was wickedness itself in the assumption that there *would* be a next time. She was allowing herself to be tempted.

A footman spotted them and came down the stairs to assist her. Illarion—*Prince Kutejnikov*, she strongly reminded herself—released her hand. 'Good day, Lady Dove.'

'Good day, your Highness.' She could not take even the tiniest step down the road of familiarity. Dove stepped down from the curricle with a strict politeness she hoped made it clear that there would be no first names, no private permissions. She promised herself she would not be like the other ladies who followed him around ballrooms and patiently waited while he danced with others. She *couldn't* be like them. It simply wasn't permissible. She was the Duke of Redruth's daughter and she was held to higher standards. Always and in all things.

He inclined his blond head, the fragments of a smile on his lips as if he knew a secret. 'Thank you for an interesting afternoon, Lady Dove.' It was done so well, Dove imagined she was the only one who noted the mocking tone beneath his propriety. Halfway up the steps, he called to her, 'Lady Dove, was your deal with the devil worth it?'

She glanced over her shoulder. She linked her gaze with his and let a coy smile take her mouth. 'Was yours?'

It was damn well worth it and he had the pages to show for it. Illarion sat in paradise, otherwise known as the back veranda of Kuban House, a glass of Stepan's homemade *samogan* to hand should he need it and papers spread before him. His thick mass of hair was piled into a bun atop his head, not unlike an eastern warrior's, a testament to how seriously he was working. He preferred his hair out of his face when he wrote. He'd discarded his coats, too, the moment he'd arrived home. The fewer distractions the better. He liked his body as free as his mind. He'd write naked out here if he could, but Stepan would kill him if he came home and found him nude in the garden. He'd tried it once, so he knew. Now he reserved that particular artistic luxury for the privacy of his chambers. Right now, shirtsleeves and trousers would have to do. He wanted to be outdoors, wanted to capture what it had felt like at the park; the feel of spring, the scent of grass and Kuban House's gardens were ideal, especially at night when the lanterns were lit.

Illarion leaned back in his chair, eyes closed, letting his mind wander through the afternoon's images: Dove walking along the shore edge, all unconscious grace, a swan princess perhaps with her platinum hair and elegant length of neck? The personification of spring and innocence? That picture conjured up a rather provocative series of subsequent images: of Dove walking the shore clad in a gossamer gown that left nothing to the male imagination; high, firm breasts with rose-tipped nipples pressed hard against the thin fabric, her bare feet scything through the long, fresh spring grass; of Spring removing her gown, her body unveiled to hidden eyes, her hands reaching up to take down her hair. Dove as Spring was the perfect juxtaposition of new innocence and womanly knowledge. She'd shown him both sides today.

The images he'd conjured from that inspiration were certainly powerful if the beginnings of his arousal were anything to go on, but Illarion was not satisfied. Any poet could depict a young virgin in the freshness of spring. Spring was the season of birth and newness, the season of the virgin and the woman. But spring wasn't entirely the right season for a woman like Dove, with her snowy looks. Physically, winter was her time and yet it was a far more difficult task to cast Dove's innocence against a season that was often symbolic of death and dormancy.

Ah. Dormancy. That was the key. His poet's brain fired. Today, winter had awakened. He recalled how the sun and a bit of temper had brought a flush to Dove's porcelain cheeks. He focused on the flush. He'd liked the colour in her cheeks, proof that his cool ice queen from the night before was still there, but that she also possessed a warm core. Fire. Ice. An ice princess awakening... That conjured a stronger image and he hastily scribbled a single word, a Russian word. *Snegurochka.* The Snow Maiden of Russian folk tales, a girl of great beauty who, according to some of the stories, had melted in the spring when she'd ventured from Father Frost's forests in pursuit of love.

He was writing furiously now, the allegory pouring from him. He wrote of *Snegurochka* trapped in spring, a season not of her making, of winter's princess far from home, surrounded by Primavera's blushing roses, her paleness a marked contrast. His mind was a blur of thought and image.

When he finished, his glass of *samogan* was untouched, the lanterns were lit. A tray of cold meats sat at his elbow, waiting for him. The servants must have brought it. He had not noticed. He'd been too caught up in all that had been revealed today. He had not thought to see so much. In truth, he'd gone today for selfish reasons, to see if she could inspire him again as she'd inspired him last night on the dance floor, to see if he could capture what had slipped away from him last night. He'd got more than he'd bargained for; he'd glimpsed a woman who was figuring out the game, figuring out that she was trapped or nearly so and something in him had started to wake. His own winter, ending. Proof of that awakening was scrawled across pages.

Footsteps clipped on the flagstones, a pair of them, not boots but shoes. Ruslan and Stepan were dressed for going out, for dancing and ballrooms and Primavera's roses. 'You're not drunk yet, I'll take that as a good sign.' Stepan noted the glass of *samogan* with a subtle lift of his brow, his gaze drifting disapprovingly to the hastily crafted topknot.

'The Huns wore their hair like this,' Illarion answered the silent reproach. There were others, too: the Samurai, the Mongols.

'Oh, to be a Hun. My greatest wish.' Stepan's tone was dry with sarcasm.

'At least you're still dressed,' Ruslan interjected, always the diplomat, always positive. Illarion had long felt that he, Stepan and Nikolay might have killed each other years ago if it hadn't been for Ruslan's cool diplomacy keeping them in check. Ruslan slapped him on the back. 'I see today's visit was profitable.' He snatched up a paper before Illarion could protect it. '"*Snegurochka*?" I like it.' To his credit, Ruslan read silently, dark eyes darting over the lines. 'It's lovely, Illarion. It could be one of your best. It has that Russian sense of fatalism, that one cannot escape destiny, and the nature allegory is sublime.' Ruslan set the paper down. 'Is it about us, Illarion? I think it is. I think *Snegurochka* represents the four of us, the four princes exiled from home.'

Illarion smiled, appreciative of his friend's praise, but the praise was tempered by Stepan's hard gaze, studying, assessing. 'It's not about us, Ruslan,' Stepan growled. 'Don't be a dimwit. It's about a woman.'

Ruslan gave Stepan a considering glance, taking the recommendation seriously and prepared his rebuttal. 'No, Stepan, look at this line here, I am pretty sure it's about us.'

Stepan was surlier than usual. 'No, it's about a woman,' he said with finality. 'Who is she, Illarion?'

'My secret muse and that's all I'm going to say,' Illarion answered staunchly. Whatever was needling Stepan was doing a good job of it. He was quite the bear this evening. Illarion grinned, much to Stepan's obvious consternation. 'A gentleman never tells.' But a gentleman did say thank you and Illarion knew just how to do it. Lady Dove had brought him to life today at the expense of exposing herself: her beliefs, her hopes, her disappointments, many of which she was just starting to recognise. It had left her confused, uncertain and sad. He knew first-hand how hard it was to let dreams go, even when they proved no longer viable or useful. He'd left a life behind, a country behind.

He would bring his *Sneguruchka*'s dream to life for just a day. He would show her that if fairy tales weren't possible in whole, they were at least possible in part. He chuckled as Stepan and Ruslan stepped out for the night. He was already imagining the look on her face when she opened the note he hadn't written yet. She would think it was an apology. But he knew better. He wasn't sorry for today in the least, he was thankful for it. He had a new poem, worthy of Pushkin himself once he tidied it up, and who knew what tomorrow might bring? For the first time in over a year, the possibilities were endless.

Chapter Six

The family carriage crawled through the evening traffic of Mayfair, bringing Dove ever closer to another supper, another ball, another evening with gentlemen she couldn't respect, gentlemen who didn't trust themselves to be liked for who they really were, gentlemen, she doubted, who even *knew* who they were any more. A ballroom full of liars. It was a rather cynical thought to start the evening on. It did not go beyond Dove's notice that it was also a rather hypocritical thought. Hadn't she scolded the Prince for being just the opposite, for being too honest? He would laugh at her if he were here now. Hours ago, she'd been scandalised by his outrageous thoughts and actions and now she was missing them. She wished she weren't. She wished she was in better control of herself and her thoughts. The truth was, she was still reeling from the afternoon.

Beside her, her mother squeezed her hand. 'Are you excited for tonight? Lady Tolliver's will be a crush.' She began reciting the guest list, offering her usual commentary on the guests. 'Percivale will be there, of course.' Her mother smiled knowingly. 'It seems he's already managed to align his schedule with yours. He arrived after the Prince had taken you out. He was sorry to miss you this afternoon, but he made it clear he was looking forward to this evening.' This announcement was followed by another squeeze of her hand. 'You're off to a fabulous start, my dear. Your father and I could not be prouder. Everything is coming off just as we hoped.'

Across the carriage her father offered a rare smile. 'Percivale is the one we're angling for. He's the whole package: wealth, title, family connections, government influence. Once he's duke, he'll have ten boroughs under his control for appointments. It was good you were gone today when he called. We don't want to make it too easy on him. A man will cherish all the more what he has to fight for.' He cast a brief, warm glance her mother's direction. They were both busy people. They were hardly ever in the same place together, but when they were, there were always secret glances, quiet smiles, as if something unseen moved between them. Dove could not imagine it ever being that way with Percivale.

Her father's focus returned to her. 'The Prince's attentions are certain to help your popularity in the short term, my dear, but I wouldn't want anyone to think we'd take him seriously. He has nothing to offer us—no real lineage, no land and, from the talk at

White's about him, the merit of what his title means is suspect. I think we need to be careful there. Do not encourage him unduly or single him out for special attentions. We need to make sure London understands he is just one of your *peloton*—another to add to the mix of the viscount from Northumberland who has already inherited, the handsome Lord Fredericks, young Alfred-Ashby, and your mother tells me there's an earl in the chase as well. A prince will add to your cache. It should be satisfactory enough to make Percivale sweat.'

Enough to make *her* sweat. Dove prickled at her father's choice of vocabulary. *Chase?* He made the pursuit of marriage sound like a fox hunt and she was the fox, the men all hounds in hot pursuit. She knew how fox hunts ended, with the fox's tail captured for a prize. She'd rather not picture her tail as the prize for these gentlemen. The image was disconcerting to say the least. But no less disconcerting was the disparaging way her father spoke of Illarion, as if he were of questionable character, a charlatan of the *ton*. This was a deeper disregard than what had been shown at the breakfast table.

Part of her wanted to defend Illarion and part of her knew better. What she *did* know made him unsuitable. He spoke his mind and that mind was full of rebellious ideas her parents would not approve of. If they knew the things he'd said today they would not tolerate him even among her *peloton*.

But most disconcerting was Percivale and what

sounded like a foregone conclusion that *he* was the chosen one. Percivale and his prosing! How would she ever manage a lifetime of that? She glanced at her parents. What would they say if she told them she found Percivale and his ten boroughs boring? It was an entirely hypothetical question. *If* she told them now they'd say she hadn't given him a proper chance, that it had only been one meeting at a ball. She needed a better moment to voice her disapproval of the match and better evidence.

Her fists clenched inside the folds of her pristine skirts. The prospect of waiting caused a sense of helplessness to rise in her. If she didn't tell them how she felt now, when? In a week? In two weeks? In three? When Percivale asked for her hand? If it was *au fait accompli*, how long would he even wait? At what point would it be *too late* for her to speak up? The line between too soon and too late was a very grey one indeed; one more thing none of her lessons had ever covered. Perhaps that was because there was no need. Dutiful daughters never rebelled, never spoke out, they did what they were told.

The carriage rolled to a stop at Tolliver House. She could hear the footman outside setting the steps. Nothing more could be said on the subject tonight. Now there was only time to endure, to get through the evening. Perhaps tomorrow would be the right time. Perhaps tomorrow she would find the courage to speak her mind.

'Remember, dear,' her mother whispered last-minute instructions at her ear. 'Draw the gentlemen out, let them talk about themselves. A man loves to show a woman he's competent.'

'And myself?' Dove replied perversely. 'Shall I talk about my drawing and my charity art school in Cornwall?'

Her mother's lips pursed in scolding reprimand. 'Dove, don't be shocking.'

'Then how shall *I* be competent?' She knew she was needling now.

'By listening, by being an encourager. Male egos are fragile things, dear. You have to prop them up,' her mother admonished as they mounted the steps.

Dove wondered what Illarion would think of such advice. His ego had seemed very much intact in spite of her attempts to crack it. She doubted he needed to have it propped up. But it was a mistake to have thought of him. She should not have done it and certainly not by first name. Doing so created a poignant reminder that Illarion had stayed with her from this afternoon much as he'd stayed with her last night as assuredly as if he was physically present.

He stayed with her through the first dances, looming in her mind as a point of comparison for the other gentlemen in her court. She found herself constantly thinking, 'What would Illarion say to that?' or 'Illarion would never…' Then she would chide herself. Did she know him so well after two meetings? This afternoon she'd argued that she did not. She needed to stop thinking of him by first name, proof that his invitation to informality had not gone entirely rejected. Proof, too, that she was not as indifferent to him as her words made her out to be. She had not slapped him solely because of his indiscretion, but hers as well. He'd been right. She had not minded that kiss nearly as much as she'd pretended.

By the middle of the evening, her court was wearing on her nerves. Not one of the gentlemen, including the coveted Strom Percivale, had made a single enquiry about *her* beyond soliciting her need for warm punch. It had been their accomplishments that had dominated the conversation, unlike Illarion, who might have been brash, but he at least had made several enquiries *about* her.

Dove was making other comparisons, too, that strayed into the dangerous realm of the physical. Illarion was tall, broad shouldered, with strong hands that took command simply through touch. These men were medium in height and mediocre in all things. Their touch didn't command, their gaze didn't ignite, their conversation didn't challenge. She couldn't envision having a heated conversation with any of them, let alone one that led to stolen kisses in a public park. *That* was the most dangerous comparison of them all. She could not imagine any level of enjoyable physical intimacy with the men on her dance card. None of them sent a thrill through her with a single touch.

Perhaps that was why debutantes weren't supposed to sneak out into gardens and kiss young men. It created all sorts of expectations that had nothing to do with titles, land and wealth, and who one's family was. In other words, none of the items parents considered valuable when steering their daughters towards 'advantageous marriages'. A young girl's idea of what constituted 'advantageous' might be quite different after a walk in the gardens. And yet, the practical side of her took her father's words seriously. The Prince might excite her with kisses, but his behaviours were unpredictable in word and deed, his credentials unreliable, his antecedents questionable. He was from a place London knew little about despite the novelty London conferred on him.

Even so, Dove found herself looking for him. By the eighth dance—a waltz with Percivale—she was wondering if he would come tonight. Would she look across the ballroom and see him striding through the crowd? Towards her? Her mind had to separate the two ideas. He *could* attend the ball without *intending* to see her. After all, he'd already spent considerable time with her today and he'd got a reddened cheek for his efforts. Why *would* he want to seek her out? She *should* hope that he didn't. She had no business fostering her curiosity over an unsuitable man and yet part of her hungered for a glimpse, for another bout, for another shocking conversation. Was this how it started with the other women, the women she'd seen trailing after him at her godmother's last night?

Dove focused on Percivale's conversation as he led her into supper—something about his grandmother's estate in Hereford and its apple orchards—and promised herself she would *not* become like those other women. She would never be desperate for a man. But she could be disappointed by one. Tonight she was disappointed by two: by Illarion, who wasn't coming, and by Percivale, because he had.

She ought to be grateful for Percivale. He was the catch of the Season and every girl in the room would kill to be her. Miss Sarah Tomlinson, especially. The girl had looked daggers at her all night, blaming her for monopolising Percivale's attentions. If Miss Tomlinson wanted Percivale, she was more than welcome to him. But Dove knew Miss Tomlinson would never step up to take him. There was a pecking order, after all. Miss Tomlinson was an earl's granddaughter, nothing more. She would never impose on a duke's daughter's claim. A naughty thought came to Dove. Maybe *she* should affect an introduction? Then it would be up to Miss Tomlinson to dazzle Percivale.

'Perhaps we might sit over there?' She gestured to Miss Tomlinson's table where two chairs were available. Percivale smiled obligingly. It was the first thing that had gone well tonight. And it was the last.

At the end of the evening, despite her best efforts, Percivale stayed glued to her side. There'd been moments of hope. He'd asked Miss Tomlinson to dance after supper, but had quickly returned to Dove's side afterwards.

'Percivale is suitably loyal to you,' her mother summed up in the carriage on the way home. 'He stayed with you as much as propriety allows.' *Clung* was more apropos. He'd been a veritable barnacle. 'You managed him beautifully, never seeming to dominate him,' her mother complimented. 'Sitting with Miss Tomlinson was brilliant. It allowed you to appear generous and yet there was no real risk of losing his attentions.'

Dove gave her a mother a cool stare. She had not thought of her overture in terms of how it would appear to others. 'I simply thought, since her family is political, that the two of them would enjoy conversation together.'

'Percivale is a smart man,' her father joined in, stretching his long legs. 'He knows there's nothing more than conversation down that road. He needs more than an earl's granddaughter can provide to have the influence he wants.' Her father's tone was smug with confident satisfaction. 'He won't stray from the Redruth fold.'

'I don't like him.' The words were out of her mouth before she could rethink the wisdom of them.

Her mother didn't even blink before she responded, a soothing smile on her lips. 'How *could* you like him? You hardly know him. You have your entire life to know him and in the knowing, respect and affection will grow. Those are things that come with building a life together, sharing experiences together. That's what will bind you together. You will make a family together, raise children together, weather life's storms together.'

Dove looked down at her hands, two thoughts coming to her simultaneously. First: they had already decided, then. It was indeed to be Percivale as she'd suspected. That filled her with a dreaded sense of finality. Her life had been predetermined for her. The enormity of what that meant swept her. She was being ushered from the shelter of Cornwall to the shelter of a husband's home without time to experience the world on her own, to test herself, to know herself, to find out who she was. Second: she was an ungrateful daughter for wanting to reject such care.

Her mother's arguments were not without merit. She'd been raised in privilege. She would marry into even greater privilege from which she could influence enormous good. How *dare* she find fault with that? And yet, Illarion's words whispered the temptation to do just that. *'I kissed you so you would know what you would be missing.'* There were other phrases, too, that rolled through her mind—*'the expense of your own happiness.'* How did she weigh her happiness against loyalty to her family?

Her mother squeezed her hand, taking her silence for acceptance and understanding. 'You may rely on us, Dove, to guide you safely.' She should be grateful for such parents, for the wealth that permitted such a lavish Season, but the hopelessness swamped her again. Wasn't there a way both could coexist without one harming the other? A way that didn't involve marriage to a man she felt nothing for? A man she had not chosen? She was not entirely naïve. She knew that the purpose of coming to London was to find a husband. But she'd always imagined that search would involve her, that she'd have a voice.

At the town house, the butler waited by the door despite the late hour, lamp in hand to light the dark hallway. 'A note came for you, Lady Dove.' He held out the silver letter salver with his other hand. She took it, studying the firm, dark handwriting in the light. Her pulse sped up as she opened the note and scanned the lines. Coolly, she handed the note to her mother. 'Prince Kutejnikov would like me to accompany him to Somerset House to the view the paintings tomorrow afternoon.'

Her mother exchanged a look with her father. Her father hesitated before giving the slightest of nods to her mother. 'Olivia, you will go with her, of course, to chaperon.'

Dove breathed a sigh of relief, not realising until then how much she equated Illarion's invitation with escape. She'd be out of the house, away from Percivale and she'd be in her element, surrounded by art. She fingered Illarion's note, a suspicion coming to her. Had the choice of Somerset House been intentional, perhaps a thoughtful apology for the shocking nature of their outing today, or had he chosen it arbitrarily because it was simply a popular public venue? After tonight, his reasons hardly mattered to her. She was grateful for the escape regardless of what form it took or what motives had prompted it. For a few hours tomorrow, she was going to be free.

Chapter Seven

'*Illarion...*'

The whisper echoed in his sleep. He was dreaming, of Katya and Kuban, of the caves of Maykop near his summer palace.

She was calling to him. 'Illarion, come...' She materialised in the darkness of the caves, vibrant and alive, with violet eyes that flashed and laughter that could captivate a room.

Illarion broke into a jog. 'Katya!' She'd been his muse once. Illarion had written wild, beautiful poetry dedicated to her. She'd been his friend, his confidante and inspiration. In many ways, he'd felt closer to her than he'd felt to anyone.

He was close now. He could see her creamy skin, silky skeins of dark hair hanging forward over her shoulders, framing luminous eyes, a beauty in death as she'd been in life. For her extraordinary looks, she'd been forgiven much by her uncle, the Tsar, even her association with him, the poet-rebel.

He reached for her, he could almost touch her.

She turned and ran deeper into the caves, her laughter drifting behind her. 'Catch me, Illarion!'

He gave chase, calling out a warning, 'Katya, wait, don't!'

They were at the heart of the cave now, a limestone pool in its centre...

The old terror gripped him. He knew what would happen next. The dream always ended this way. Maybe this time it would be different...maybe this time he would find the words...

He always said that. It never mattered. He always failed.

Katya turned to him, this time with haunted eyes, the vibrancy gone from her. She looked as she had just two years into her marriage; she wore a tragic beauty now, her spirit a shadow of its former self. It was worn down by a marriage that had stifled her, imprisoned her—a marriage that had benefitted the crown of Kuban, but not her. She reached out a hand to him.

'Katya, come to me. Step away from the water.'

His voice was hoarse, his throat was tight. He edged close to her, not wanting to frighten her.

'Will you take me away? We can run away, Illarion. We can go somewhere no one knows us, where he can't find me.'

She grabbed the fabric of her bodice in both hands and rent it down the centre, exposing white, perfect breasts. No, not perfect. Illarion froze.

'*See what he has done?*' There was an angry red brand at her right breast in the shape of a U.

'*He already suspects you and I are lovers. Why not make it real in truth? You were right, I should not have married Ustinov. I should have found a way to resist.*'

Illarion swallowed hard against his anger. He would kill that bastard of a husband who had done this to her, who had wrecked this woman.

He nearly had her. '*Step away, Katya. Come to me.*' He repeated his command, reached out his hand. '*I will protect you.*'

He would promise her anything, no matter how wild. He'd never got this close before.

'*I will challenge Ustinov.*' He was a good duellist— too good, in some opinions, from too much practice.

But the idea terrified her. It was the wrong answer.

She stepped backwards, the milky water of the limestone pool with its sharp, protruding stalagmites lapping at her hem.

'*He will kill you. I cannot risk you, Illarion, you're all I have left.*' Her eyes went dark, a shadow crossed her face. '*It is hopeless. There's no way out, Illarion, not for me. The only freedom is death.*'

Illarion went cold. He wished he'd never written those words. '*No!*'

He was too late. She held out her arms and let herself fall...

'*Katya!*'

The sound of his own voice woke Illarion; his body sweating, his heart pounding. He had failed again. He sat up, hands trembling as he reached for the water beside his bed. He couldn't pour it. The carafe crashed to the floor, shattering.

There was pounding on the door, Ruslan calling, 'Illarion, are you all right?' Ruslan pushed his way in, his robe unbelted, his hair unruly from sleep. 'What's happened, another nightmare?'

'Glass.' Illarion managed an incoherent warning.

'Yes,' Ruslan soothed. 'I heard the crash. I'll be careful. Let's get you something to drink, something stronger than water.' He hunted around until he found the decanter of *samogan* on the desk and poured a glass. Illarion felt like a child as Ruslan brought him the drink, keeping his own hand around his to steady the tumbler. Ruslan sat beside him, letting him drink in silence.

'Was it Katya again?' he asked quietly after a while.

'I couldn't save her.' The old recriminations flooded back, the early grief, the early guilt when he'd heard the news. She'd gone to the caves alone, his presence was a manifestation unique to the dream, and drowned in the limestone pool. 'I should have found a way to help her, to prevent the marriage from happening in the first place.' General Ustinov was known as a brute. But the Kubanian Tsar had needed the alliance with the military commander to put down the threat of a coup. He'd sold Katya, his niece, to make the alliance.

'No one could,' Ruslan offered. 'The peace of the country depended on the match.'

'But it was my poetry,' Illarion began, 'that encouraged her to think of rebelling.' In the end, he'd feared it had been his poetry that had inspired her suicide. 'If I had not written "Freedom", she would still be alive.' *'The only freedom is death.'* The last line. The fatal line. The Tsar believed it. The Tsar had blamed him publicly for Katya's death, had renounced him as the royal poet laureate, calling his poetry inciteful and dangerous.

Ruslan sat with him until dawn, until the fears of the night had passed and he could hear London waking up outside his window. Modern London didn't believe in curses. But Illarion did. He'd failed Katya and he was cursed for it. His poetry had caused a woman to take her life—not just any woman, but his best friend. It didn't matter that he'd not intended it. His need for a muse was urgent now. In a few hours, he had a date with destiny, a *new* destiny. He was more convinced than ever it was the only way to put the past behind him. To stop the nightmares.

Now *this* was the London Dove had *dreamed* of! A drive to Somerset House, an afternoon spent leisurely touring the Royal Academy's art exhibition on the arm of a gentleman who wasn't attempting to calculate her net worth or peek down her bodice. Although, to be honest, Illarion *not* calculating her net worth did make her a bit nervous. If he wasn't doing that, what was he doing with her? Illarion—she'd given up *not* thinking about him by first name—could have the attention of any woman in any room and, for the moment, he'd chosen her.

Today, he was on his very best behaviour, which somehow managed to disappoint her. There were no pointed conversations or audacious comments—yet—as they strolled the galleries. The omission of his outrageous remarks was a very small shade on an otherwise perfect outing, a far different outing than the one yesterday. Dove smiled to herself and thought, *apology accepted.*

Beyond the windows of Somerset House, the Thames sparkled beneath blue skies as they toured the exhibit in the north wing. Around them, the crowd ebbed easily, making it possible to stop where they willed to take in art that appealed. At the Constable oil of Salisbury Cathedral, the crowd thickened and they had to wait for good viewing; a wait that was entirely justified in Dove's opinion. 'He's mastered it again, so perfectly!' Dove exclaimed as they moved closer to the painting and she could study the details. 'Look at how he's captured the weather.' She pointed discreetly to the dark cloud peeking above and be-tween the high leaves of the trees. 'A storm is com-ing. The picnickers in the right corner are unaware, they still have the sun. But not for long.' She smiled, enjoying her story. 'They will have to hurry. One can almost see the clouds moving across the sky.'

Illarion nodded, his gaze thoughtfully on the canvas. 'There is irony in attempting to capture transience. Your Constable seeks to trap change into some sort of permanence on canvas, I think.'

'Don't poets do the same thing?' She tossed him a smile full of friendly challenge. 'Except they capture a moment with words instead of oils.'

His blue gaze contemplated her, making her feel as if he were capturing *her*. They might have been alone in the crowded room in that moment. '*Touché*, Lady Dove. We do indeed. How insightful.'

'You're having a good time.' It was a statement, not a question, but it wasn't without a certain element of surprise on her part. He was enjoying this, Dove realised. He was enjoying *her*. And she was enjoying *him*.

'I am, aren't you? You seemed somewhat amazed that this should be the case.' He grinned and they began to stroll once more past minor works that didn't require their concentration or commentary.

'Except for my father, I don't know many gentlemen who enjoy art so thoroughly.' Dove could not imagine discussing Constable with any of her court. Lord Fredericks would stare at her and say 'quite so, quite so' and she certainly couldn't imagine strolling here with Percivale, who would only come to be seen. She cautioned herself to be fair. He wasn't the only one who simply came to be seen. *Most* people came for strictly that reason. But not her. Not Illarion. They'd actually come to enjoy the art. She slanted a quiet look in Illarion's direction, taking him in with a new view. They had something in common now.

'You know something of the artists' world, Lady Dove. You mentioned yesterday that you draw. Do you paint as well?' he ventured, impressing her further.

'I draw, mainly. Pencils and charcoal. I paint a little. Nothing like this.' She was suddenly reticent, shy about her talent.

'I would like to see your work some time,' he offered, perhaps to be polite. Then his eyes sparked. 'I know, we should have an artists' picnic. You can bring your sketching and I can bring my notebook. We could lie beneath the sky and indulge our creativity.' Dove smiled at the image his words created. It sounded lovely and impossible. Such a suggestion was far too private. She said nothing, wanting to savour the idea of such an outing instead of ruining it with practicalities like chaperons. Her mother was here somewhere, trailing behind them. It seemed they'd left her at the last picture.

'Does your whole family enjoy art, then?' Illarion asked.

'Yes. My mother used to paint. I don't think anyone can live in Cornwall and not love art. The countryside is full of artistic potential. There's a wildness to it, a natural beauty that begs to be captured: cliffs, rivers, the sea. And there are gardens. We can grow the most amazing plants in Cornwall.' She paused. She was getting too excited about home. 'I'm sorry, I was rambling.'

'Not at all.' Illarion's eyes crinkled at the corners. 'I would like to see Cornwall. I think it is a place that inspires and a man, especially a poet, is always looking for sources of inspiration.'

'I think art is an important piece of expression,' Dove offered, 'even if one does it badly. It means something to the artist.' She paused, thinking of the children she'd left behind in Cornwall. The gallery, seeing all the paintings, had made her nostalgic. 'I have a small art school at home where I teach the children in the village.' It was not something she'd talked about since coming to London, but it seemed right to share it in this moment.

Illarion's face filled with a smile. 'That sounds wonderful, a place where children can learn to express themselves at an early age. Not only expression, but inspiration. You're helping them to see the inspiration around them in their daily lives, helping them to appreciate nature through that expression. Perhaps you are teaching the next Constable.'

She blushed at that. 'It isn't much. I only pass on what I know, what I've learned from my tutors.' But she was touched that he understood the goals behind her pet project. Her school was so much more than just the physical act of painting or drawing.

He didn't let her argue against his praise. 'It's more than they'd have otherwise. Never underestimate the power of a gift, no matter how small.'

They'd reached the end of the gallery; he guided her outside to one of the verandas overlooking the river and gestured towards a table set with white linen, a vase of white roses in full bloom and chairs for three, a reminder that they were not entirely alone. Her mother would be joining them. 'I took the liberty of arranging for refreshment.' He held out her chair and gave her a melting smile. Today, he was redefining the term 'Prince Charming'.

She gave a nod towards the white roses with a teasing goad. 'No lilies today?' She liked this Prince Charming, but she missed the sharp-edged man who pricked her temper and her conscience.

'White roses suit you. You, too, have layers, I am discovering.' He evaded a direct answer, plucking a rose from the vase and presented it to her with a flourish that was half-mocking gallantry and half-seriousness. 'A token of transient beauty, like Constable's weather.' Their eyes held, something subtle passed between them before he looked beyond her shoulder and straightened. She knew without turning that he'd spotted her mother coming towards them. In that instant, Dove resented her mother's arrival. It would break the spell. There would be no more private riddles about lilies and roses, no more discussion of her art school. He held her gaze for a last, lingering moment as if he, too, felt the loss. 'To transience, my dear,' he murmured, rising from his chair to help her mother and direct the arrival of the tiered tray of cakes and sandwiches and the tea. 'Lady Redruth, come and sit. We have the most splendid view of the Thames and the best of weather in which to enjoy it.'

Dove heard the teasing laughter beneath his words and knew the mention of weather was for her. Even surrounded by others, he'd managed a type of privacy for them alone. What a skill that was and how intoxicating even if she knew it shouldn't be. She really must try harder to resist his charm. Nothing could come of this interlude except memories, which of course assumed the opposite—that she wanted something to come of it. What would that something be? She had the afternoon to ponder it, to watch him in action as he continued to dazzle effortlessly.

Chapter Eight

Oh, he was smooth! She couldn't help but admire the way he talked with her mother, the way he greeted everyone who passed by their table. He seemed to know everyone and their table became a social hub. Before she realised it, they were holding court, or rather the Prince was. People *wanted* to be with him, he was a magnet. And no wonder. Dove noted how he knew something personal about each passer-by. He'd ask after a favourite horse, or a beloved relative. No one was beneath his notice or attention; not the ageing aunts who'd been pressed into chaperon duty to earn their keep, not the spinsters whom society had overlooked, not the enterprising mothers who had dragged their daughters over to meet her and her mother, but in reality had come to the table to see him. He was generous with them all.

Extra chairs were brought over, the tiered tea tray was refilled twice and still the people came. Gentle-

men with ladies on their arms strolled by to exchange
a brief word, the women eyeing her with calculated
speculation. Dove could see the question in their
eyes: what was she doing with the Season's most coveted bachelor? There was speculation in the gentlemen's eyes as well. What was the Prince doing with
the Season's most anticipated debutante? She could
almost hear their thoughts: hadn't she been intended
for someone more traditional? Someone more *English*? Had everyone known, then? Was she the only
one who hadn't truly understood what her debut had
meant? Society had already decided her future when
she had not even grasped it.

There was a certain tension beneath the gentlemen's bonhomie. Dove slid her glance towards Illarion as recognition flared. The men were wary of
him. He didn't belong, not quite, despite the fact that
he was like them in many ways. He had wealth, he
had a title, dubious as it might be. Still, he wasn't one
of them. He was an outsider, not entirely accepted
because he was different. Did Illarion understand
that? It put his clothing at her ball into a new light.
Had his choice of evening attire been a small rebellion on his part? A chance to thumb his nose at society with its rules?

If such things bothered Illarion, he didn't show it.
But the realisation gave her yet another lens through
which to view him, this time as a man far from home.
A man alone in a new world. Not unlike herself. Each
day she was here, Cornwall seemed further away,

taking her true self with it. Did he feel that way about Kuban? She had not believed him yesterday when he'd said he knew something of homesickness. Today, she thought she might have erred. She might have erred in other ways, too. His attraction was not just the physical impact of his looks—although some women would never look further—it was in how he made people *feel*. Despite their wariness, people couldn't help but like him, at least for the moment. It was hard to dislike someone who showed an interest in you. It had worked with her, after all, hadn't it?

The flow of guests past their table fell off, giving Dove a moment of quiet. Her fingers itched to pick up a pencil and draw him, to see beyond the planes and lines of the straight nose, the strong jaw, beyond the leonine lengths of his champagne-coloured hair. If she could draw him, she could know him.

A shadow fell across their table, the brief respite interrupted by Percivale himself. 'Ah, I thought I'd find you here at the centre of attention,' he effused, offering a short bow that encompassed all of them, although it was not clear if his words were meant as a compliment to her or a reprimand to Illarion. Of all the men who had come by the table, Percivale's wariness towards Illarion was the most palpable. 'You seem to be at the centre of everything these days, Kutejnikov.' Ah, so he had meant to snub Illarion with his remark. It was a further snub to forgo any reference to Illarion's title. 'You must be enjoying your first Season in London.' Another reference to Illarion's status as an outsider to the elite circles of the *ton* where everyone had known everyone for generations. His gaze drifted over the crumbly remains of the oft-filled tea tray.

'I apologise for not having anything to offer you.' Illarion's tone was generous, overlooking the insult. 'But as you can see, you've caught us at the end of our refreshment.' Translation: *you are late to the party, old chap.* The tray had been replenished several times already, but Illarion made no move to refill it now. Something competitive and primal sprang up between the two men.

'No bother.' Percivale dismissed the tray as unimportant. 'I only stopped by to pay my respects.' His gaze moved to her, his blue eyes lacking the lively flame of Illarion's. They were empty, simply blue and nothing more. 'I hope you enjoyed the exhibit, Lady Dove?'

She opened her mouth to reply, but he went on without stopping. 'You didn't find looking at all the art too tedious? There are so many pictures on the walls they all start to look alike.' There was another strike against him. She'd been unable to imagine sharing the exhibit with Percivale and she'd been right. While Illarion had planned an outing that would please her, Percivale didn't even know she enjoyed art. She could spend hours looking at the paintings, studying each line, each colour choice, each brush stroke, but he dismissed each individual work collectively within seconds. If he was a smart

man, he would stop here. But Percivale wasn't done
with his self-immolation.

'Such a to-do every year over paintings. It's ridiculous the Royal Academy insists on creating a
profession out of being an artist. A hobby is one
thing, tolerable even. But encouraging it as a career
in this day and age? It's almost irresponsible.' He was
speaking to Illarion now. 'I'm a scientist myself. In-
ventions, steam, industrialisation, that's where true
innovation lies.'

It took all her willpower not to argue that art
was a form of human expression, a form of innovation that captured the essence of the human experience. But Dove needn't have worried. Illarion was
all too ready to make the argument on her behalf.
'I think some might disagree with you, Percivale.
Lady Dove, herself, is a fine artist. She draws, did
you know?'

'A fine hobby for a woman, something to occupy
her time and her mind.' Percivale nodded, oblivious to the caution, the clue, Illarion had tossed him.
Dove, however, was not oblivious. Did Percivale
think such remarks made him sound liberated? Illarion was making Percivale look like a fool. No,
she amended. Illarion had given him a last lifeline
to retract his tactless comment and Percivale had
eschewed it.

'Lady Dove was sharing with me that she runs a
school in Cornwall for children where she teaches
them painting and drawing.' Illarion added, 'So that

they might have new channels of expression available to them. *I* think it's quite noble of her.'

'To be sure, Lady Dove is generous to those less fortunate,' Percivale dismissed with a smile that bordered on condescending. 'Do you have much industry where you're from, Kutejnikov?' The comment was meant as an insult against Kuban and its reported isolation, bordered by the Turks and not much else.

'No,' Illarion answered evenly with a misleading smile that implied friendship where there was none. 'Unlike England, we have eschewed the ugliness of coal mines and factory cities for the natural beauty of nature.' On that note, Illarion rose and offered an arm to her and to her mother. 'Lady Dove, Lady Redruth, shall we go? I told my driver to bring the carriage around at four. He'll be waiting for us. Lord Percivale, if you will excuse us?' It was all masterfully done. One way to win an argument was to simply leave it. She would have to remember the tactic. It was a small satisfaction to be able to walk away while Lord Percivale was still picking his jaw up from the floor.

The Prince was making a perfect muddle of the Season! The man had no breeding. He'd dismissed a future duke, for heaven's sake. What sort of gentleman behaved like that? Percivale was just glad no one had been about to see it. It had been humiliating. Never one to voice an opinion the majority might find unpopular, Percival took consolation in the fact that he wasn't alone in these thoughts.

By the time he arrived at White's to fortify himself for another evening out amongst the *ton*, others had gathered to express the same sentiment. 'The damned foreigner didn't know the least about how it's supposed to work,' one gentlemen announced with authority.

'He thinks he's better than us,' said another.

'It's not just that,' came a man from the corner, a young baronet newly up from the country, hoping to catch a bride with little more than his looks. 'He's taken all the ladies' attentions. The ladies aren't interested in us when he's nearby.' That remark got a response. The volume in the club rose as men shared their experiences: the women loved his hair, his blue eyes, the way he danced, his accent.

One of Percivale's close friends, young Viscount Heatherly, nudged him. 'What are your thoughts, Percivale? He's been spending time in Lady Dove's court.'

Percivale shrugged as if he wasn't bothered. 'Lady Dove is popular, everyone spends time in her court. Even you.' He elbowed his friend good naturedly. He was smart enough to avoid giving an outward show of fear.

'He took her to the Academy today, I hear,' Heatherly pressed.

'Yes, I know. I saw them and stopped to chat.' Never mind he'd been dismissed. Heatherly and these chaps didn't need to know that. All they needed to know was he was not bothered by the Prince's attentions towards his intended. Everyone knew Lady Dove was his, *destined* for him even. Everyone knew grand families married grand families and they were two of the grandest. It would be the height of insecurity if he worried aloud. Besides, he was confident in his own appeal. He was attractive and he'd just become more so. A note had arrived that morning informing him that his ageing uncle was sickly and taking a turn for the worse. The title of Ormond was closer than ever. He'd meant to share the news with Lady Dove today, until Kutejnikov had ruined his plans.

Lady Dove Sanford-Wallis and her dowry was *his*. To be sure, he didn't like discovering that she'd gone driving with the Prince yesterday and out with him again today. It had all been very proper. Her mother had been along. But two days in a row? Percivale knew what the Prince wanted—her money, like every other man in London. Rumour had it the Prince had some wealth of his own, but no land to go with it. He was an exiled upstart. What better way to establish himself than to marry a woman of substance, acquire some land through her and even some social standing, before his popularity ran out or something unsavoury was discovered? Percivale was confident in one thing: the Prince would dig his own grave as so many who didn't truly belong in society did. It was the circle of *ton*nish life. Under no circumstance would he panic over the Kubanian upstart.

Percivale looked around the club, listening to the rising conversations of discontent. It was always intriguing to him to watch society work and it was definitely at work now, an organism recognising a foreign subject and labouring to expel it. Did the Prince understand London's gentlemen had just declared war on Illarion Kutejnikov?

Chapter Nine

Apparently Percivale hadn't taken his dismissal at the Academy well, Illarion mused from his place on Dove's left side as her court gathered during intermission at the Hamptons' musicale. Since the Academy art show, Percivale had been *glued* to Dove. The young scion spent copious amounts of the evening flashing dagger glares in Illarion's direction. Not that such looks intimidated Illarion. It wasn't the first time Illarion had made an enemy over a woman. Neither was it the first time ballrooms had become battlefields where a pretty one was concerned. Illarion knew how to play that game. Too well. It would take more than thunderous stares from an ego-bruised young nobleman to send him scurrying in the other direction.

Tonight, Percivale was going on about an upcoming debate in Parliament. Percivale caught his eye, his raised eyebrow an attempt to call attention to his superiority as if to say here was a man who cared about England, who spent his days pursuing the work of his country, as opposed to Illarion, a prince from a foreign land who spent his days doing who knew what?

Illarion met Percivale's gaze with a broad, easy smile. Percivale had guessed wrong if he thought such tactics would succeed in driving him from Dove's side. In fact, Percivale's tactics had done just the opposite. Illarion was determined to stand his ground.

He would have done so on principle alone. He would never back down to a man like Percivale. His reputation as a bold lover demanded it. But he had practical reasons, too. He'd found his muse. He was writing again, meaningful poems that went beyond the drivel he'd managed to pen since he'd arrived. There were other reasons, too. He was not in the habit of abandoning a damsel in distress and tonight Dove looked as if she could use a champion. Something had happened. Something was wrong.

His gaze slid to Dove standing between him and Percivale. The average onlooker would notice nothing. She was poised as always and had obviously been well schooled in hiding any upset she might feel. She looked stunning, turned out in a white-satin gown with hints of ice-blue undertones that played to the platinum depths of her hair. While the other girls looked like a spring bouquet in their pastel yellow and pinks, Dove looked calm and collected. Where the other girls looked like flowers on the verge of

wilting as the night wore on, Dove remained fresh
and cool, untouched by the heat of the evening. But
Illarion knew differently. It was there behind her
eyes, in the faint furrow in her brow that deepened
the longer Percivale spoke.

Since the Academy he'd been playing with the
metaphor of an iceberg and the idea that an iceberg
hid so much of itself below the surface. His haughty
debutante was like that iceberg. There was more to
her than first impressions implied. Dove Sanford-
Wallis *loved* art; she ran an art school for village
children; she understood what art—any art—offered
to the human soul; she missed her home. Because
of his own experience, he understood why leaving
home had been difficult for her. Like him, she'd not
only left the familiar geography of home, she'd left
people. Homes could be replaced, the way his friend,
Nikolay, was rebuilding his through his Russian riding school. But one could not replace people.

Percivale was still going on. Illarion allowed a
small glance of empathy in Dove's direction. The
fringes of a smile played on her lips. Didn't Percivale
know one *did not* offer details on such things at an
evening out? The man had taken up the entire intermission with his prosing. The men in Dove's court
only stayed for her. Was Percivale aware of that? *She*
had drawn them. They stayed for her. The men tolerated him because of Dove. Across the circle, young
Alfred-Ashby idly shifted from foot to foot, as did
several of the others. Did Dove see it? Illarion won-

dered. Did she understand this was what life would be like married to Strom Percivale, future Duke of Ormond, commander of ten seats in the House? Political powerhouse he might be, but he needed a strong hostess beside him. Perhaps she *did* understand and that was the source of her discontent.

He needed to get her alone. Illarion was damned if he'd spend the evening listening to an attractive but mediocre Italian soprano with a dubious accent for nothing. He'd come tonight to challenge Percivale, certainly, but he'd also come to see Dove. A muse wasn't a muse if he couldn't spend time with her, to be inspired by her and, if the truth be told, to protect her. Dove not only inspired him with her sharp wit, but the more he knew of her, the more he liked her, this heiress who taught children to draw. He did not want to see her sacrificed into a loveless marriage. He wanted to show her she didn't have to settle for such a decision. That was the problem with innocence, it was like being blind. So many girls did not fully understand what they were getting into. How could they? Dove stirred him and, in return, he felt an obligation to protect her.

Protect her? For what purpose? He knew what he was protecting Dove from, but that prompted the question of 'for'. What was he saving her for? What happened to her if she didn't marry the likes of Percivale and take up her place in society? It meant she could be his muse a bit longer. But that wasn't protection, was it? It was selfish to keep her from Percivale when he had nothing to offer her as an alternative, yet Illarion couldn't resist. The twin temptations of challenging and championing were too much.

Lady Hampton begin ushering guests back to their seats in the music room; Intermission was over. Rule number one of any ballroom battle: don't leave the room until you get what you came for. It was time to separate Dove from the crowd. This would be the tricky part with Percivale nearby likely hoping for the same thing. He'd extricated more difficult women than one debutante from a crowd before. There'd been the *excellent* Italian soprano in Vienna, the French ambassador's wife, the Hapsburg Princess— needless to say, he was something of an expert. Although this would be the first time he'd attempted to extricate a woman of Dove's calibre.

He was not in the habit of stealing off with virginal debutantes. Too risky. If one was caught with the notorious wife of an ambassador, so be it. One weathered the scandal, which lasted maybe three days until it was superseded by something else, and moved on. There was no moving on from being caught with a duke's daughter. The only move was to the altar, which seemed to be the one place neither he nor Dove were interested in going.

Illarion set his gambit in play. 'Lady Dove, I have seats where the acoustics are excellent. It would be an honour if you would join me for the second half of the performance.' Illarion boldly put a hand to her back, ready to escort her, hoping she'd take the hint and start moving. One way to settle any question was to walk away while still waiting for an answer, especially if that answer might not be the one you want. It was exactly what he'd done in Kuban. He'd walked away and kept going until he hit London. Tonight, he just had to walk to the next room.

Fortunately, Dove was an eager study. 'Thank you, your Highness, I am enjoying the music very much. Are you?' She might have been overly bright in her response, but it was another successful trick to extricating oneself; using conversation to define the size of your circle. With her question, the circle had just shrunk to two, much to Percivale's glaring dismay. Gentlemen muttered disappointment behind them as Illarion moved Dove into the conservatory, leading her to two seats in the back by the garden doors. They were ignoble seats, to be sure. Hardly the finest in the house. Lady Hampton had seated him back here, out of the way, where one would not be noticed. Illarion suspected Percivale, who was fast friends with Lady Hampton, had something to do with that. But Percivale had overlooked the charms of these seats, located so close to the French doors.

'Are the acoustics truly any better back here?' Dove whispered, settling her ice-blue skirts.

'Depends on whether or not you like the music.' Illarion lowered his voice. 'When I said the acoustics were better, I meant it was quieter.' He gestured with a nod towards the French doors. 'If you felt faint during the performance, we could manage to take

the air unobtrusively.' Then he added, 'It's been difficult to get you alone these past few days.'

His admission caught her by surprise. Her eyes
widened slightly. 'Have you wanted to? I heard…'
She paused, rethinking her word choice, no doubt
to avoid coming across as jealous or gossipy. 'I
mean, you've been busy.' She sounded cooler, more
in control like the woman he'd encountered on the
dance floor that first night. 'You had a reading at
the Countess of Somersby's. You've had quite a few
there, I hear.'

Ah, so she knew. He'd done a reading of a new,
highly erotic piece that he considered not half bad
at the intellectual all-male salon held by the Dowa-
ger Countess of Somersby. Most of London knew,
the poem wasn't a secret any more than the Countess's licentiousness was. But somehow, Dove knowing he'd done such a thing took the shine off it. The
poem was called 'Primavera', the culmination of one
of the poems he'd drafted that first day by the Long
Water, the product of the heated images he'd conjured in the gardens of Kuban House. He wondered
how Dove would feel if he told her she had inspired
it? Exposed? Embarrassed? Empowered? Perhaps a
little of all three. Maybe someday he'd tell her. Tonight he'd stay with more mundane topics. 'I wanted
to talk with you about your art school. There was so
little time to speak of it at Somerset House.'

'My art school?' Her question was rife with wary
cynicism. 'Most men don't want to talk about my art

school.' Unless they wanted something badly, was the implied message.

'Most gentlemen are not artists themselves.' It was true, he did want to hear about the school, although Illarion suspected he'd talk to her about any number of things if it meant getting her alone in the moonlight, having a chance to watch her come alive, to set aside the cool mask she wore night after night in the ballrooms. That was the woman who inspired him, the woman the rest of the *ton* didn't get to see. But he also wanted to make sure she was all right. Perhaps it was nothing after all. She seemed better now that they were alone.

Dove slanted him a coy smile that was misleadingly worldly as the Italian soprano took the stage. 'If it's my art school you want to hear about, be prepared. I might feel faint right before the second aria.'

Good heavens, what was she doing? Accepting an invitation to walk alone with a man? Her response shocked Dove. She knew better. She should *not* be encouraging this radical Prince who whispered rebellion in her ear. But here she was, agreeing to go out into the gardens with him for reasons she didn't entirely understand except that they seemed a preferable alternative to sitting here listening to the soprano. The problem with her reasoning was that Illarion had become a preferable alternative to so many things and to so many people: to Alfred-Ashby,

to Fredericks, most of all, to Percivale. He was the
real threat these days.

Several rows in front, Percivale's blond head took
his seat. Not for the first time, Dove wondered why
she couldn't like him. Everything would be easier
if she did. What wasn't there to like? He was good
looking, titled, wealthy, all the things she was raised
to respect and *expect* in a proper husband, yet she
could not fathom herself married to him. Why? What
was wrong with her that she wanted to avoid that
fate? That she was willing to risk her parents' disappointment by sneaking out with Illarion? Her parents would not approve of her going into the gardens
when they heard of it. And they *would* hear of it.
Her godmother, her chaperon tonight, although Lady
Burton was sitting only rows away with old friends,
would tell them.

The dark-haired soprano began the first aria.
She still had time to back out, but Dove knew she
wouldn't. The clock on her freedom was ticking.
Percivale had called today to speak with her father
about his uncle's feeble health. Time was running
out. If she couldn't turn back time, she had to focus
on making each remaining minute count.

Getting to the gardens was far too easy. Sitting
in the back of the room had its merits and she gave
herself credit for doing a passable job of waving
her fan and leaning on Illarion's arm should anyone have been watching. 'You might have a career
in theatre if this debutante thing doesn't work out.'

Illarion laughed as they reached the freedom of the gardens.

Dove laughed, too. 'The soprano, she was terrible. Do you really think she was from Italy? I can't imagine her appeal.'

'I think she appeals mostly to men. I heard Lord Hampton was the one who arranged for her to sing,' he offered.

Dove slid him a look, ignoring the other implication. 'Lord Hampton is tone deaf, then.'

'And his wife is blind,' Illarion alluded cryptically as they walked the cobbled paths. 'A perfect pair.' He gestured to the sky and Dove followed his arm up to the stars. 'There's another perfect pair; Polaris and the Plough, as you say in England.'

Dove looked but didn't find it immediately. Illarion leaned close with more instruction. He smelled of patchouli, exotic and exciting. 'To the left a bit, there! Do you see it, Polaris, the brightest star in the sky.'

'I have it now.' She lifted her finger to trace the lines of the constellation. 'Do you not call it the Plough in Kuban?'

'No, we call it the Great Bear. Bears are important symbols in Russian folk culture. To have one in the sky looking down on us makes sense.'

'You're a poet and an astronomer?' she teased, part of her thrilling to learn another piece of him.

Illarion shook his head. 'A poet is a little bit of everything. I think he has to be in order to write about the world and its emotions. A poet has to see connections between the external world and the internal soul.'

She was quiet before she spoke again, pondering the depths of the remark. 'I think a good artist must see that connection, too, in order to capture a face or a scene. I do not have that, I think. My life has been sheltered.' By extension, her art had been limited, too. She tilted her face to the sky, her eyes searching. 'What else is up there, I wonder?'

'Everything. Secrets, planets, maybe even worlds we haven't found yet. The sky is eternity,' Illarion murmured. She was aware of him close behind her, of the slight movement it had taken to draw her close, his arms wrapped about her waist. His back was conveniently to the conservatory, blocking any view of her. No one could see his hands about her. He began to talk, a quiet murmur for her alone. 'Our skies are clear in Kuban. At night, the sky is covered in stars, like brilliants on dark blue velvet, twinkling and teasing with their mysteries.'

'There's too much smoke in the city for clear skies very often,' Dove admitted. 'There are clear skies in Cornwall, too. One night, I took the children out to a meadow for an evening picnic and we painted the stars.' She'd never been touched like this, never held like this. It was both natural and exciting. On the one hand, it felt right to be here in his arms looking at the sky. On the other hand, it conjured up hopes—would he try to kiss her again? Would she allow it this time?

'You miss Cornwall. I would never have guessed the sophisticated miss I'd waltzed with at Lady Burton's was a country girl at heart,' he teased.

She nodded. 'I do. As do you, I think. You miss Kuban. Whenever you talk of it, you say "we" as if you still belong there, as if London isn't your home yet.' They had more in common than she first realised. London wasn't her home yet either. They both clung desperately to the homes of their childhood, the only homes they'd known. Perhaps, like her, he had not given up his home entirely at will either.

'Kuban is the only home I've known.' Illarion sighed and she enjoyed the feel of him against her, the smell of him as she listened. He spun tales for her straight from his memories, painting word pictures for her of summers spent at the summer palace with its fountains and parks. And she fell in love with the beauty of Kuban: boating on the lakes, fishing in the rivers; autumns spent hiking the mountains until snow fell; winters spent indoors near elaborately tiled *kachelofen* staying warm and listening to stories while wolves howled outside. He told her of Maslenitsa, the holiday that signalled the end of winter and the coming of spring, and always the food; the honey cakes and the *piroshkis*.

'*Piroshkis* are peasant food, some say.' Illarion described the hot, spicy meat wrapped in a pastry. 'But in Kuban we are hardy folk, not everyone is so lofty. My friend Nikolay Baklanov's family are Cossacks from the Steppes, what some would call not

true royalty in the sense that they are not from the
great families of St Petersburg.' He gave her a history
then, explaining how Kuban was a new province,
only recently settled by Russia to protect territorial
claims and to push Russia's interest in Turkey. 'We
are three generations old.'

'And your family? Are they Cossacks, too?' Dove
asked, breathless from his tales. Did he understand
what a gift he'd given her tonight? The sharing had
been honest and heartfelt, so different than the drawing room tittle-tattle that ruled her days. It was yet
another surprise in an evening full of them. When
she'd anticipated the evening, it had been with dread
and fear of boredom. It might have started that way,
but it was not ending that way.

'No, we are from St Petersburg originally. I'm too
blond to be a Cossack.' Illarion laughed. My family
sought to win the Tsar's favour by being the first
to settle in Kuban. It worked. My grandfather was
made a prince and his family was given a position
of status in the new royal court with all the riches
and estates that went with such a title. It was an ad-
dictive lifestyle. But to keep that status, to sustain
that addiction, one has to stay co-operative. That is
easier said than done at times.' There was a mystery behind those last words, but tonight was not the
night to probe it.

'I envy you.' Dove sighed. 'You've seen so much,
you've had so many experiences. I have seen little
and that is not likely to change. I did not under-

stand that until I came here and saw what it was really like—a handing off of sorts, a changing of the guard. I know it's meant to keep me safe, to keep the world out. But that's not how I see it. It's meant to keep me in.' Her voice broke and she stopped for fear she'd break down entirely.

'Dove, what has happened? I could tell tonight that something was not right,' Illarion whispered and the temptation to tell him was too great. When had he become her friend? Her confidante? The one she wanted to run to?

'Percivale met with my father to share that his uncle is ill, perhaps for the last time. Percivale will become Ormond soon.' She waited for him to see the implications of that. He did not disappoint. Of course, a prince like himself would understand the intricacies of inheriting and mourning.

'He will want to marry before his uncle passes. If he does not marry before, he'll have to wait until after mourning. It would delay him.'

'Yes.' Dove felt the panic rise in her when she allowed herself to think about how that affected her. She wouldn't have even the Season of her childish fairy tales. They would marry in June, barely a month after her debut, or sooner if his uncle showed signs of worsening. 'I know it's silly, but I have these images of being awakened in the middle of the night and rushed downstairs in my nightclothes to marry Percivale in the drawing room before his uncle breathes his last.'

'Every girl dreams of her wedding being a beautiful occasion,' Illarion prompted. He wasn't empathising with her, she knew, he was forcing her to admit to the real fear.

She shook her head. 'It's not the lack of a grand wedding that panics me, it's the suddenness, the not knowing. My life hangs by a thread.' It was her very own sword of Damocles. She tried to explain it was her freedom being cut without warning, being bundled into a life not of her making without a chance to protest, that terrified her.

Illarion had gone still while she spoke, his words quiet and urgent when she finished. 'Then you will have to speak up before it's too late or what you fear, Dove, will absolutely come to pass.'

She gave a bleak laugh. 'That's not the reassurance I hoped for.'

He turned her to face him, tipping her chin up to meet his gaze. 'No, but it's the honesty I've promised you.' From inside, the soprano had been replaced by a string quartet. Strains of a Vivaldi Adagio wafted out into the garden. 'Dance with me, Dove, beneath the stars and forget about Percivale for a night.'

His hand was warm and natural at her back as if it belonged there, as if *she* belonged there, with him. It was a slippery slope to seduction, then. She didn't stop him from moving her into an improvised waltz, she didn't stop him when he whispered provocative rebellion in her ear. 'You don't have to choose Percivale. It *can* be different.' She certainly didn't stop him when his mouth took hers in a kiss designed to show her how different it could be.

She was ready for him this time, hungry for him even in ways she'd not anticipated. Her lips opened for him, her arms reaching about his neck, the form of their waltz giving way to a more intimate posture, their bodies melding as the kiss deepened. She felt the hard planes of him beneath his clothes, the strong press of his hand at the back of her neck, the sensual flick of his tongue tasting her in slow teasing strokes that brought heat low in her belly and a dampness between her thighs.

'Illarion.' She ventured his name in a tiny, breathless gasp, as if saying his name, that one single word, expressed the sum of her feelings. This was what she'd dreamed of when she'd thought of her Season, of being swept away, of seeing her future in a single kiss.

'You deserve *this*,' Illarion whispered, hushing her with another kiss, another bout of intoxication. She breathed in the scent of him, savoured the touch of him, his hands on her, her hands on him; it was too easy to let her senses overwhelm her thinking, especially when thinking was too dangerous here in the garden. A woman might do anything if she believed those words, if she believed that kiss. It would change everything.

If he cried foul, it would change everything. Percivale crushed the remains of his cheroot under a heel with some force as he watched the scene in the garden. He'd come out for a smoke and this was what he'd found: Lady Dove waltzing with Prince Kutejnikov; Prince Kutejnikov *kissing* her with little regard for restraint! The damnable thing about it was that he could do nothing. If he called attention to it, Lady Dove would be compromised. She would be required to marry the Prince and that was precisely not what Percivale wanted. She was lovely and fine, well bred and precisely what he wanted in a duchess. She would run his home and raise his children, his heir, and do him proud at every turn. Although, at this particular turn, she'd momentarily been led astray by the guile of a more experienced man with no honour. But he wondered, watching her with the Prince, if she would ever gaze upon him with that same look, as if the stars were in his eyes instead of the sky. Fear of losing came to Percivale, who had never been denied anything in the entirety of his perfect life, for the first time. Something must be done about the Prince. Surely Lady Dove wasn't the first woman he'd led astray. Heatherly and the others were right. The Prince must be stopped. He posed a danger to them all. But it must be done carefully, quietly, so as not to alienate the women folk who were so desperately taken with him, even if it was being done to protect them.

Chapter Ten

White's was crowded for this time of day. Everyone, apparently, had got wind that there'd be vodka tasting this afternoon. For many, the certainty of drink among manly company had trumped the idea of tea and cakes under the watchful eyes of the *ton*'s matchmaking mamas.

Men pressed around Illarion as he held up a glass of clear liquid and called for attention with a provocative line. 'Vodka is like a good woman, pure to the eye and soft when it goes down.' Men chuckled, adding a few bawdy comments of their own before Stepan called them to order for a more academic explanation.

Illarion sat back and watched his friend work. He'd done his job by getting the group started; now Stepan could do his magic. He was hoping to convince White's victualler to import vodka, along with several other gentlemen present today as well. Stepan, it seemed, had decided if he couldn't be in Kuban, he was going to bring Kuban to London.

Well, to each their own, Illarion silently toasted his friend. They all had to make peace with leaving. Prince Nikolay Baklanov sat across from him, making a rare appearance in order to support Stepan's venture. These days, Nikolay was busy with his new wife and new riding academy. Nikolay was happy. He had found his peace. Illarion envied him. The rest of them were still looking for it. Illarion wondered if he would ever find it. After a year, perhaps he'd been wrong in thinking a change of scenery would help him exorcise the past. Perhaps nothing would. After last night in the Hampton gardens he was more aware than ever how closely Dove's situation paralleled Katya's. What had started as the seeking of a muse to help with the exorcism of past demons had stirred the demons to life instead of squashing them to death.

Of course, not everything was parallel. He'd not kissed Katya, had not written an erotic poem about her. Katya had been his muse, but never his lover. That was where the two situations diverged. With Dove, he wanted more than a muse, more than a friendship. He'd never deliberately attempted to lead Katya away from her decision. Perhaps that had been his mistake. Perhaps he should have. Perhaps he should not have stood by as an empathetic shoulder to cry on, but nothing more. He was attempting to atone for that with Dove. He was showing her what she was sacrificing. That, too, was a dangerous choice. He would have to assume responsibility for the consequences should she decide to refuse Percivale.

Illarion held his glass to the light, playing along with the others, testing the vodka's luminescence while his thoughts ran elsewhere, another sensual poem taking shape in his mind: *vodka like a woman, pure in the light, soft in the night...a creamy swallow of sweet on the tongue.* It was a bit too superficial for his taste, proof that his writer's block still persisted. But it was the sort of poem the Countess of Somersby would appreciate. The Countess made no demure about what she wanted from him—the novelty of a Russian lover in her bed. He could be her consort for the Season.

It was precisely the sort of liaison society expected him to make, the dashing, rakish Prince with the licentious widow. It would allow society to continue to romanticise him, to tolerate him without having to truly accept him. He could be a Russian Byron and bed all the merry widows he liked, just as long as he stayed away from their pure-bred English virgins.

It was also the sort of liaison he'd been looking for when the Season had begun, something physically consuming. He had no doubt the Countess was a liberated bed partner who could keep his body and mind busy until August. She was well read, intelligent and not without her own brand of power. But the Countess did not inspire him. She was too cynical, too worldly. She did not need him. While she might appreciate the sensual vodka poem forming in his head, it was not the Countess who inspired it, or anything else he'd written lately. *Vodka, clear and pure, quicksilver like her eyes.* No, the Countess could be his lover, but not his muse, even if he were interested. There was a difference between the two.

In Kuban, he'd often had both at the same time in two different women. A lover who took care of his body and a muse who took care of his soul, the caretaker of his spirit's flame, the thing that lived at the core of himself. His body merely housed that flame. Never had he found women who could combine both roles. Which was not to say he had not found passion with a muse, or two, or three. He had indeed taken several to bed over the years, but those had been spontaneous occasions with no expectation of a long-term attachment.

It was not the sort of spontaneity he could enjoy with Lady Dove. To take her to bed would require an understanding of the matrimonial sort. He did not deal in those, but he couldn't deny the physical pull of her. He'd been attracted to her looks since the first night in Lady Burton's ballroom. That attraction had only deepened as their association lengthened. Last night in the garden had been proof of that. She'd been exquisite, her face tilted to the stars, her eyes the colour of moonlight, her body warm and aroused yet innocent. Just thinking of awakening that innocence, the possibility of bedding her was tempting. He realised with a rather visceral intensity that he wanted to be her first lover, the lover who showed her passion's promise, that he could not bear the idea of someone else having that opportunity, of having *her*.

When they'd danced, he'd held a moonbeam. There was poetry in that image. It was laying in fragments on sheets of paper in his room. How long would his moonbeam last? Already, she understood her fate too well, as did he. Percivale and society would not let her play the moonbeam for long. Marriage to Percivale would crush her, slowly, accidentally even, over the years, wearing down her joy, her dreams, until she was a shadow of her former self, her ebullience lost. Illarion swallowed down the last of his vodka. What would it take to save her from that fate?

Around him the men started to applaud, bringing his thoughts back to the present. The vodka tasting was going well. Nikolay had his sword out, balancing a full glass on the flat of the blade while Stepan and Ruslan each held an end steady. It was an old Cossack ritual of manhood to drink a glass from a blade without spilling or cutting oneself. Nikolay was just about to drink when the door to White's opened, a group of gentlemen entered laughing, walking sticks swinging, expressions freezing, good humour evaporating when they laid eyes on the group. Viscount Heatherly and Percivale were at the centre. 'Well, what do we have here?' The derision in Heatherly's tone was thinly disguised.

'Vodka tasting.' Ruslan came forward with a tray

of glasses, sweeping aside any acknowledgement of hostility. 'Join us. Prince Baklanov is about to demonstrate an old Cossack tradition.'

The group ignored the offer, letting the immaculate Heatherly speak for them. 'I understand vodka is nothing more than fermented potatoes, the food of serfs and Irishmen.' This got a cold round of laughter from the group. Illarion's gaze drifted over Percivale. Heatherly might be the one engaging, but Percivale made no move to intervene and put a stop to it. Perhaps Percivale had orchestrated this, put Heatherly up to it as he might have put Lady Hampton up the seating arrangement last night. That was the way of the *ton*—indirectness. It prevented Illarion from outright accusing Percivale of any wrongdoing.

Well, he simply wasn't going play that game. Illarion rose and stepped towards the newcomers. This wasn't about vodka, not really. It was about him. 'You're mistaken, Lord Heatherly. Vodka is the drink of all Russians.' He held his arms out wide and proceeded to quote, 'Prince Vladimir in the tenth century remarked, "Drinking is the joy of all Rusi. We cannot do without it."'

'Here, here!' Nikolay seconded, clinking glasses with anyone near him, rousing the quieted group surrounding Stepan, many of whom were looking uneasy, perhaps reconsidering their association. 'I dare say we're not alone in that.' Illarion felt Nikolay's presence at his shoulder—Nikolay the warrior, Nikolay who would rather fight than think if given the choice. Illarion wondered where the Cossack sword had ended up. 'Englishmen are so desperate for their brandy they've been known to bring it in illegally.' Nikolay didn't even pretend to be polite. No one was allowed to insult the motherland in his presence. Nikolay remained fiercely patriotic in spite of exile, believing fully that one could hate one's Tsar, but not one's country.

Something dangerous glinted in Heatherly's eyes as they shifted to Nikolay. 'It could be liquid ambrosia and I still wouldn't drink it with the likes of you. I don't drink with men who claim to be one thing, but are quite another. How interesting that Amesbury died with you and the others here in hot pursuit. Is that what passes as princely behaviour in your country? Running a duke to death?'

'That sounds dangerously close to a slur against my character and my wife's. Would you care to make one or do you insist on hiding behind your insinuations?' Nikolay snarled, still heated over the venomous gossip that surrounded his marriage to the Russian ambassador's daughter, Klara Grigorieva. Illarion put a hand on Nikolay's chest. If Heatherly wasn't careful, there would be blood spilled and it would likely be his. He needed to separate Percivale from the group and take care of the real problem. He gestured towards a table by the window. 'Percivale, a word?'

Percivale was not an unattractive man: tallish, a strong jaw, trademark guinea-gold hair and blue eyes, the kind of looks the English treasured. What went on behind those eyes was anyone's guess. He was something of an emotional vacuum. 'You've behaved inappropriately towards Lady Dove Sanford-Wallis,' Percivale ground out in low tones, showing more feeling than Illarion had seen him display to date. Illarion understood the insults directed at Nikolay now. Percivale had not wanted to publicly implicate the lady in question. Far easier to cast aspersions with a net that caught them all instead of singling him out, so he'd had Heatherly do the dirty work. And why not? Illarion had seen Heatherly shoot at Manton's. The man seldom missed. One would think twice about challenging Heatherly even against the most damning of slander.

Illarion crossed his arms over his chest. 'Are you the lady's champion? Has she come to you with a complaint?'

'She is innocent. She does not understand what a man like you is capable of. I am here to see that she never does.'

'A man like me?' Illarion couldn't resist goading Percivale a little further. 'What sort of man might that be? A royal prince of the house of Kuban, a man with a title that outranks any you currently possess, although I did hear that your uncle had taken a turn for the worse. I am completely a gentleman in all ways according to English standards.'

'A foreigner and a rake,' Percivale snarled. 'You are a prince with no kingdom. That makes you a fortune hunter in my book. You're hardly a prince at all.

A prince would never have done what you did. You were with her *alone* last night. I saw you dancing in the Hamptons' garden. Dancing!' He spat the word as if it were filth in his mouth.

Illarion assessed the situation. Percivale had seen them, likely not just the dancing from the vituperation with which he spoke the word. To his credit, the young man seemed genuinely horrified.

'Apparently you stayed long enough to watch. Did you enjoy that? Some men do.' He saw Percivale's nostrils flare with the implication that coming upon them had been an act of voyeurism. It was a harsh goad, but if Percivale wanted to impugn his honour and sling slanderous barbs, he needed to be prepared for the same in return. Percivale was jealous and there was nothing the man could do without ruining his own chances at winning her. 'You're in quite the pickle. You can't tell anyone what you saw for fear of losing her,' Illarion reminded him.

'I can tell *you*,' Percivale retorted. 'Consider yourself warned. I will see you dead before I allow her to fall into the hands of a scheming foreigner. Dove Sanford-Wallis is mine. I will not be so polite about it next time.' He turned on his heel, collected Heatherly and strode towards the door.

'Are we going to let him go?' Nikolay materialised beside him. 'A sabre slice has a way of changing one's opinions.'

'We will not be cutting anyone today.' Illarion blew out an angry breath. Percivale was not to be underestimated. He commanded the *ton*; he dictated who they associated with, who was received and invited. His remarks could put the princes beyond the pale of society, as he'd demonstrated today. Through Heatherly, he'd dealt Nikolay's fledgling riding school a dangerous blow by unearthing the unsavoury details of Amesbury's death and Nikolay's association with it.

Illarion had seen such games before in the Kubanian court. While he could understand it, he could not tolerate it. He needed to take Dove out of Percivale's orbit. The best way to accomplish that was to keep her too busy to receive the man. But unmarried girls didn't go about with eligible bachelors without a chaperon. He was going to need a lady's help and there was only one that he trusted. 'Nikolay, I need Klara to call on the Duchess of Redruth.'

'Redruth? What the hell are we plotting over here?' Stepan inserted himself between them with an angry whisper. 'Do you know who Redruth is? Next to Ormond, he controls more seats in Parliament than anyone else. Now, what the hell do you want with the Duchess? Tell me you are not having an affair with her? I didn't think she was the sort. Redruth seemed a decent chap the one time I met him.'

'It's not the Duchess, it's the daughter,' Nikolay interrupted, trying to smooth things over, but only making them worse. Illarion cringed and Nikolay stepped back, making excuses about needing to re-join the vodka group.

No one ever accused Stepan of being slow. He crossed his arms. 'Dove Sanford-Wallis? Let me guess, *she* is your new muse?' He grabbed Illar-ion by the arm and dragged him to a quiet corner. 'Good God, Illarion, what are you thinking? Tell me you haven't seduced her yet? You can't seduce her, you know that? You shouldn't even look at her. The betting book lays odds she's promised to…' Ste-pan stopped his worried tirade, the rest of the pieces falling into place for him. 'Percivale.' He pushed a hand through his dark hair. 'Is that what this after-noon was really about? What did you do to warrant Heatherly all but calling Nikolay out?'

'Lady Dove doesn't want to marry Percivale. She's being forced to it by her parents. She doesn't want any of this,' Illarion tried to explain, but Stepan was too fast.

'You have to stop seeing her, immediately. This is not Kuban, Illarion. You can't go about protest-ing and breaking up marriage matches, or writing reckless poetry.'

'It's not reckless,' Illarion said. He hated it when Stepan dismissed his work as frivolous.

Stepan leaned forwards, his voice hushed. 'A woman in Kuban killed herself over one of your poems. Do you want that to happen here?'

'I didn't mean for Katya…' Illarion's voice broke with anger and emotion. 'How dare you of all peo-

ple, *my friend*, suggest the Tsar in all his corruption
was correct that I prompted Katya to suicide? I had
no idea what she intended.' That was the fear that
drove his nightmares, the fear that had driven him
from home—that *he* had killed Katya. She had become a casualty of his war against the marital injus-
tices of Kuban. 'If you were not my friend, I would
call you out for that.'

Stepan lifted a brow. 'Like you did the others?'
Illarion had fought a series of duels before he fled
Kuban, duels for his honour, for Katya's posthumous
name. He'd won them all, but he hadn't really won.
Winning had not changed the accusations, it had
only made people more circumspect as to where they
voiced their opinions. 'Illarion, this is not how we
make friends. London is supposed to be a new start
for all of us. But you are intent on repeating the past.
Let this girl go. She is not your problem.'

'She inspires me.' What if he lost Dove and he
couldn't write again? What if he stepped away and
she married Percivale?

'You can find another muse, one that isn't so much
trouble.' Stepan blew out a breath. 'What happens
when you tell she has a choice and she actually be-
lieves you? What can you offer her?'

'I don't know,' Illarion admitted.

Stepan was quiet. 'You *need* to know before you
take things any further. It's not fair to her. "With
great power comes great responsibility,"' he quoted.
'She has to know what her choices really are and

what they really mean. Life outside the *ton* isn't for everyone, especially a duke's daughter who's been raised to it.'

To which Illarion answered with equal determination, '"The only thing necessary for the triumph of evil is for good men to do nothing."' That was the albatross of Kuban, the millstone that hung about his neck and threatened to drag him down. He'd stood aside and done nothing for Katya. As a result, Ustinov had driven her to her death. It would not happen again, not on his watch.

Stepan sighed. 'What do you mean to do since you don't mean to follow my direction?'

Illarion grinned. 'I mean to take Lady Dove on a picnic.' In the interim, he'd deal Percivale some indirectness of his own, a little poem, perhaps, with a few references only Percivale would understand.

Chapter Eleven

The invitation arrived the next day, sent most properly by Princess Klara Grigorieva Baklanova, requesting the attendance of Lady Dove Sanford-Wallis at a Russian-style picnic to celebrate the beginning of summer as it would be done in St Petersburg. It was all very decorously arranged. The Princess and her husband called for Dove the following afternoon in a black lacquered open-air landau, the Princess dressed in a summery carriage ensemble of robin's egg blue embroidered with yellow flowers, the Prince turned out in English driving clothes, his dark hair pulled back neatly, respectably. That was indeed the word for it: respectable. There were no grounds on which the Duchess of Redruth could find fault with the invitation without insulting the Princess. And yet, Dove knew the occasion had Illarion's stamp all over it. He had planned this, he had put the newly wed Russian Princess up to it—all for her, which prompted numerous questions, most of which began with *why*.

The drive out to Hampstead Heath was pleasant, the weather good and the Baklanovs made excellent company. 'The others will meet us there,' Princess Klara explained, her gaze sliding warmly to her husband. They were a couple obviously in love. They made no secret of holding hands and Dove did not miss the Prince's thumb rolling gently over his wife's knuckles as she spoke. The simple affection of the gesture made Dove's heart clench. She wanted to be cherished the way Prince Nikolay cherished his wife. Such love was possible. The Baklanovs proved it.

Was that why Illarion was doing this? Was this another way of showing her the possibilities of life beyond Percivale and her parents' choices? His kiss, their dance, his arms about her and his words in her ear were still warm in her memory. A reminder of how she felt when she was with him and a reminder of how she did *not* feel with Percivale.

She studied the Baklanovs. There was more between them than kisses. It was more than kisses she craved from Illarion. He wanted to *know* her and she wanted to be *known* by him. She wanted to know him in return, and perhaps, she hoped, he would want to share himself with her. She'd never felt that intensely drawn to another person in her entire life. Certainly not with Percivale. Then came the most wicked thought of them all: *perhaps she never would feel like that with anyone except Illarion.*

Illarion. Percivale. The situation had changed drastically since it had begun. In the beginning, it had been about ideas: the loss of her freedom, the thought of marriage to a man she didn't love, leaving her home, the craving of adventure. It had not been about choosing between Illarion and Percivale. It had been about choosing freedom over entrapment. But at some point, it had become about choosing one man over another. Illarion was her freedom. Percivale was her jailer. Those were dangerous thoughts indeed, especially when she had no claim to Illarion. There was no guarantee *he* would choose her. And yet, here he was arranging for a picnic, a chance for them to be alone. Together.

'Lady Dove, you're a thousand miles from here, is everything all right?' Klara asked.

'I was wondering why Prince Kutejnikov is doing this,' Dove admitted. She had ideas, some of which left her warmer than others. Was he merely showing her life beyond Percivale or was he showing her himself? If Klara knew the answer, she was of no help. She only smiled and pointed in the nearing distance as a white canopy came into view. 'Look, they have everything set up!'

'Everything' was an understatement. An entire camp had been laid out. Dove noticed the details as the carriage came to a halt. Chaise longues, rugs and tables had been set up beneath the wide canopy and servants bustled about with hampers of food. 'We'll never eat that much!' Dove exclaimed.

'You've never seen these boys eat.' Klara laughed, letting Nikolay help her down. 'Besides, it's a point of Russian pride to have lots of food at a picnic.'

Nikolay kissed his bride's cheek. 'All of my favourites, I hope.' Then Illarion was there and Dove forgot all about the affectionate Baklanovs. His hair was pulled back in his usual black bow and he was dressed for the warm spring outdoors in buff breeches, tall boots and a loose white shirt open at the neck. His jacket and waistcoat had already been discarded. He swept her a gallant bow. 'Lady Dove, welcome to our camp. We've been busy.'

'I can see that.' She laughed, relaxing in the festive atmosphere.

'Whenever Nikolay and Klara undertake something it's like a military operation—enormous but well organised.' Illarion kept her hand in his as he led her about the encampment. 'We'll have games.' He gestured towards the archery butts and shooting targets. 'Klara's outrageously good with a pistol. Do *you* do any weaponry?' He cocked a curious brow her way.

Of course the perfect Klara with the perfect husband did guns. One might be intimidated by that. Dove merely laughed. She was in too good of a mood to care. 'What do you think? No, I don't "do" any weaponry.'

Illarion smiled back. 'Then I'll teach you.' Something in those words warmed her and set butterflies fluttering in her stomach, as if he meant to teach her more than archery or shooting. He continued the tour. 'We'll eat. Afterwards I can write and you can draw.'

Just as he'd promised. An artists' picnic. There was only one problem. 'I didn't bring anything.'

His eyes danced. 'I did. But you'll have to wait until after lunch for your surprise,' he teased. 'Then we'll walk. Perhaps we'll find early strawberries. Now, let me introduce you to everyone.' They'd come full circle and 'everyone' turned out to be two men: 'Stepan and Ruslan, two of my best friends.' Stepan was tall, with short dark hair, sharp eyes and a stern demeanour. Ruslan was slender, not quite as tall as the others. He sported a thick gold wave of hair and kind, intelligent eyes with a hint of sadness where Stepan's had been sharp.

It was clear the four men were devoted to each other, like brothers, Dove imagined, watching them ready their pistols and good-naturedly bantering with each other. If her brothers had lived, they would have been of an age with these men. She shoved the image of four little crosses, four little boys who had come before her, aside. This afternoon was not made for sadness.

The princes let Klara shoot first. Dove was impressed. She'd never seen a woman use firearms before and Klara was indeed skilled, hitting the centre of the target. Illarion shot last. He offered his pistol to Dove. 'Would you like to try?'

Dove shook her head. 'Too loud. I'll save myself for archery. It's quieter.' Illarion nodded and stepped up to the line. She couldn't help but notice the manly grace of him. Shooting was far more of an art than she'd thought. She noted the steady strength of Illarion's arm as he extended it, the unimpeachable stillness of his body as he sighted the target. He breathed in, exhaled and fired. His shot was perfect, piercing Klara's with deadly accuracy.

Nikolay whistled. 'That's why you're the best.' He slapped Illarion on the back.

'You're still better shooting off horseback.' Illarion was modest in his victory, but Dove didn't miss the warning glance he shot at Nikolay as if he feared Nikolay would say too much. He held out a hand to Dove. 'Let's try your luck with a bow.' He selected a weapon from the table and led her to the butts, standing behind her as he arranged the bow in her hands, offering instructions.

'Relax,' Illarion spoke softly in her ear. Did he have any idea how impossible it was to do that with him so close? With his body pressed to hers, his hands over hers as they nocked the arrow? This wasn't archery, it was seduction. 'Easy now.' Together, they drew back the arrow. 'And, let fly.' The arrow released, flew and hit the outer ring of the target. Respectable for a first shot. Dove found she liked archery, even when Illarion stepped away and let her shoot on her own. There was a freedom in letting the arrow loose and watching it soar.

Knives were next. She and Klara stood on the sidelines, watching the men throw and argue, nei-

ther of them having a taste for blades, although Illarion had offered to teach her to throw. 'They're like
boys.' Klara laughed as Nikolay and Stepan debated
a throw. 'I like to see them like this, happy and playing.' There was a yelp from the group and Stepan
went down, Nikolay tackling him, followed by a cry
from Nikolay. 'Illarion, grab his legs!'

Dove gasped at the roughness, but Klara assured
her, 'It's always like this, Nikolay and Illarion against
Ruslan and Stepan. The two hotheads against the
two cooler minds.'

Dove shaded her eyes. 'They do this often?' She'd
never seen men behave like that before.

'More often than you think. They've been friends
since childhood, inseparable, Nikolay tells me.' Klara
grew serious. 'They're all each other has, you know.
They left everything behind in Kuban except each
other. They couldn't bear to be parted. I think leaving
was hardest on Nik and Illarion. They had no choice.'
Klara paused, perhaps waiting for her to understand
that what was being shared was important. 'Nik had
done things in Kuban, things that could not be forgiven.'

Dove waited for Klara to say more, but Klara
Baklanova was no gossip. She guarded her husband's
back in all ways. 'And Illarion?' Was Klara imply-
ing that Illarion, too, had done things that could not
be forgiven? By whom? What?

Klara would not tell. 'They can't go back, Lady
Dove. You should know that.'

Questions swarmed through Dove's mind. Why? Why couldn't they go back? Why did Klara think she needed to know? There was no time for questions. The wrestling had ended as suddenly as it had begun. The four men tramped over, arms draped across each other's shoulders.

Illarion's hair had come loose and he was smiling, looking at ease and terribly handsome. 'I'm starved. Let's eat.'

They sat on the rugs beneath the shade of the canopy. Dove helped Klara unload the baskets, Illarion narrating each of the treats brought forth: tomatoes, cucumbers, bread, cold salmon, cheese... 'And my favourite, mushroom *piroshki*.' Illarion took a pastry and unwrapped it, handing it to her. 'Take a bite.'

Dove bit in to the flaky pastry, letting the rich insides fill her mouth. Her eyes went wide as she savoured it. 'I've never tasted anything so good.' She could see her response pleased him and she was touched. Illarion had *wanted* her to like it.

'Now try these.' Illarion assembled her a plate with two delicate crêpes. *'Blinchiki.'*

Her plate was never empty. Illarion kept it full, selecting a little of everything, serving her tiny bites. 'So you can taste it all without getting too full,' he explained, casting a mock scold in Nikolay's direction. Nikolay had piled his plate high and was plowing through quantities of food at record speed. 'There's an art to picnicking, one must slowly graze and discuss.' Everyone laughed. It was the most pleasant afternoon Dove had ever spent, sitting under the canopy, eating and talking as Illarion and his friends regaled her with tales of Kuban and sometimes St Petersburg, where Klara had grown up.

'So this is a real holiday?' Dove asked, finishing her third *blinchiki*. She'd suspected Illarion had made it up as an excuse to have a picnic with her.

'We only have eighty days of summer up north.' Klara settled against Nikolay, getting comfortable. The look on her husband's face suggested he was growing tired of lunch and had other things on his mind. 'We celebrate every one of them. White Nights, we call them, because the sun doesn't set until after midnight. The celebrations go back to Peter the Great, he's the one who started the tradition. One year, I was allowed to stay up for a midnight river cruise to watch the sunset.'

'Sunset at midnight? I don't believe it.' Dove was incredulous. Under the circumstances she might have felt like an outsider. They all had Russia in common. She'd never left Cornwall. But they weren't telling the stories to leave her out. They were telling her the stories to draw her in, to give her a piece of them. A yearning started to blossom. This was what life could be like, not merely a life of freedom, but a life with Illarion, among his friends.

Nikolay shifted and got to his feet, helping Klara rise. 'I think we'll take a walk.' Stepan and Ruslan rose, too, making noises about a walk of their own. Dove noticed they went in a different direction. Nikolay was not in the mood for company.

'Your friends are nice.' Dove said once they were alone. After a day spent surrounded by others, there was a slight awkwardness to the aloneness.

'They are everything to me.' Illarion reached for his canvas bag, the one that carried his travelling desk.

'Are they why you left Kuban? Klara said the four of you couldn't stand to be separated.' Dove ventured tentatively. So many of their conversations had focused on her. They'd spent very little time talking about him. Perhaps today that would change.

'In a way, yes.' Illarion seemed ill at ease with the subject as if it made him nervous. 'Here, I have something for you.' He pulled a small travelling case of art supplies from his bag and gave it to her. 'I thought you might want to draw some memories of today.'

He was changing the subject. For now, Dove let him. She took the case and ran a hand over the smooth surface, aware of his eyes on hers, aware of the closeness of him, his body folded cross-legged across from her on the rug, mere inches between them. 'It's beautiful.' Her voice was bit choked. Even if she didn't draw anything today, she would remember this outing every time she looked at this. 'It's the most thoughtful gift anyone has ever given me. Truly.' So much more thoughtful than flowers or bonbons. This gift was about her, it had been picked out especially for her. The realisation brought her full circle back to the question that had started the day.

Dove set the box aside. 'Why are you doing this? This picnic, this box, meeting your friends.' *Giving me a glimpse of your soul.* What he couldn't, or wouldn't, tell her about Kuban, he was showing her the best way he could.

'What am I doing, Dove?' The back of his hand skimmed the curve of her cheek. His voice was low and private for her alone.

She gathered her courage. In her gut, she knew what he was doing. But to say it out loud would take bravery. If she was wrong, she would feel foolish. Would he laugh at her? No, Illarion was not like that. She let her eyes meet his. 'You are seducing me.'

He did not laugh. His gaze did not waver. His hand drifted to the column of her throat. 'And if I am?' He didn't deny it.

Her mouth went dry. She cleared her throat to speak. 'I would have to ask myself what you want.' His mouth brushed hers in the gentlest of kisses.

'That should be obvious, Dove.' His hands worked the pins free in her hair, his voice at her ear. 'I want you.'

Chapter Twelve

Wanted, yearned, desired her in so many ways and on so many levels—levels that had been ratcheted to a delicious tension throughout the afternoon, until desire had become nothing short of craving. Illarion nipped at her ear, his teeth sinking a tiny bite into the tender skin. 'I've wanted you since the moment you stepped down from the landau.' She'd taken his breath away, the sun in her platinum hair, the cool beauty of her in the white-linen carriage ensemble, blue forget-me-nots embroidered delicately, brightly at the hem, a reminder that she was his *Snegurochka* come to life, the winter Princess walking amongst spring. When she'd slipped her hand into his, the possessive thrill of 'mine' had coursed through him. That had merely been the start of the wanting. Teaching her archery had done nothing to ease his growing need. Watching her with his friends; listening to their stories, eating their food, her eyes bright with interest, had been intoxicating. Mere wanting had become craving.

'Why me, Illarion?' She framed his face between her hands, her eyes questioning, yet full of that quicksilver desire he loved—loved knowing he put it there, that it was there for him, because of him, and it was there for the first time. He was the only one who'd conjured it for her. Dove wanted *him*, she was hungry, too, but she resisted, part of her uncertain why he would want her.

'Because you have brought me to life.' Illarion kissed her mouth, bearing her back to the cushions. What he wanted to do required more than kneeling allowed. 'I would do the same for you, if you would allow it.' God, he hoped she'd allow it. He was ravening for her, for her little gasps of delight when he touched her, for the quicksilver desire in her eyes when he kissed her. And yet, he must curb his desire, must not scare her away with the force of his want. He wanted to show her the possibilities of pleasure. More than that, the wolf in him cried out, he wanted her for himself. He wanted to drown himself in her so that his guilt might be washed away, his nightmares might be cast out, so that he might write again, fully and without fear, as he used to. If he could bury himself in her, he could be free from his plagues.

And that wasn't fair, his better self called from the depths of his conscience. This was supposed to be about her. He was supposed to save her. Perhaps he could save them both. He dropped a kiss in the feminine hollow at the base of her neck, his eyes lingering intently on hers, willing her to give permission. 'May I, Dove? May I bring you to life?'

'Yes,' she breathed, 'you may. Bring me to life, Illarion.' She would not be sorry, he would make sure of it. He bent her knees, letting her skirts fall back, revealing bare thighs above the silk of her stockings. He kissed the soft skin, small, teasing kisses that made her sigh; each touch, each kiss drawing ever closer to the core of her. He could hear her breathy gasps change to long sighs of anticipation; he could smell the intoxicating musk of her arousal, his body tight with an arousal of its own, desire driving him hard. To bring pleasure was a pleasure of its own. He sought her core first with his thumb, rolling it over the tiny nub hidden in her folds, letting the first waves of pleasure lap at her senses, letting her body accustom itself.

'Do you like it, Dove? Do you want more?' How erotic it was to look up at a woman, to see the rise of her breasts, to gauge the rapidity of her breathing, her enjoyment. The length of a woman's body was a sensuous map of curves and hills.

'Yes, more, please.' The long sighs had become moans. Her body beginning to seek its own 'more', hips lifting against his hand. Illarion braced her then, his hands on either side of her hips, his mouth blowing against her core, tasting her in licks and nips, her desire driving her; her breath catching in broken gasps now, her words no more than exclamations. Gone were the slow waves of pleasure. She bucked against him, looking for release, once, twice, and then he felt her shatter, gone to pieces against his mouth, against his hands in a final cry.

She was stunning in her pleasure, her hair falling about her shoulders, her eyes glistening with wonderment and discovery, bewilderment, too, that this pleasure existed and it could be hers. In those moments, he felt it, too—the wonderment that came with claiming climax and in providing it. He could not recall the last time giving such pleasure had been so profound for him. Perhaps that was the magic of Dove; she made the profane beautiful again, the dead alive again.

Illarion stretched out beside her, propped up on an elbow; all the better to see her, his inner wolf prompted. There was satiation in her gaze, that dreamy, drowsy quality a woman wears after she's been well pleasured. A rivulet of pride went through him. He'd done that. He'd put that look there. Him and no one else.

'Does that happen every time?' Dove asked candidly and some of his satisfaction faltered.

'No,' he answered her with equal candour. 'Sometimes never. A man needs a certain knowledge, a certain skill.' Already he could feel the shade of Percivale intruding on their pleasure. A stab of jealous arrogance went through him. He did not want her thinking she could have this with any man, yet what did it mean that he wanted her to have this only with him?

'A poem of the body.' Dove smiled sleepily at him.

'Yes, something like that.' Illarion pushed a strand of hair out her face, letting his hand skim her cheek. 'You're beautiful.' And trusting and innocent despite what they'd done. She was full of ideals, her convictions untried. He had to be so very careful not to ruin her.

'Thank you for today.' Dove captured his hand and laced her fingers through it where it lay against her cheek. Her touch was warm and the simple gesture spoke of intimacy. 'I enjoyed seeing your world, at least a slice of it. You're a lucky man in your friends.'

'We would die for each other,' Illarion said. 'Stepan risked much to get Nikolay out of the country. We could not let him go alone.'

'And you, too, I think?' Dove's eyes searched his face, studying him. 'Nikolay was not the only one who had to leave if I understand correctly.'

He had to tell her. This was the piece his conscience grappled with. He could not expect her to give all and not to give some of himself in return. Only he feared, if she really knew him and what he'd done, that she would leave him. She would know he was the sum of her parents' fears for good reason. He was dangerous. 'I encouraged the people of Kuban to stand up against unjust marriage laws. Our Tsar didn't care for it.' They were mild words for what he'd done and for what the Tsar had thought, but they weren't untrue.

'What kind of laws?' They were talking softly now, just the two of them lying close on the pillows, the afternoon lazy around them.

It was easier to talk about the laws in general than to talk about his exile. 'Laws that require nobles to marry for the good the kingdom. Our Tsar must sanction each marriage. It started merely as coming forward and asking for approval, a formality. But it has become much more than that. The Tsar and the great families arrange every marriage now. No one comes forward any more, each match is presented to the family. The choice to refuse is an illusion. Refusal can result in a family being stripped of royal favour, of their worldly possessions. The more pristine the daughter is, the better the marriage alliance for the family can be. Families have gone to great lengths to ensure a daughter's purity.' That was as far he'd go with what he'd witnessed.

'It is different than here in intensity, then, but not in intent.' Dove was thoughtful. 'I think it was right that you stood up to that. People should be able to choose their own futures, their own mates.' Her grey eyes held his, revealing the depths of her emotions. 'Perhaps that time will come if people like you are willing to fight for it.'

'Will you fight for it, Dove?'

She dropped her gaze. 'I don't know how. It's more complicated than saying no. Refusing hurts my parents, shames them. How can I do that to them?'

Debate welled up in Illarion. He wanted to argue. 'Your life is no small consideration.' Could she not see that her freedom had value? 'You do not have to give your life for them.'

'Don't I?' Dove's answer was quick and selfless, showing a maturity beyond her innocent years. 'They've given their lives for me. Should I not reciprocate?' She puckered her brow here, deep in thought. 'Do you know why I don't have close friends? Because I was sheltered. I lived in isolation. My parents were my friends, the only people I associated with, except when we went to church on Sundays. There were visits from cousins during the summers, but I never returned those visits, I never went to their estates. I was the last of five children, Illarion.'

A suspicion began to take cold hold in his stomach. 'Five? I thought you were an only child.' Hadn't the gossip about her debut suggested she was Redruth's only offspring? But she had not said youngest, only last.

'I had four older brothers.' Sadness tinged her sleepy gaze. 'I never knew any of them. They were all dead before I was born; two from random fevers, one at birth, one stopped breathing in his cradle after two perfectly fine months of life.' Her voice caught.

Illarion drew her to him. He wanted her to stop, wanted to spare her the pain. 'You don't have to say any more.'

'Yes, I do,' she murmured against his shoulder. 'I

need you to understand that it can't be yes or no for me. It is so much more complicated than that. I owe my parents. I am the one who survived. I am the one who must make good on their hopes, on their legacy. I am the only one who can do it.' He heard the anger in her words—for her parents, for *him* because he wanted her to reconsider, and for herself, because she could find no legitimate grounds on which to reconsider her choice.

She pulled back from him. 'What becomes of me if I refuse Percivale? Refusing him costs me everything.' Except her freedom.

'What becomes of you if you accept him?' Illarion challenged softly but carefully.

'Illarion, don't. Do you think I haven't thought of that?' she whispered. He let the argument go because he had no answer either. She smiled, perhaps in apology, and stood up, her hands starting to work her hair back into some order, a sure signal that the interlude was over. 'Perhaps we might draw and write a little before the others come back?' she suggested.

It was as good a solution as any. They settled in on their respective pillows, Dove with her new art case open on her lap, a private smile on her lips as she took out a pencil, he with a fresh tablet, his head full of ideas. At least the ideas came more easily these days, even if the poetry to express them still struggled.

They weren't going to resolve the Percivale situation today. Or ever. The thought brought an uneasiness to Illarion's gut. *He would not lose her.* The refrain had taken up residence in his mind after his declaration to Stepan. Only now, he wondered if it meant something different. Once, it had meant encouraging her to stand up for herself so that another woman did not suffer Katya's fate. Percivale would not hurt her the way Ustinov had hurt Katya. Was it possible he wanted her to reject Percivale for more personal reasons, selfish reasons? Was it possible he wanted her for himself?

He studied her from his paper. The goodness in Dove would be her undoing. She would sacrifice herself for her family. Is that what her family expected of her? Had her parents been an arranged match as well? Did they know nothing of love and its importance? That conclusion didn't ring true. Dove had been well loved, well raised, most definitely cherished. She had not learned the art of *agape* on her own. How ironic that parents who had loved her would force her to make a loveless marriage. It might do to learn a bit more about the Duke of Redruth's own marriage. Perhaps there was a clue in that to help Dove with her decisions. Or, a clue to help him with his. He would have to ask Ruslan to assist.

'You're staring at me,' Dove caught him out.

'You're lovely,' he answered easily. 'You're my muse.'

She blushed at that, thinking he was teasing her. 'I think you say that to all the girls.'

Illarion grinned. 'No, Dove, just to you. You're the only one.' And for the first time ever, Illarion realised he meant it. Now what the hell did he do about it?

Chapter Thirteen

The best aspect of Venetian breakfasts were the sweets. Dove bit into a delicious *bigne cioccolato* and let the chocolate crème fill her mouth. Other than that, however, Lady Camden's Venetian breakfast was hard pressed to compete with yesterday's Russian picnic. For one, Illarion wasn't here, at least not physically. That he was on her mind constantly, however, was a sign of how thoroughly yesterday's experience had shaken her. Even a day later, it took only the slightest effort to call forth the echoes of passion—her heart racing, her body throbbing in remembrance of how it had felt to shatter, to feel herself come apart and then slowly come back together again. She would remember that feeling, those moments, always. She loved him for the memory and she hated him for it. He'd given her very intimate pleasure quite deliberately so that she *would* remember. Remember it or remember *him*?

This was where the confusion began. He'd called

her his muse. He'd given her intimacy. He'd urged her to speak up for herself, to refuse a marriage not of her own making. Why? Because he wanted to pursue her? Or because he simply wanted her to recognise the possibilities? The costs? Originally, she'd assumed the latter, but after the picnic and the Hamptons' gardens and all that he'd shared about himself, she felt there was something more. Or was it just her? Was she imposing more on the situation because of how *she* felt? Did she think he felt something more simply because she did?

That confusion spawned more confusion. How *did* she feel about Illarion? Did her growing affections stem from how she felt about him personally or from what he represented to her? This was to say nothing of how she perceived *his* feelings for *her*. Dove reached for a second *bigne*. If one couldn't resolve one's confusion with logic and clear thinking, perhaps it was possible to confound the confusion with chocolate instead. In the end, did answers to those questions even matter? What if she decided she *was* falling for the Prince? What if he decided he was falling for her? It had already been established by her parents that he was not an eligible suitor. A future between them wasn't possible.

He wasn't Percivale. In society's eyes he was only a handsome man with a reputation that bordered on rakishness. He would be popular for a while, a novelty. Those sorts of men weren't entitled to dukes' daughters, especially if they were outsiders, no matter how much money they had. Never mind that he made her laugh, made her think, made her feel valued, made her aware of herself, made her *feel*, all of which were very dangerous reactions. She wasn't supposed to feel, wasn't supposed to question the order of her life. But Illarion had made her do both.

The girls around her made small talk, chatting about dresses and fabrics and their favourite gentlemen. Dove wished she felt that carefree. The girls chatted as if they didn't know what waited for them: marriage to the highest bidder. Or perhaps they *did* know. If so, how could they be so glib about being treated like prettily dressed cattle? Worse, how could they *celebrate* that? Was she the only one who saw the injustice of it? The limitation?

'Did anyone read the society pages this morning?' Eliza Brantley, a debutante out for her second Season, leaned forward, catching the girls' attention with a sly look. She pulled a folded sheet of newsprint from her bodice and spread it out, mischief in her eye. '*He's* published a new poem.'

'Who?' A girl dressed in pink leaned forward, breathless at the anticipation of gossip.

'The Prince of Poems, who else? Don't you know anything, Sally?' Eliza scolded with a laugh.

The Prince of Poems? Is that what they were calling him these days? Dove set aside the second *bigne*.

'This one is called "Jealousy",' Eliza said in hushed tones not meant to be overheard by the mamas gathered at the other table. 'It's so romantic. It's about men competing for a woman's affection,' Eliza prefaced with a wicked smile and began to read. '"She can belong to only one…"'

Eliza finished reading to an applause of sighs. 'I wish Mr Adamson and Mr Gilbert felt that way about me,' Sally said wistfully. 'Sometimes I think they do and other times, I think they're more concerned about pleasing my father.'

'How lovely to think the gentlemen feel the same way as we do, after all,' another girl gushed. 'We feel we have to compete for their attentions, while all the time *they* are competing for ours.'

'Why do we have to compete at all?' Dove broke in, unable to stand it any longer.

Sally stared at her, uncomprehending. 'Whatever do you mean?'

'I mean, why force a marriage?' Dove explained. 'Why not marry someone of *our* choosing instead of our parents'? For that matter, why marry now? Why not demand a Grand Tour like your brothers? Why not see the world before settling down?' She was warming to the subject, but her audience was all horrified confusion. The girls looked back at her with blank expressions.

Eliza Brantley's shrewd gaze knew precisely what she meant, though, but there was no help from that quarter. She wanted to talk about the Prince. 'I wonder who the Prince wrote this about? Does anyone care to speculate, ladies?'

'Do you think it's about the Countess of Somersby?'

Sally Rinehart whispered, eyes round. '*I* would be melting for him if he would look my way even once!' That was all it took to open a floodgate all the girls could involve with. Sally's comment was followed by a chorus of, 'He's so handsome.'

'I love his hair. Those eyes!'

'Those shoulders!'

'My cousin danced with him once and she said he waltzes like a god. She felt so dainty in his arms, like a real pocket Venus.' The girls oohed and aahed over the description, more than one pair of eyes going hazy with the image.

'Lady Dove has danced with him.' Eliza smiled coyly. 'Maybe she'd tell us what it's like.'

Dove panicked. For a moment only the dance beneath the stars came to mind, a secret dance. Eliza couldn't possibly know about that. She must mean the dance at the debut ball. Eliza had been there.

'He's arrogant,' Dove said. 'His conversation is… different.' Even saying that much felt like telling a secret. She didn't want to share Illarion with them. He was hers. It was a silly notion, nearly as silly as these moonstruck girls gasping about his shoulders as if a man's shoulders defined him.

'His accent is so attractive. The way he says his *r*'s makes me faint,' a girl in lavender put in eagerly. Dove wanted to scream that it wasn't his accent that made him attractive. It was his topics, his choice of words, the way he thought about the world, his way of framing the discussion to call out and expose one's opinions, one's self, that made conversation different. His conversations had meaning. These girls wouldn't understand that.

'I suppose his accent is indeed part of his appeal,' Dove said neutrally, retreating from the field. Despite the excellent *bignes*, it was time to leave. The Venetian breakfast had lost its appeal.

Dove wished she could leave Illarion's poem behind as easily as she left the gathering. In the silence of the carriage the poem's lines and Eliza's comment kept niggling. *Who* was it about? It didn't have to be about anyone, but Dove felt it was.

Spring's green dragon pits its fire against the strength of the surly bear, fresh from winter's sleep, new-woken to life, hunger raging. The maid cannot belong to both. Perhaps the maid does not want to belong to either. It is not hers to choose her champion.

Her mind fixed on the image of the bear. Polaris, the Plough, the bear... She was certain the bear was meant to represent Russia or a Russian in the poem. Perhaps Illarion himself? If so, Spring's green dragon had to be someone. Green could symbolise someone untried but the poem's title firmly suggested the colour represented envy. Perhaps both. Spring's jealous, untried dragon, then. What did the dragon do? Breathe fire. *Fire*. She thought of Percivale's dissertation on fire-making that first night.

Her stomach clenched. Percivale! The dragon was Percivale. That left the maid. She was too easy. The maid was her.

Perhaps the maid does not want to belong to either. It is not hers to choose her champion.

In retrospect, it was so clearly her, the allusion to her situation—a maid torn between two suitors. Was that how he saw himself? A suitor? There was the message, too; a woman had a choice if she was brave enough to take it and that choice didn't have to include a man.

The carriage came to a halt in front of Redruth House as the fullness of revelation struck her. 'Jealousy' was about the three of them. The *bignes* churned in her stomach. How dare he? Did Illarion not understand the risk to her? To himself? The embarrassment for Percivale if anyone recognised the allegorical nature of the poem? For all his poor humour, Percivale was a powerful enemy. Not in a violent, dangerous sense, but socially. Where he led, the *ton* followed. If Percivale understood the poem, Illarion would have awakened a sleeping dragon in truth. If Percivale felt threatened, if he thought he could lose her, he would feel the need to hurry his suit. The *bignes* sat heavy in her stomach. Dear heavens, what had Illarion done? He'd called all three of them out. He'd pushed them all to the end game.

The carriage door opened and she followed her

mother out. Another carriage was parked at the kerb. 'It looks like we have company, my dear.' Lady Redruth smiled knowingly. 'It's a good thing your father was home this afternoon. I have a feeling today might be a very auspicious day.'

Dove's fists clenched in her skirts. Only one man in London drove a blue-painted high-perch phaeton drawn by two matched greys. The dragon was not only awake, he was *here*.

There was always the hope the men would be closeted away in her father's study and miss them coming in, but Dove wasn't that lucky today. They were lying in wait in the small receiving room at the top of the stairs. At the first sound of heels on the stairs, her father was in the doorway, beckoning for them to join the men.

'Lady Redruth, Lady Dove, it's always a pleasure.' Percivale rose, all effusive politeness. There was an exchange of greetings and small talk, but the air was pregnant with unspoken words.

'Might we walk in the garden, Lady Dove? I've been wanting to see your father's new roses,' Percivale asked as soon as a decent interval of small talk had passed.

There was no refusing, not with her parents both giving permission. She did her best to get it over quickly. She led him straight to the roses and gave the dissertation on the new rose. 'Father and my godmother grafted it this winter. They're calling it the Redruth. It's white tinged with pink on the outer rims of the petals to give the petals texture and depth,' she explained, trying to forestall any further non-rose-related conversation. But Percivale was in no hurry.

'Yes, I remember the roses from your debut. They were all hers, weren't they? Not these roses, however. Those were ivory. Very traditional, a classic beauty like the woman they honoured,' Percivale complimented broadly.

'Yes. The French White.' She didn't offer anything more. Her throat was tight, her stomach tighter. Percivale gestured to the bench. 'Sit, Lady Dove. We must talk plainly.' There was an edge of new steel in his voice. 'I have something to discuss, something I hope you will be happy to hear. Once I was sure you would be, but these days I am not so certain.'

Dove folded her hands in her lap and waited for him to go on. He was looking for reassurance and she had none to give him. 'As you may know, I have long held your family in great esteem. As you may also know, my uncle is in failing health, which brings my responsibilities ever closer. I had thought to wait to marry, but circumstances have changed, although the target of my affections has not. I find it imperative that I marry immediately so that I may firmly take up the reins of the dukedom when my uncle passes.'

He knelt before her on one bended knee, taking her hand in his. It was a pretty gesture, one that when viewed through the drawing-room windows would look gallant and handsome. Percivale, as always, was the picture of perfection with his well-tailored clothes, immaculate grooming and gold hair. But the gesture left her empty. She did not thrill to his touch, although she did panic. She knew what was coming. 'What I am asking, Lady Dove, is would you be willing to do me the honour of being my Duchess?' Not his wife, but his Duchess. What had Illarion said? *I don't let the title wear me.* Was that what Percivale saw when he looked at her? A duchess? Not a wife, not an artist, but the embodiment of a lineage?

He took her silence as a sign of surprise. 'I understand it is short notice. I had hoped to wait until the end of July to give you a Season. I do not think my uncle has that long.'

'How much time does he have?' Dove tried to be delicate. But she needed to know. How much time did *she* have?

'A month, perhaps, the doctors say.' Percivale shook his head. 'He could linger for the summer, of course. These things are not set in stone.' Dove offered him a comforting smile. She could see that the news upset him. She recalled hearing that he and his uncle were close and she felt callous for having asked. But as dreaded as the interview was, it was not unexpected, nor had such situations been unanticipated in her training. A young lady with a fortune must be prepared to refuse marriage proposals and she did have that skill in her arsenal. She ought to look demure, honoured, perhaps slightly sad. She should have practised in the mirror. But she'd never dreamed she'd need to refuse a future duke. There hadn't been room in the fairy tale for that.

Knowing what to do wasn't the same as actually doing it. Knowing also did nothing to calm the panic that churned in her stomach. Did Percivale see it? She felt as if she might cast up her accounts on her father's new roses. Did she look it? She managed a soft smile, managed to meet his blue eyes, 'You do me a great honour, even if it comes as a surprise. But because it is a surprise, I would beg you for whatever time you have to spare. I need time to acclimate myself to the idea of marriage so soon after my debut, time to gather a trousseau.' She tried for a smile of modest shyness. 'Surely you can imagine the enormity of being a duchess at eighteen?' She prayed he wouldn't ask for more reasons. What would she say if he wanted details? If he made her defend her position? Or worse, what if he knew the real reason she hesitated and called her out on it? How much easier it would all be if she could muster up some liking for Percivale, some tolerance for what he stood for. But he was the gateway to a life she didn't want. She could not accept him without accepting what he represented.

He squeezed her hand. 'I certainly can. If it were up to me, I would give you all the time you needed.'

'May I think it over and give you my response?' She rose, forcing him to stand. It occurred to her that he would simply argue her into it until she had no objections left if she remained seated.

Disappointment dashed across his features. 'You may, Lady Dove.' He paused. 'May I ask you a question? Does your reticence have anything to do with another's attentions?' He stammered slightly, embarrassed by what he perceived as his own bluntness, but he courageously forged on. 'Are you certain your affections are not engaged elsewhere?' For a moment, Dove saw the potential of him, everything Strom Percivale could, but would not, be. Society had bred it out of him.

Dove answered as best she could. 'I assure you, my family's affections hold you in the highest regard as always.'

'And yours, Lady Dove?' he pressed, not swayed by the pretty words. He'd seen the poem, then. Worse, he'd understood it. Perhaps the poem, more than his ailing uncle, had prompted the visit and his need for haste.

'My affection for you has never wavered in its intensity.' It was true, in so far as it went. The intensity of her affection towards him had never amounted to much previously and it amounted to just as little now. Her smiling reassurance mollified him.

'I am honoured and relieved to hear it. I confess I had fears that a man of unseemly character had turned your head. I would not want to see you at the mercy of a fortune hunter.'

The words made her bristle. Did he think she was so helpless? And yet, she felt guilty for such uncharitable thoughts. He was trying to be nice. 'I assure you nothing of the sort has taken place. Even if it had, I am more than capable of taking care of myself.'

'But you shouldn't have to, Lady Dove. That is what a husband is for. What, if I may be so bold, I am for.' He bent over her hand. 'I shall await your word, Lady Dove. Until then, I am always your champion.' His eyes held hers for a moment longer than necessary. She did not think Percivale had chosen those words by accident.

Chapter Fourteen

How did she get out of this? It was the one question that went around in Dove's head as her maid, Mary, dressed her for the evening. How did she refuse Percivale and still remain loyal to herself *and* her family? His proposal this afternoon had moved that dilemma from hypothetical consideration to reality. 'You're quiet tonight, miss,' her maid commented, finishing with her hair. 'Thinking about your new dress?' Mary smiled. 'Or maybe you're thinking about the handsome gentlemen you'll dance with tonight?'

'Perhaps.' Dove tried for a smile in the mirror, enough to convince Mary she was right. 'Shall we try that gown now?' Dove rose, eager to distract Mary. She stepped into her gown, letting Mary lace it up. This gown had a white-organza overskirt that floated over a silk underskirt, the collection of skirts slightly fuller than current fashion and tied with a wide bright blue sash at the waist, making it look impossibly tiny. Mary settled the usual pearls at her throat and turned her towards the mirror. 'You look like a fairy-tale princess, miss.'

A single thought came to Dove as she surveyed the reflection. She did look like an innocent princess straight from a fairy tale. But she didn't feel like one. London had indeed stripped the scales from her eyes. Illarion's bold remark about being deflowered by the city seemed years ago instead of days. The girl who had chided him for such audacity didn't exist any more. Beneath the white gown lay a less inno-cent woman who understood the machinations of the Season, who understood she was a commodity to be bought and sold. To remain silent meant to be complicit in that game.

The door opened, startling Dove out of her thoughts. Her mother entered, dressed for the eve-ning and all smiles, a small blue-velvet box in her hand. 'Darling, you look lovely!' she exclaimed, taking in the effect of the new gown. 'The fuller skirts are breathtaking and these will be perfect.' Her mother opened the lid to reveal two perfect pearl earrings dangling from dainty diamonds.

'Grandmother's earrings,' Dove said wistfully. How long had she yearned for this moment? Grow-ing up, she'd coveted her grandmother's earrings, hardly able to wait for the day she'd make her debut and be able to wear them.

Her mother's face glowed with pride. 'I remem-ber when you were little. You used to sit on my bed when I dressed for an evening and play in my jewel case.'

Dove smiled at the memory. It was one of her favourites from childhood. The box had smelled like cedar and lavender when she lifted the lid. It had held a thousand treasures to a little girl's eye. How many nights had she sat on her mother's bed going through her jewel case, dreaming of the day when it would be her turn to dress in fine gowns and put on the earrings? Now that the moment had come, it was too late. That dream was dead. It would be easier if it wasn't, easier if she could just accept what would happen.

Her mother took the earrings out of the box and clipped them on Dove's ears. 'Beautiful. Grandmother would have been so proud.' She took Dove's hands, her smile softening. 'Some day soon you may have your own daughter to pass them on to and you can tell her about the night you first wore them.' She paused. 'Your father tells me Percivale has made his official offer.' They had not talked about what had happened in garden. Percivale had left and she'd gone up to her room to rest. Apparently, her mother and father had such confidence in her that they were not concerned Percivale had returned inside without securing an acceptance.

When she said nothing, her mother continued with a gentle prompt. 'Percivale told your father you asked for some time.'

'It's too soon.' Dove began the arguments she'd

carefully rehearsed in her room. 'I've been out less than a month. I won't have the experience I need to be a duchess at eighteen with not even one Season to my name.'

'My dear girl, come sit.' Her mother led Dove to the edge of the bed. 'Is that what you're worried about? Not enough experience? Percivale understands that. He will show you everything you need to know.' She squeezed Dove's hand in reassurance and for a moment Dove wanted to collapse in her mother's arms and spill out everything; her hopes, her fears, her feelings for Illarion. She wanted to ask; Had her mother ever felt this way? Had her mother been this conflicted? But she didn't dare. Her mother would be so disappointed.

'What if I don't want to be shown? What if I want to discover my life on my own? I wonder if Percivale would wait for a year? Let me have my Season? I don't think waiting until after mourning is a bad idea if it comes to that.'

Her mother gave her a serious look, choosing her words delicately. 'There are other issues, too, Dove. He is too much of a gentleman to speak of it, but there are practicalities, too. He's the only Ormond male. He does not have the luxury of a year, Dove. He has to look to his nursery, secure his succession. Is that what worries you? You will be a good mother. I've seen you with the village children.'

Her? A good mother? At nineteen? After only a few months of marriage and even fewer weeks of a

Season? 'It's not that I don't want children.' She could imagine sitting in a field surrounded by children at her lap with drawing tablets and pencils, laughing as they worked. But those children had champagne hair and blue eyes. 'I just don't want them now.' Certainly not next summer, Dove thought.

'Once you hold your child in your arms, Dove, you will be ready and glad, whenever it happens,' her mother assured her. But her mother had been twenty-eight when she was born. She'd had years to settle into married life, to settle into a husband, a title. She'd had years to hold other babies that had come before her. Her mother had craved the child she'd been. 'What would you do for a year, anyway?'

Dove gathered her courage. If she didn't say it now, it would be too late. 'I'd like to travel and draw.'

Her mother relaxed, some of the shrewdness leaving her gaze. 'Oh, is that all? You and Percivale will travel for your wedding trip. We can arrange for you to go to Bath to see your aunts, maybe up to Scotland to visit your cousins. Percivale may have other ideas. Perhaps the Lake District. It's lovely in the summer.'

'No, not Bath. Not Scotland,' Dove said slowly. 'I'd like to go to France and Italy. I'd like to study in Florence with a drawing teacher.' Saying the words made her feel powerful, made the prospect of doing such a thing seem real for the first time. A dream was born in that moment, a new dream to replace the one she'd lost weeks ago. She would study abroad. Despite her panic over Percivale, a burst of elation took her. She wanted to shout her new dream to the world. She wanted to throw open the doors to her little balcony and cry out to London, 'I want to go to Florence and draw!'

Most of all, she wanted to tell Illarion. She wanted him to go with her. It would be glorious; the two of them bashing around Europe with his poetry and her pencils. There could be more picnics, more pleasure. That was the dream now...

'Italy?' Her mother sounded dismayed. 'I don't think Percivale would let you go as far as that. Perhaps you could suggest a honeymoon in France, though? He would likely give you that. He *is* eager to please you, dear. Everything will come out right, you'll see.'

'How do you know that? How do you know you can spend the rest of your life with someone?' If she had the answer to that, she might just have the direction she needed to make her decision.

Her mother's brow knit. She shook her head. 'You just know. You feel it, right here.' Her mother's hand went to her heart. 'Society helps, your parents help, they know who will suit best. But ultimately, *you* know. You feel a certain way when they're near like nothing can harm you, that you're safe. More than that, you feel invincible, that nothing can stand against you as long as that person stands with you.'

It was at once the right answer and the wrong answer. Dove recognised the feeling her mother described. Now she knew for sure. It was not merely

girlish infatuation she felt for Illarion. She was falling in love with him, the most unsuitable of men.
And she had to see him at once.

A knock on his chamber door brought a growl
from Illarion. He was in the middle of refining '*Snegurochka*' and didn't wish to be disturbed. To that
extent he'd rejected every invitation in the salver
downstairs and opted to stay in tonight. He was completely 'in', too—he hadn't left his chambers nearly
all day. A quick glance at the clock suggested it was
nearing midnight, an odd time for a call especially
when no one was expected. Or wanted.

'Your Highness, you have a guest. Are you receiving?' a footman enquired with all the bland aplomb
an excellent English servant might exhibit in the middle of day; there was no blinking of sleep-blurred
eyes although the 'guest' most likely had woken the
fellow from a light doze in the foyer as he waited
for Stepan and Ruslan to come home. Illarion had
to give the footman credit for composure. It wasn't
every day a footman had to deliver midnight mes-
sages to a prince who worked in the nude. Even his
work 'attire', or lack of it, had failed to knock the
bland neutrality from the footman's face.

'No.' Illarion waved an impatient hand. 'I'm working. I am not to be disturbed.'

The footman bowed deferentially. 'Very good,
your Highness. I will just tell her…'

'Her? There's a woman here at midnight?' Illarion

rose, coming around the work table in a rush of surprise and concern. 'Is it Klara?' His first thought was for Nikolay, that his wife had come because Nikolay was in trouble or hurt.

'No, your Highness, it is not Prince Baklanov's wife.'

Illarion halted in relief and ran through the list of women who would be bold enough to come to his home at night. Who could it be? The Countess? The thought was met with dismay. If she was here, he knew what she'd come for. He was about to instruct the footman to send the woman away when the rapid clip of low-heeled slippers sounded on the stairs, the white fabric of ballgown skirts shimmered in the darkness of the corridor. Those skirts pushed past the footman into the room, revealing unmistakable platinum hair coiffed in pearls and flashing silver eyes. Not in a thousand chances would he have guessed the caller downstairs was Dove Sanford-Wallis.

'Lady Dove, what are you doing here?' Illarion's words were beyond inadequate to express his shock. What could have possibly happened to bring her here of all places—the home of not one, but *three* unwed men? She knew the rules better than anyone. She had no excuse, which meant she had a *reason*.

A kaleidoscope of questions swirled through his mind. Why was she here? What had happened to bring her? Who knew she'd come? There were other thoughts, too; practical thoughts like how quickly he needed to get her out of here and how stealthily that needed to happen if she was to be protected. But beneath that instinctive reaction to protect her, to send her away, there was a part of him that wasn't obsessed with the danger of her being here. That part of him was *glad* she was here. She looked beautiful in her signature white, and troubled; troubled enough to run to him in his lair. For all his poet's vocabulary and intuition, Illarion could only manage the most basic of thoughts, the most basic of questions. 'Do you know how scandalous this is?'

She answered him with a slow nod, silver-grey eyes saucer-wide, indicating she was fully cognisant of what she'd done. Two simultaneous thoughts struck Illarion. She was in trouble and he was naked. A hot rose-red flush crept up her pale cheeks as she recognised it too, her teeth biting into the fullness of her bottom lip. Her emotions being so thoroughly on display was a telltale sign of just how upset she was. Dove usually kept herself in perfect, emotional check. But not tonight. Tonight, whatever was bothering her had bothered her enough to risk scandal by coming to a man's rooms, enough to risk ruination.

Illarion strode casually across the room to retrieve his banyan. There was no reason to rush and feign a modesty or embarrassment he didn't feel. He liked being naked and most women liked him naked, too. Besides, it was too late to change the fact that he was probably Dove's *first* naked man. She might as well look her fill. Who knew when she'd get another chance? Illarion shrugged into the banyan, unhurried. 'I like to work naked. I think better. Clothes are so confining,' he explained.

'I must apologise for barging in on you like this.' Dove's recovery was laudable. She tried to look as if nothing unusual had happened; that she visited men at home after midnight, men in their altogether, all the time. But he knew better. She'd slapped him over a kiss. Protocol was everything to her. Except when she was with him. She'd slipped out to a garden with him. She'd come here... Yes, and look where that had led: to standing in a naked man's bedroom.

'I trust you have a good reason.' Illarion trusted she'd also have the good sense to hold on to the reason until he dismissed the footman. The servants at Kuban House were trustworthy in the extreme, but Illarion felt that trustworthiness had been tempted enough for one evening. 'Perhaps we should go downstairs.'

'I'd rather stay here, if we could.'

'All right,' Illarion acceded. Why not? The damage was already done. She was here, where she shouldn't be. It hardly mattered if they were in the rose salon or his bedroom at this point. Scandal was scandal, the degrees of it stopped being relevant after a point.

Illarion studied Dove as the footman busied himself around the room, stirring up the fire and trying to tidy. She was determined and desperate. It was there in her eyes, in the set of her jaw, as if nothing mattered any longer except moving forward. It gave her face a frantic strength, a reckless courage. The footman continued to putter around the room unnecessarily. There was very little anyone needed in a sitting room this late at night, except brandy, and Illarion noted, the decanters were full. Illarion finally dismissed him outright. 'Please, return to your post and wait for the others to return.' Which would hopefully be hours from now. By then he would have Dove's problems resolved and Dove safely escorted back home where she belonged. Illarion didn't relish having to explain this to Stepan.

'Now…' Illarion sat beside her on the sofa and reached for her hands, finding them cold '…tell me everything. Why are you here?'

'Percivale proposed today.'

Now *he* felt cold. He could lose her in truth. 'It was not unexpected.' He said it as much for himself. 'How soon?' How much time did he have left with her? Damn the ailing uncle. He might have been able to manage a year if it hadn't been for the uncle.

Dove shook her head. 'No date has been set. I told him I needed time, that everything was happening so fast.' Illarion gave a dry chuckle at that. He saw some dark humour in imagining the upstanding Percivale thinking he'd overwhelmed Lady Dove with his ardour in a whirlwind romance.

'It's not funny,' Dove scolded. 'There is no time, as you well know.' Desperation took her features. 'I don't know what to tell him.'

That was the real surprise. 'Yes, you do.' Wasn't it obvious to her?

She leaned forward. 'No, I don't. Do I say yes and simply accept him? Put all of this drama behind me and embrace what I was meant to be? Or do I refuse him?' She didn't bother to list the consequences of that. The look on her face said those consequences were too dire to mention. Beneath those words was lay a question: *If I say no to Percivale, will you be there for me?* He wanted her, but it was not fair to mislead her, to make her think that he'd be enough if she walked away from Percivale.

'Choose for yourself, Dove. Don't let a man or a title become more important.' It killed him to say it. He wanted to shout that he would protect her. But how could he do that? He had a chamber in a house on loan from Dimitri Petrovich. It was a far cry from what he could have offered her in Kuban. Never mind that in Kuban, she would have been beneath his marital notice. How ironic that the roles were reversed here, where he was the one of questionable note?

What did he have to offer a woman like Dove? He'd never thought of it before. In Kuban he'd never had to. He had palaces and jewels and summer homes. Fine horses and carriages, clothes for every season that filled wardrobes. Here, he had only himself; a man plagued by nightmares of a dead woman, a woman he might have driven to suicide; a man who could barely write drivel, who had a spark of inspiration only because of her.

Dove was restless in her anger. She rose from the sofa and paced the room. 'I don't want to choose. Not yet.' She stopped and picked up a paper with a few lines written on it. 'This is your fault. You should not have published that poem about us. He knows it's about him even if London doesn't.'

'His uncle would still be dying. His uncle was failing before the poem came out,' he answered coolly, but it stung that she accused him.

'You called me out, too, when you attacked him,' Dove continued. 'You put me in a position where I have to decide! I'm not ready.' That was the true source of her anger. She had to decide. She wanted him to decide for her.

'I can't give you what you want, Dove,' he said slowly. 'I won't decide for you. You would hate me for it some day.' Especially if he chose wrong and how could he not? All three of her options might turn out disastrous in the end. 'This has to be your responsibility. I can't give you reassurance that it will turn out all right no matter what you choose.' There was, in fact, damn little he could give her, his shimmering white Princess, his *Snegurochka*. His heart did a sad little flop at the realisation. He had never felt so helpless before, so powerless. Yet to assert his power would be to decide for her. He could, however, offer her comfort.

He went to her, taking her in his arms as he had in the Hamptons' gardens. This was as much for him as it was for her. *He* needed to hold her, to touch her, to breath in the lavender scent of her hair, the light rose fragrance of her soap. 'Whatever you choose, Dove, you will not be alone. I won't allow it.' Even if she chose Percivale. He would be like the French troubadours of old, following the courts of married women if it came to that. He had the power to make sure it didn't.

You could change her mind. You could make her choose you. Temptation rode him hard. It would be so easy, and so delicious, to kiss her throat, to suck at her earlobe and hear her gasp, to feel her body start to rouse.

If you want her, will you not fight for her? Will you cede the field so easily? Time was, you never backed down. Don't stand aside. You stood aside in Kuban. You know how that ended.

Illarion pressed his lips to the column of her neck. 'You smell like the very best of English gardens,' he whispered, feeling her pulse jump beneath his lips.

She turned in his arms, her voice husky, her body pressed to his. 'Then come pluck me, Illarion, while I am in full bloom.'

Chapter Fifteen

He kissed her hard and full, loving her with his mouth, with the press of his body, letting her know the extent of his desire, obvious beneath the thin fabric of his banyan. 'Look at me, Dove.' Illarion broke from her, stepping back and sliding the garment from his body. This was slow and deliberate, nothing at all like the hasty shock of catching him unawares. Now she could look on him in honest consideration and she did. He watched her eyes roam over his body. He revelled in her gasp, the appreciation in her eyes at the sight of his bare chest. This was an aphrodisiac all its own, to be worshiped by Dove. When had a woman last looked on him in such unhurried adoration? When had it meant so much?

'I had not known a man could be so beautiful. I thought surely the Greeks were exaggerating.' Dove's voice was breathless. She reached out a finger and trailed it along a ridge of muscle downward to his hip. The proximity of her hand to his phallus made it restless. He guided Dove's hand to the hardness of him, unable to wait any longer. A streak of silver curiosity gleamed in her eyes as she made contact, unafraid of his maleness. His Dove was a bold one, a woman made for passion. Her hand closed around him, sliding along his length, ascertaining his need, reconciling her awe with her curiosity.

He let her stroke until he couldn't allow the pleasure without ruining her own. 'Now it's my turn.' His voice was gravelly with desire. 'Give me your back, Dove.' He worked the laces, slipping it from her to reveal the delicate slope of her shoulders, the feminine flare of hip, the sensual bell of rounded buttocks. 'Oh, God,' he murmured his reverence, dropping a kiss at the notch where neck met shoulder. 'You're beautiful, Dove. Far lovelier than I. Let me see you, all of you, as you saw me.'

He turned her out from him, letting his eyes honour her. His gaze swept the small, high breasts, the tapered waist, the silver pelt between her thighs. She was beauty personified and his blood thrummed with the age-old call of possession. *His. His.* She was his—his to claim, his to protect. He reached for her, his hand slipping loose the pins from her hair, the last vestiges of bondage.

'You, too,' she whispered, her hands going to the leather strip holding his bun in place. 'You look like an ancient warrior.'

Illarion laughed. 'Stepan thinks it's girlish.'

Dove moved into him, pressing to him skin to

skin, her hand wrapped about his phallus once more. 'Stepan has never seen you like this. He would never think such a thing.' *Sin wrapped in satin.* He'd not been wrong. Illarion kissed her mouth. 'My sweet, innocent, Dove, I do believe you are a temptress, after all.'

She looked up at him with wondering eyes that belonged both to the innocent and the courtesan. '*Do I tempt you, Illarion?*'

She drew her thumb over the tip of his phallus as if to test the assumption and he groaned. 'In so many ways, Dove. You can't even begin to know.'

She tempted him, this man who could have any woman. Those were heady words, nearly as heady as feeling the proof of his desire in her hand, against her lips, against her body as he moved her backwards to his bed and laid her down. The enormity of these moments swept her as she looked up at him from the pillows. Oh, sweet heavens, she was naked with the man she loved! And it was beautiful. 'Like Adam and Eve in the garden,' she murmured. With a few exceptions; mainly, Adam likely didn't have the appearance of a Norse god and she had not come here tonight with the conscious intention of making love. Why had she come here? She could answer that only with abstract ideas; she'd been looking for escape, for reassurance, for hope. But now those ideas had taken on a more concrete aspect. How better to escape, to hope, to seek reassurance than in the arms of a man she trusted? A man who understood her? A man who knew the way to freedom, to pleasure? A subconscious part of her discerned the very real probability that only Illarion was uniquely positioned to give all of that to her, that this might be her only chance to experience true passion. Tonight, and tonight alone, there were no titles, no expectations, no social pressures, nothing between them but skin and desire. This might not have been the intended outcome of her visit, but that didn't make it any less right.

Dove trembled with anticipation as the bed took his weight and he came down beside her. She was not afraid, not with Illarion's blue eyes holding hers, not with his warm touch on her body, his hand moving her breast, his thumb passing over the peak of her nipple until it was taut. She could feel the now-familiar ache pool low in her stomach as her desire gathered, just as it had that afternoon at the picnic, and her body quickened. Each touch, each caress played on her sensitive skin until her nerves were raw with wanting him, wanting more.

He moved over her then, his knee between her thighs, urging them apart, his mouth moving down her body, her breasts, her navel, blowing soft puffs against her skin. Her body gave a delicious shiver, knowing the path his mouth would take, wanting the pleasure that would follow. Her legs opened in welcome. At the first stroke of his thumb, the first lick of his tongue, she sighed into the pleasure, falling into

the soft heat of his touch against her skin, building
the fire in her to a slow, steady burning. She arched
into him, like a cat and he gave a playful growl. 'You
like that, my vixen.'

'I could do this all night,' Dove murmured, but it
was her downfall. He was not content to let her. His
tongue deepened its work. Her hands gripped the
thick depths of his hair, irrationally torn between
tearing him away from her and anchoring him there
so that he could never leave. The soft fire became an
inferno, swallowing her whole until all the world was
reduced to the sounds of her cries, and afterwards
the feel of his head on her belly, his breath coming
fast as if the pleasure had been his as well.

He let her recover, but not rest. She'd no sooner
regained a sense of equilibrium than his hand was
between her thighs, coaxing her to arousal again,
his mouth at her ear. 'You're ready for me now.' He
whispered his intentions, securing her permission. It
was a kind gesture, made with those blue eyes boring
into hers. 'Are you sure, Dove? There are other ways
to pleasure ourselves. We can still play.'

She tugged him to her, raising her hips to meet
his, a gesture designed to show him this was beyond
play. In a world of uncertainty, this was the one thing
she was certain of. How dare he give her a choice
now when she could barely manage speech, let alone
cogent thought. 'I want this pleasure, with *you*,' she
whispered fiercely. 'And I want it now.'

He kissed her then, his body finding its space between her thighs. She lifted her legs, instinctively wrapping them around them about his waist; they seemed to belong there as much as he seemed to belong here with her. She felt the press of his phallus, the nudge of its head against her entrance. The nudge became a push, his body going taut above her in an effort of restraint. She could feel her own body, wet and tight, responding to his invasion. She gave an involuntary cry.

He covered her mouth with a kiss, his body stilling, the pushing stopped. 'Relax, *golubushka*. We will go slow,' he murmured, the husk of his voice hinting at the willpower the effort cost him. He eased from her and then returned in a slow slide that claimed her inch by steady inch until he was fully sheathed, her body stretching and flowing around him, an intruder no more but a welcome guest.

Then it began. Slowly at first, with the most infinitesimal of strokes, easing and teasing, as her body took up the rhythm. Each entrance now becoming a thrust, her body joining him, finding the mutual pleasure so that it was no longer his body pleasuring hers, but their bodies seeking pleasure together. Dove moaned, each stroke, each rocking of their bodies, taking them closer to the edge that waited beyond. But Illarion was not content to simply race towards the ledge and crash over it. He was like the tide, pushing them towards the shore and then drawing them back, only to push them forward once more; each time inching closer to the implosion point so that when he did allow their wave to crest, it was with a shattering clarity that went beyond her previous satisfaction, leaving her breathless, bodiless. She was fragments of sensations, scattered on a beach. She would eventually put all those pieces back together, but, as with anything once shattered and then reassembled, she knew in her heart she would never be quite the same again. She was changed, perhaps for the better.

Illarion was gentle with her, mindful of his weight. He moved beside her, taking her into the crook of his arm so that her head rested against the hollow of his shoulder, letting her body soak up the heat of him in the aftermath of lovemaking. As intimate as that had been, there was an intimacy to this that went beyond in its own way. To lay quiet and naked was a new luxury.

'I was right. When I first saw you, I thought your hair would be an avalanche if freed from its pins,' he murmured.

'I am like snow?' She was drowsy. Lovemaking had depleted her, or perhaps *repleted* was the better word. Dove felt contentedly full and complete, the way one feels after an exceptionally good meal.

'Not snow, you're like *Snegurochka*.' Illarion ran his hand up and down her arm in a slow motion, raising gentle goose bumps in its wake. 'In Russian folklore we have tales of a winter maiden. There are different stories about who she is, but I like the one where she's a snow maiden. She has blue eyes, red lips and fair hair. Some say she's the daughter of Spring and Frost and she lives in her father's woods where it's always winter.'

She laughed softly. 'Two out of three isn't bad. I haven't the blue eyes.'

'You are my silver-eyed *Snegurochka*.' His. She liked the sound of that. In these drowsy, happy moments, it didn't matter how impossible that was.

'What does *Snegurochka* do?'

'Well, like many things in fairy tales where people aspire to what they are not, she sees the other girls playing and she wants to be a real girl. She's lonely. Depending on the tale, she wants to play, or to fall in love. She wants to go out into the world beyond her father's winter forest. But when she goes out to play with the other girls, it grows dark. The girls light a fire and take turns jumping over it and shouting the names of their true loves. *Snegurochka* does the same but she is snow.' Illarion's words trailed off, letting Dove fill in the ending of the story.

Dove sat up in disappointment. 'She dies? That's a horrible story. What kind of moral is that? Freedom kills?'

'It's not so bad as all that.' Illarion chuckled sitting up with her. '*Snegurochka* is immortal. She returns to her father's forest and never ventures forth again.' He tapped Dove on the nose with a finger. 'And the lesson, my cheeky miss, as with so many Russian tales, is that one cannot escape their fate.

She was made to be a child of ice and winter. Nothing more, nothing less.'

She let him draw her back down beside him. She wiggled, finding that perfect place once more against his shoulder. 'Or perhaps the moral is that joy is not for ever, but for only the moment.' Dove sighed. 'I don't think I like the tale.' Not at all. The parallels were too obvious. What if…? A stab of fear took her and she voiced it in slow halting words before courage deserted her. 'Illarion, is this your way of telling me to marry Percivale?' To forget him, to not seek to be that which she was not intended to be. She was not to toy with fate.

Illarion shifted to his side to face her full on, body to body, his merry blue gaze solemn in a way she'd never seen it before. 'Dove, you must believe above all else that I would *never* compel someone to marry where they did not wish.'

Dove swallowed hard. 'Because of your politics? Because of Kuban?' It wasn't the answer she was looking for. She was naked with a man, she'd given him all she had to give. After what had transpired between them, she was hoping for something more personal than a political agenda.

'No, Dove. Because of Katya. Because a woman died when I did nothing.' *Katya.* The word was a blow to her stomach. A woman, perhaps a lover? Certainly a woman he'd cared about. Dove thought she might be sick. She'd misread this entire situation. She'd thought… Oh, she'd thought a million things, not the least being that Illarion felt about her the way she felt about him. Whatever he felt for her, it wasn't the same. Dove threw her legs over the side of the bed. She just wanted to get up, get dressed, get home. This had been a terrible mistake and she had only herself to blame. This was what happened when she stepped out of the box she was meant to live in. *Snegurochka* indeed!

Her feet hit the floor. Illarion's hand closed about her arm. 'Where are you going? His grip was hard. 'Will you get back in bed and let me explain?'

'Please, you don't need to. I understand.' She would not cry. Not yet. She was just another woman in a string of women for him, someone who meant something in the moment but not beyond and she had known that. She'd just conveniently forgotten.

'All right, then I will get *out* of bed and explain it to you.' Illarion slid out beside her. He handed her his banyan. 'Put this on and sit down,' he ordered. She was already wounded, she might as well stay for the salt, too, especially when Illarion seemed intent on it.

She sat on the sofa where he'd first had thoughts of her. She remembered him telling her. It was indeed narrow. Dove gathered the folds of the banyan around her, feeling dwarfed inside it, the sleeves hanging well past her wrists, but she sat and waited. Illarion sat across from her, a throw across his lap for modesty's sake. 'Katya was my friend and when she needed me, I did not help her. She was not, as you think, my lover, or even my mistress. She was

engaged to a powerful general in the military, a man
known for his cruelty. She was the Tsar's cousin and
her marriage would bring peace to a situation that
was on the brink of a state coup. Katya was a wild
spirit, the sort men like the general take pleasure in
breaking.'

The gruffness faded from his voice, replaced with
tenderness as he told her about Katya. 'She was a
woman every man fell in love with at once…' It was a
heartbreaking story, this vibrant girl squashed under
the tyrannical hand of her husband. Dove heard the
anger overcome the tenderness. Instinctively, despite
her own hurt, she reached a hand out to Illarion, hat-
ing how it pained him to tell the tale.

When he finished, she felt silly and shallow. 'My
own situation is not at all bad.' Dove said quietly.
'Percivale is not a bad man. He would never hurt me.'
He merely represented all that she feared: a life of
bland mediocrity, a life devoid of passion in exchange
for following the rules. And yet, there was a price for
that, too. Katya had married to save a country. But
she'd lost herself in the process. Dove didn't want to
think of the ways Katya had been hurt. Dove had far
less at stake. Why couldn't she like Percivale? Why
did she have to be stubborn?

'He would not hurt you intentionally. Don't you
see,' Illarion pressed softly. 'Katya's story is extreme.
But marrying Percivale is no less dangerous. You risk
the same unhappiness. Anyone who marries away
from their own choices does.' He paused, deciding

how to continue. 'In Kuban, some parents place their daughters in nunneries when they're eleven and they encounter no men until their weddings have been arranged. If a man visits the convent, the girls are blindfolded until he leaves. There was even one wedding I attended where the bride was blindfolded until the vows were performed.'

'That's barbaric,' Dove gasped. 'Why don't they run away?'

'The same reason you don't, Dove,' Illarion said with a gentle sharpness. She'd known her answer even as she'd asked the question. She didn't run because she couldn't. Where would she go? What would become of her? Because she, like those girls, needed a champion in a system that didn't let them fight for themselves.

'You were there. Why didn't you try to stop it?' There was a hint of accusation in the question.

'I did try.' Illarion answered solemnly. 'The girl had been young, scared, the blindfold soaked with her tears while all around her there was praise for her parents and the virtuous daughter they'd raised. I saw no virtue in that. I penned my poem "Freedom" that very night. I read it at court the next day. Within two days, Katya was dead and Kuban was on the brink of revolt. The Tsar used her death as a means of putting down the revolt and the poet responsible for it. He did a good job, Dove. I haven't been able to write since, not like that, not until I met you.'

Dove sat in silence, absorbing, processing. No wonder he was so careful with her. Illarion Kutejnikov, this bold, audacious man who spoke his mind and tempted her to act on her convictions, was afraid. Afraid of his power, afraid of his feelings. And yet, that fear had not stopped him, not completely. He fought against that fear, he fought for her. 'Thank you.' He'd given her an enormous gift tonight in revealing so much of himself, even at the risk of making himself vulnerable. She smiled at him. 'Your secrets are safe with me.' She whispered the words he'd once spoken to her.

He touched her face. 'And you are safe with me, Dove. Whatever you decide, I will keep you safe.' Not merely secrets. But herself. Her person, her soul. The words moved her, perhaps too much because she wished they were true. 'Let's get you dressed and then we have to get you home.' He ran a hand through his hair. 'How did you get here, anyway?'

'I walked.' She saw the belated concern on his face and hastened to assure him, 'No one saw me.'

Illarion raised an eyebrow in doubt. 'Dressed in white? You are a beacon in the dark.'

'No one knows I was coming. I told my parents I had a headache and that I was going home with a friend. They will be at the ball all night. My father has meetings. He and his friends have been closeted behind closed doors the entire evening with some important Parliament business.' She leaned towards him, concern shadowing her eyes. 'You're safe. I promise.' Was he worried she'd compromise him?

It was odd to think of it that way. Usually it was the men who did the compromising.

Illarion pulled on a pair of trousers. 'I'm not worried about me, *golubushka*, I'm worried about you. You can't go wandering around Mayfair at night alone.'

'*Golubushka*? What does that mean?' He'd called her that during lovemaking, too.

He came to her, his hands working the laces she couldn't reach. 'It means "darling". There, that should do. Are you ready?'

She was many things in that moment—confused, happy, sad, sleepy—but she was *not* ready. She didn't want to leave this room. Coming here might have provided her with clarity, but it had certainly not made her decision any easier. That brought her up short. Had she made her decision, then? Had she truly decided she would accept Percivale's offer and walk away from Illarion? All because she was too afraid to tell her parents what she wanted? Dove put a hand on his arm. 'What happens next, Illarion?'

'I don't know.' He held the door for her and gestured to the backstairs. 'I suspect it depends on you.' And it did. She'd wanted her independence and now she had it, if she was brave enough to claim it. She'd never understood until tonight how difficult it would be to do that. Taking responsibility for her decision meant accepting the consequences of it too. She could not blame her future happiness or disappointment on anyone else but herself.

Chapter Sixteen

The issue of what to do *with* Dove, what to do *for* Dove, had kept Illarion awake the rest of the night. The problem with virgins was that there was always a 'next'. One could not make love to an innocent and walk away. Had Dove realised that yet? He could not walk away from her, even if he wanted to, which he most certainly did not. Did she understand how hard it had been last night not to give her advice? To keep from telling her to refuse Percivale? To choose him instead? If he had told her to after they'd made love, she would have done it. But that was not what he wanted for Dove. He didn't want her to feel marriage to a man was her only choice. That cut against the grain of all he stood for and it made him a hypocrite. It also gave him extraordinary pause. He wanted to *marry* Dove? How had that slipped into his consciousness? He knew how. It was all Nikolay's fault. Nikolay and Klara with their incessant hand holding and moon eyes showing him a different sort of marriage was possible.

Illarion headed downstairs to breakfast, hoping food would clear his mind. Nikolay and Klara proved that marriage could be more than alliance. Their happiness proved that he was right. Marriage could be about love with the right person. Lucky for them, they'd found the right person. Dove might be the right person for him, but that begged the question, was *he* the right person for Dove? Marriage to him might be more of a sacrifice than marriage to Percivale, depending on how one weighed the costs; one more reason why he didn't want her to feel she had to choose between the two of them.

Illarion stepped into the breakfast room to find Stepan and Ruslan already there. He offered them a brief smile and turned to fill his plate with fresh blini and berries.

'Sleep well?' Stepan scowled over his coffee mug.

'Good morning to you, too.' Illarion helped himself to cold salmon and took his seat. Ruslan's gaze slid between the two of them in anticipation and Illarion frowned. Oh, hell, Stepan knew.

'I hear your *muse* was here.'

Illarion did not care for the implication in Stepan's tone, that Dove was something less savoury than an inspiration. 'I will thank you to keep a civil tongue in your head when you speak of Lady Dove.'

'*I* will thank you to keep a civil cock in your trousers!' Stepan banged a fist on the table. The china tea cups jumped. Illarion did not. 'A Cossack may do as he likes, but he must take responsibility for his actions.'

Illarion met Stepan's outrage with the blue steel of his gaze. He rose from his chair, hands braced on the table. 'How dare you quote the Kubanian motto to me. I know it full well. Do I not take responsibility for Katya? Do you think I don't take responsibility for Dove, never mind that it was she who came here?' He was, however, going to have words with the footman. Dove deserved her privacy. 'Do not sit there and act as if I played the rake.'

Stepan shook with barely contained fury. 'You made love to a virgin, the daughter of a duke, in this house. Do you know how many rules you broke?' All of them. He knew precisely how many rules he'd broken. He'd do it again.

Ruslan intervened. 'No one knows, Stepan.'

'The footman knows,' Stepan responded tersely. 'Do you know how this will look if word gets out? It won't do our reputations any good. What do you mean to do about this? Are you willing to marry her?'

'If she'll have me,' Illarion replied boldly. The words were as much of a surprise to him as they were to Stepan.

'If she'll have you? She's already *had* you.'

'She can't marry him,' Ruslan interrupted. 'He's not respectable. It's all over White's. Heatherly and

Percivale have been talking.' Ruslan shook his head. 'It's just rumours this time. But what they're saying is not exactly untrue.'

'What are they saying?' Illarion took his seat, but it was hard to sit with so much emotion roiling through him.

'That you've got nothing to offer a bride. No family, no property. That your title means nothing, quite possibly you don't even possess it any more and, even if you did, it's empty since there's nothing to go with it.'

Ruslan was right. It wasn't untrue. It was just presented in a way that looked very unattractive. But Ruslan wasn't done. 'They're saying you're a fortune hunter, that your interest in Lady Dove is for her money and land. She can provide everything you lack.' The very things Dove had decried in the gentlemen who populated her court. He hoped Dove didn't hear those rumours. If she did, he hoped she didn't believe them.

'Then I've got to be respectable,' Illarion answered. Respectable wasn't something he knew much about. 'How do I start?'

Stepan glowered. But Ruslan smiled and took something from his pocket. 'You can start with this.'

'A key?' Illarion took it and turned it over in his hand. 'What is this to?'

Ruslan laughed. 'To your future, should you want it. I've been investing in prime real estate while you've been out wooing the ladies. Number Two

Portland Square—you won't find a better address in Mayfair.'

Illarion nodded. 'I don't suppose you might also have a small manor in Cornwall in your pocket?' Dove would like that—a place to draw, a place to be near her family.

'Not today, but I could find something.' Ruslan rose from the table, leaving Stepan and Illarion alone.

'Do you really want to marry her?' Stepan asked, his temper quieting. 'I thought you were rankly against marriage. Or did you say that because I made you angry?'

Stepan was giving him a chance to retract his statement, but Illarion would not back down. The more he thought about the idea, the more he liked it. 'I want to marry her, but I want it to be her choice. She needs to understand what it means to be with me. There are things I cannot give her, that money will never buy her.' Social status, the idea that she might no longer be accepted, incurring the disappointment of her family. His money could not change those things. Dove had no idea what it meant to lose them. He had to make her understand what exile looked like because that's what she'd experience if she chose him, or even if she didn't. Striking out for herself would have the same social consequences.

Stepan nodded solemnly. 'Nikolay is holding a riding demonstration tonight. Perhaps you should bring her and she can see what it means to live between worlds.' It was the perfect place to start. She could see the 'bad news' of life with him up close. He pocketed Ruslan's key. He would save that for later—the house would be the good news to the bad news, as it were.

The riding school was located on Leicester Square in Soho, a square that had seen better days, as evidenced by the big houses and large lots—something that didn't exist in cramped London any more. At one time, Leicester Square had been a popular neighbourhood for the well-to-do, but as the caprices of landownership and city planning had them move west to Mayfair, the large mansions had been broken down into multiple residences, many becoming boarding houses until years of decline had created a neighbourhood of immigrants. French aristocracy who had fled with nothing more than their titles, their pride and their heads intact, Polish inventors, German composers, men with ideas if not money, men and families who hoped Leicester Square was a temporary resting place as their fortunes climbed. But until then, this was home. Small businesses had sprung up; bistros that cooked food from homelands across Europe; bookstores selling texts in the languages from home, a world within a world, a world Dove had not known existed.

Dove found Soho intoxicating: the smells of cooking food, the sounds of different tongues and the sights of different clothing. It was as if she'd left London behind her. Here, Illarion's tunic, the

one he'd worn to the ball, would not be out of place.
Here, *she* was the one out of place. Illarion had said
to wear something plain. She'd chosen a round gown
of celestial blue with only a bit of lace trimming the
bodice and a cashmere shawl of blue flowers on a
white field. The gown was simple, not plain. She
saw the difference now as they passed crowds of the
working and middle class on their way home from
the day. The women wore plain wool dresses in dark
colours, making her blue appear all the brighter.
She was, without doubt, conspicuous. On her own,
she might have been frightened as opposed to in-
toxicated by the newness of her surroundings, but
with Illarion beside her, it did not cross her mind
to be afraid.

'Nikolay's riding school is there on the left.' Illarion directed her attention to a large home still
entirely intact, turning his team towards the kerb
where other carriages had begun to line up, some
of them personal, but most of them were city hacks.
Even more people came on foot. 'It looks like he has
a good turn-out for the exhibition tonight.'

Illarion had been cryptic about the outing. His
invitation had indicated that Prince Baklanov was
hosting a riding event, chaperoned by Klara Baklanova. The credentials of the evening were as impec-
cably presented as those for the picnic.

'Will you tell me what the exhibition is?' Dove
demanded playfully as he swung her down.

'It's a demonstration of Russian horseback riding,

mostly military in nature. Nikolay stands on a horse's back, rides two horses at once, things like that.'

'You are teasing me! No one can do those things.' Dove laughed. 'I am not that gullible. What are we really seeing?'

'You are seeing exactly what I told you.' Illarion chuckled at her disbelief. He was at ease tonight and that put her at ease. Any awkwardness over last night's intimacy vanished in the wake of his good humour. Perhaps there was no need for awkwardness, which would imply an embarrassment and regret she did not feel. She'd awakened pleasantly sore, but she was not sorry, even if she wasn't sure what it meant. If she'd thought making love would settle the question, she'd been wrong. The question was still there.

Inside, the viewing gallery was full of spectators, but Nikolay had set aside seats for them beside his wife in the front row. As they made their way down front, Illarion's hand always at her back, Dove noted the audience. These were not the *ton*. These were horsemen, expatriates of varying occupations. Certainly, there were likely some gentry among them, country baronets with an interest in horses, in town for a few weeks for horse racing before returning to their farms. No wonder Illarion had been sparse with his details. A suspicion began to take bloom. Illarion had brought her here for a reason.

The show was all Illarion had predicted and more. Never had she seen such skills performed on horseback. Nikolay and his riders had been incredible and Dove was loath to see the evening end. This was far more fun than a Mayfair ball. When she said as much to Illarion, he bent close to her ear. 'There's more to come. Do you want to go to a party?' Ah, Dove thought. He was still testing her. Did he think she'd refuse? Did he think he could frighten her off with this glimpse into his 'Russian life'? Or, came the wicked thought, did he think to entice her? Was this another layer of seduction?

The experiment was…enlightening and deuced enjoyable, as the English would say. When Illarion had come up with the idea of showing Dove what life would be like outside the *ton*, he'd not been sure of the reaction he'd get. Part of him feared it would frighten her away, even as much as he knew the necessity for it. Better for her to know now than to find out too late. But Dove had not scared. She'd embraced the evening from the moment he'd driven out of Mayfair. She was still embracing it as they joined Nikolay's group at Mikhail's, a bistro that served Russian food. She'd devoured the *piroshki*, much to Mikhail's delight, and drank down vodka at a rather alarming rate. She'd joined the dancing without hesitation, letting him lead her through the steps of the country dances. She twirled now with a wide smile on her mouth, laughing with her partner, a young Russian officer attached to the embassy.

Nikolay took a seat next to him and slid him a

glass of vodka. 'You're generous.' He nodded to where Dove danced.

Illarion shrugged. 'Being with me all night will not help her see the world I intend to show her.'

Nikolay chuckled at that. 'Did you really bring her here to talk her out of her decision or to talk her into it? Why would anyone want *ton*nish life when they could have this? I tried this with Klara and it didn't work. It only encouraged her, thank goodness.' He grinned happily.

'A life in between, you mean?' Illarion said seriously. Nikolay had opted for that: a life split between the upper-class living offered by Klara's father, Alexei Grigoriev, and the streets of Soho where he could be his own man.

'There's nothing wrong with it.' Nikolay was defensive. Illarion had not meant to insult him. It suited Nikolay. He might be a prince, but he'd also been a cavalry officer. He was used to living rough on the border campaigns. He was not a man who would survive long if limited to prowling ballrooms. He was not Dove. How long would places like Mikhail's hold any allure for her?

'You're not Lady Dove, daughter of a duke,' Illarion reminded him. 'She knows nothing but luxury. She hasn't the faintest idea how to do without it.' That was what worried him the most. Lady Dove was a rebel in theory. She had no idea what it would cost her. Luxury was embedded in everything she did, in ways she probably wasn't even aware of.

'If luxury is so important to her, she can marry Percivale and be done with it,' Nikolay offered matter of factly. 'She would have accepted his offer days ago.'

He levelled Illarion with a long, dark stare. 'You're getting in pretty deep for a woman who was only supposed to be your muse. I hear Ruslan gave you the keys to a town house.'

'My politics demand it,' Illarion answered automatically. 'You would do the same. You and I are opposed to women being forced to marry against their will for the sake of alliances. It's what we risked everything for back in Kuban.'

Nikolay laughed and took a long drink. 'Your politics? Is that what we're calling it these days? Your *sexual* politics, perhaps. I'd buy that.' He rotated his glass thoughtfully in his hand. 'You have a fortune in the bank. You can see to her luxury.' He finished off his drink and winked, 'For political reasons, of course.'

Nikolay leaned in close. 'You know you can't take her to bed without marriage, Illarion? Not a girl like that.' Something must have moved in his expression. Nikolay gripped his arm. 'You already did. Damn. Humour me for a moment as I risk sounding like Stepan, but Percivale will kill you if her father doesn't do it first, or you don't get her to altar before it all comes out.' Nikolay tightened his grip, his voice dropping. 'Is that what you want, an excuse to face Percivale at twenty paces?'

'Murder or matrimony? I doubt it will come to

murder. I don't seek out duels on purpose,' Illarion replied with quiet iron. But the idea held some merit. Percivale was attempting to slander him.

Nikolay was grim. 'If it comes to either, call me. I'll be your second.' Illarion smiled. That was the difference between Nikolay and Stepan. Stepan would rail at him until dawn for taking such a risk. But Nikolay would nod his acceptance and offer to be his witness, no questions asked.

The dance ended, the music swinging into another tune. Illarion brightened as he recognised it. 'Hopak!' he cried. 'Shall we?' There was nothing like a lively Hopak full of squats and bends and leg kicks to remind him of nights spent dancing in Kuban. He linked arms with Nikolay and dragged him to the centre of the floor with a laugh to join the other men.

Chapter Seventeen

The Hopak, danced in its purest form, was a man's dance. Dove stood beside Klara Baklanova, her cheeks flushed, her body sweating from the dancing, as she clapped along with the crowd surrounding the dancers. What had started as group of men dancing had become just two: Nikolay and Illarion. The two of them sprang into the air, legs spread, hands touching toes as they leapt, only to land and conduct a series of fast squats and leg kicks. Nikolay was impressive, but Dove had eyes only for Illarion. His hair had come loose from the black silk bow he'd worn earlier. In fact, much of what he'd worn earlier was gone; his coat, his waistcoat, his cravat, all lying around the bistro somewhere, she supposed. It didn't seem important at the moment. The gentleman who had collected her in Mayfair was gone, replaced by a man who was more primal, more natural than any man she'd ever met. The gentleman-Prince Illarion

Kutejnikov played at being had slowly been replaced by this man over the course of the night, she realised. It had started slowly at the riding exhibition as he'd exchanged a few words in Russian with those sitting around them, until he'd spoken more Russian than English by the time they'd arrived at the bistro, and then the clothes had started coming off, the hair had started coming down.

She didn't mind, not one bit. While the Mayfair Prince was captivating in his own right, this man was positively riveting. She loved the sound of the Russian language spoken around her, the spicy taste of the food, eaten with her hands, the smooth, cool vodka as it washed down the *piroshki*. Most of all, she loved watching him in his element.

Illarion danced by her, flashing her a wide grin as he passed, arms flung wide. Tonight, she was seeing *him* for the first time. Oh, she didn't doubt that she'd seen the real him prior to this, only she knew now that what she'd seen was a slice, a carefully doled-out slice—enough to make him interesting to the *ton*, but not nearly enough to reveal the sum of who he was. He passed by again, this time grabbing her hand and pulling her into the dance as the music shifted into a polka. Her heart whispered a warning even as it sped up in the excitement of being with him. This man was dangerous. This was a man she wanted for ever.

Illarion whirled her about the floor and she laughed with reckless abandon as they wove in and out of couples. It was amazing no one crashed when everyone was dancing as fast as they were. 'This is madness!' Dove cried, delighting in the speed and trusting entirely in the competence of Illarion to lead them through the throng of dancers without mishap. Her own hair had fallen down, her pins finally giving up the battle.

Illarion laughed with her, pulling her close. 'The madness is the best part.'

The madness ended too soon. It was midnight and, while early for a ball, it was late to be out for a riding exhibition. They said their goodbyes to Nikolay and Klara and Dove reluctantly stepped up into the coach. 'I feel like Cinderella leaving the ball,' she said wistfully as the coach pulled away from the kerb. 'I would have liked to have danced all night.' The others would. They'd been the first to leave.

Illarion grinned and stretched his legs out from the seat opposite her. His discarded clothing lay in a pile beside him. 'I wasn't sure you'd like it.'

'Did you want me to? I haven't figured that part out yet.' Dove voiced the suspicion she'd been harbouring all night. 'You brought me tonight to teach me a lesson. But I don't think I learned the one you intended.' She felt Illarion's thoughtful gaze study her.

'Tell me, what did you learn?'

'That I need to be free. That I was right in wanting to see the world. No matter what it costs.'

'You don't know what it costs.' Illarion's voice was stern, almost scolding. She was not going to take that from him, not tonight when he'd been the one to open her eyes. How dare he think he could give her such a gift and then snatch it away. Even after last night, he doubted she knew her own mind. She would show him, *prove* to him, that she was so much more than a pretty, rich girl.

'My parents treat me as if I am a child and make all my decisions for me. I am not a babe in arms.' She moved across the small distance between them, sliding next to him on the seat. She could feel the heat rolling off his body, a reminder of how vital, how alive he was. She reached for him, cupping his jaw with her hand, drawing his gaze to her, forcing him to see her and what she intended. 'I am not a child, Illarion,' she whispered. Her eyes dropped to his mouth. 'I know my own mind and I know I want this. I want you. I want the man I saw tonight.' She moved into him, taking his mouth with hers. She tasted the vodka on his tongue, smelled the mingled scents of exerted man and patchouli.

She wanted, she wanted, she wanted. The words were a litany in her head, pushing her onwards towards more recklessness in a night that had been full of rashness. Her hands framed his face, pushing back the thick fall of his hair. She was kissing him again, but this time she was not alone. His mouth answered hers. The invitation had been accepted. He nipped at her lips with a fierce growl. She nipped back, her mouth duelling with his. Tonight, *she* would be the one to give him something to growl about. Tonight she would give him pleasure.

Dove kissed him on the mouth, her hand cupped his jaw, she deepened the kiss, her tongue exploring him until Illarion groaned. 'Where does a duke's daughter learn to kiss like that?'

She gave a coy smile. 'I had a very good teacher.' She'd kissed him the way he kissed her, with everything he had, as if that kiss was the most important thing in the world. 'Let's see, what else do you like? How about this?' Her mouth moved to his ear, her teeth sinking delicately into the tender piece of his lobe. She pressed him back against the carriage seat, straddling him, her hand moving between them to his trousers. She found him roused and ready, her hand slipping over the shape of his erection. She moulded him, shaped him. His hips slid down the seat to grant her better access. But it wasn't enough for her, not tonight. Tonight she wanted to touch him, no holds barred.

'Shall I put my mouth on you, Illarion?' she whispered, already slipping down to kneel in front of him, watching his eyes go dark at her words. 'It's what you want, isn't it? For me to put my mouth on you like do for me.'

'Yes.' He gave her the word in a hoarse rasp.

Her hands trembled as she worked the fastenings of his trousers, her pulse beating fast with vodka and arousal. She had him free, hot, hard and long in her hand, the heat of him astonishing to hold. With a last wicked glance upwards, she braced his legs apart and bent to him, taking him inch by hot inch and then retreating, her mouth approximating what he'd done with her, to her. She tasted him with her tongue. She licked him then, a long flickering caress across his tender head, gratified when his hips twitched, his body wriggling down in his seat as he let the sweet decadence of the moment take him, thrill him. His response emboldened her, it fed the excitement of what she could do to him. That excitement overrode any sense of decorum. Her mouth closed over him fully and a moan escaped him—a sound part pleasure, and part pain. Through lidded eyes, she saw his hands dig into the seat for balance. She licked him as he shuddered. Her hand found the flesh hidden behind his straining phallus and she squeezed gently, provocatively, until his moans became bays. She felt his body gather and clench, reaching its limits, driving itself towards release.

He cried out, perhaps in warning, just before he spent and she caught him in her hand, warm and pulsing and alive. The sight of him, head thrown back, the cords of his neck taut, eyes shut against pleasure, was a primal one of man undone. He was at his best, at his most vulnerable, in these moments and *she'd* brought him to it. The intensity of the moment awed her. This was intimacy at its finest; to watch a man come apart, to see the pleasure rack him.

'Do you see what you do to me?' Illarion's voice was a hoarse rasp.

She *did* see. Illarion Kutejnikov climaxed with his blue eyes open, perhaps specifically for that purpose. He *wanted* her to see the pleasure take him, wanted her to see what they did together mattered to him. In seeing that, she also saw him exposed. She was his weakness, odd thought though it was, that this man of strength and confidence, this man who had the *ton* at his feet, should have any vulnerabilities. A sense of pride surged through her as she rested her head against his thigh. She was breathing hard, too. This had taken a toll on her as well. His hand played softly in her hair. 'My dear girl, you do know how to play with fire.' She smiled up at him and took the handkerchief he offered.

Something flickered in his eyes. 'We were talking about tonight before we got distracted.'

She took the seat across from him. 'I think you were about to tell me what I was supposed to learn from tonight.' She'd learned quite a lot, about herself and about him. She'd learned that she could enjoy life beyond the ballrooms of Mayfair. She could, in fact, enjoy many things as long as he was with her. Perhaps enjoy them enough to stand up to her parents if the need arose.

'I wanted you to see the life between,' Illarion said bluntly. 'Nikolay and Klara have her father's connections but they are not necessarily received on their own. They are not recruited into the higher echelons of society. Klara gave all those aspirations up when she married Nik.' Illarion paused. 'She was promised to a duke, just as you are.'

'What are you trying to tell me, Illarion? If tonight was supposed to be a warning to scare me off, it failed miserably.' As did Klara's story. If living 'between' was good enough for Klara, it was good enough for her. 'Do you think I am so silly as to crave society's attention? To care what society thinks?'

'It may matter to you some day.' Illarion looked out the window and sighed. 'We are nearly home. Thank you for a lovely evening. I *am* glad you enjoyed it.'

'I do not think you finished saying what you meant to say.' Dove was not eager to get out of the cab with their conversation incomplete. There was a mystery lurking here. Why had tonight mattered so much to him?

Illarion gave a half-smile. 'We will finish this conversation tomorrow. Klara will call for you at noon to do some shopping.'

'Shopping?' The last thing she wanted to do was shop.

Illarion laughed. 'Not really. You'll have to wait until tomorrow to find out, *golubushka*.'

Chapter Eighteen

Portland Square, Number Two.
Noon.
I have something to discuss.

Dove fingered the folded note Klara had given her, feeling the form of the key hidden within its folds. For a man known for his poetry, the note was terse and short. But for all its brevity it still had the power to make her pulse quicken.

She was coming to suspect it would always be that way with him. Even when he left her, the sound of his name in a conversation or the slightest whiff of patchouli would recall him to her. She would never be free of him, one more unintended consequence of her rash gambit. And this visit to Portland Square another.

Dove wrapped her pink shawl about her shoulders, thankful for the company of Klara in the open-air landau. Klara's presence had saved her the need to lie to her parents. Number Two was easily located, the whitewash and the black shutters made it stand out from its brick and sandstone counterparts. Dove looked up from beneath the brim of her hat at the four storeys of paned and shuttered windows. The home was impressive, fit for a duke, or, Dove thought with a shiver of anticipation, a prince. Although, why this particular Prince needed a town house was beyond her. Actually, she could imagine a few reasons, all of which left a knot of butterflies fluttering around her stomach. Men needed homes for one reason: to set up housekeeping and nurseries. Was that what he meant to discuss last night?

Dove climbed the front stairs slowly, behind Klara, smoothing her hand over her belly in the hopes of settling the butterflies. Had Illarion meant to propose? How odd when he'd made it clear to her that he thought marriage was a prison. She had, too, for that matter, only, she wasn't sure she believed that any more. Marriage to a man like Illarion would be different than marriage to Percivale. And yet, she felt as if marriage would be an imposition. Illarion didn't *want* to marry.

The shiny, black-lacquer door opened before she could knock. Illarion ushered her inside with a sweep of his hand. 'Come in. Welcome…home.' He glanced at Klara. 'Thank you for bringing her.' It was a po-lite dismissal. He meant for them to be here alone. A trill of anticipation went through her.

She gave him an odd look. There was something different about him today. He'd dressed carefully in a dark blue jacket and buff breeches, his hair immaculate in its black bow, his cravat crisply tied in an Osbaldeston knot. A heavy ring set with a sapphire adorned his hand. But that was nothing new. He was always well turned-out. What was new was the tension about him. The ease he usually exhibited, as if nothing mattered, was missing. Today, Illarion was nervous. How curious. But it did nothing to ease the nerves in her own stomach. His nerves became her nerves.

'We need to talk, Dove, but first, let me give you a tour.' Inside, the town house did not disappoint from the black and white marble tiles of the floor to the high ceilings and the majestic sweep of the staircase leading upstairs.

'This is spectacular,' Dove commented, and meant it. The entrance rivalled her father's own home.

Illarion smiled, pleased. 'You haven't seen anything yet. Allow me to show you around.' He ushered her up the staircase, a guiding hand at her back. The first stop was the main drawing room, done in exquisite wallpaper of hand-painted Chinese silk. Doors opened to a music room that carried out the oriental theme with peacocks, adorning the space in lush teals and blues. The dining room with its long table could seat twenty, easily. There was a library, a lady's writing room in soft rose. Chintz would look lovely in there; soft and feminine. She could already picture a vase of white roses on the small white hearth. The light was excellent here, it was a place where she could draw. At that thought, she had to take herself firmly in hand. She was *not* to mentally decorate the space. It was akin to naming strays. It made the space too personal.

'Shall we go upstairs?' Illarion gestured towards the stairs leading to the third floor. 'There are six bedrooms, but there's only one I want to show you.'

'I can't imagine anything rivalling what we've already seen. The house is so…exotic.' Each room was a story representing a different place in the world: the Far East in the drawing room and conservatory, the grand French style in the dining room, the English garden in the lady's sitting room. One need never leave the house to see the world if one decorated just right.

Illarion just grinned smugly, pushing open the door to the suite. 'Tell me what you think now.' He stood back and let her enter, let her stare. With the exception of the dining room, the house was empty, but here an enormous, carved four-poster bed dominated the centre of the room. It was lodged against the far wall between two long windows and draped in the most sumptuous collection of silks she'd ever seen: burnished golds, teals, deep plums, dark blues, a splash of red. Silken pillows were piled high at the head, a lush purple throw draped haphazardly at the foot. It was a sultan's bed.

'I had it brought in last night,' Illarion supplied. 'I wanted you to see the room with a bed in it.'

The comment was the most curious remark of all. As intrigued as she was by the splendour of the house, her patience was stretching thin. 'What is the meaning of all this, Illarion?'

'I've been thinking it's time to have a place of my own.' He let her look one last time before leading her out of the magical room. 'I can't live at Kuban House for ever. Dimitri and Evie will be wanting it back some time and it's time for me to start my London life in truth.' The butterflies in her stomach were replaced by a sense of disappointment. He wanted the house for him, that was all. She should have been relieved. He wanted her opinion on a house, nothing more. Of course he'd been wanting a home of his own.

'There's one last room to show you.' He took her back to the first floor where a set of over-wide double doors remained unopened. 'It's not as grand as your godmother's.' He winked as he threw them open and Dove gasped. Ballrooms by nature didn't have the intimate ambiance of a bedroom, but what this one lacked in intimacy, it made up for in elegance.

'It's *as* grand, it's grander,' Dove gasped. Beneath her feet, the polished floor gleamed, but it was what hung overhead that claimed her attention. Four chandeliers suspended from a ceiling of painted clouds and cherubs done in the style of Raphael.

'They were hand-blown in Venice, I'm told,' Illarion offered. 'They're not from Metternich himself, but perhaps they'll do?' He gave her a wink, seeming more relaxed than he had been since her arrival. 'I take it you approve of the house?'

'More than approve,' Dove said breathlessly, moving about the room to study the chandeliers from various angles.

'I see you are already planning balls.' Illarion chuckled, sweeping up behind her and turning her in his arms. 'Perhaps we should try out the dance floor first.'

'What are you doing?' She gave a startled laugh as he moved her into the steps of a tuneless waltz.

'Avoiding buyer's remorse.' His mouth was close at her ear. 'Can't be buying a ballroom that doesn't work now, can we?'

We. What a lovely word. For a moment she gave herself over to the fantasy of it—of them dancing in their own ballroom, of life being a waltz, every day full of laughter and smiles.

At the end of the ballroom, he brought them to a halt in front of the doors leading out to the wide veranda and a view of the gardens beyond. 'Do you like it, truly, Dove?' He was a little breathless. 'Can you see yourself here? With me?'

The words took her by dangerous surprise. The butterflies were back. 'What do you mean, Illarion?'

Illarion dropped to a knee before her, taking her hands in his, his blue eyes serious and earnest. 'I am asking you to marry me, Dove, to live here with me, for ever.'

The fierceness of his grip on her hands was testimony to how serious he was. This was no joke. Illarion Kutejnikov, Prince of Kuban, was asking her to marry him. And Dove didn't know what to say.

'I will take you around the world for our honeymoon,' Illarion tempted. 'We'll furnish this house from our travels. We'll be gone for years if you want. You can draw and when we come home, we'll hang your drawings all over the house to remind us of our great adventures.'

He was bargaining with her again. Offering what she wanted in exchange for something he supposedly wanted. What a temptation it was to say yes, to ignore the undercurrents of his proposal. With one small word, she'd have everything she'd ever wanted: adventure, freedom and the passion of Illarion in her bed. Her earlier thought returned. Marriage to Illarion would not be like marriage to Percivale. It was everything she wanted. Almost. Was it everything *he* wanted?

She was obligated to ask the hard question. 'Why are you doing this? You said you didn't want to marry. What has changed your mind?' A thought came to her that perhaps he felt duty bound to offer for her. She did not want him that way. It would destroy her to be the only one in love. Dove pulled her hands away from his. This would be easier if he weren't touching her. She tried not to think of the big bed upstairs, or the rose sitting room with the excellent light.

'It occurs to me that I can give you a way out from Percivale.'

'You want to *save* me?' A noble but not romantic sentiment. And the words hurt. She knew he did not mean to hurt, but they did. 'I think marriage needs a little more than that to recommend it, don't you?' If he made such a sacrifice now, would he hate her for it later? Unless it wasn't a sacrifice at all. Unless it was something he wanted, too? 'I'm sorry, Illarion, I don't think leaping from one forced marriage to another is a very good idea.' She understood the purpose of last night in vivid clarity. He'd wanted her to see what life would be like with *him*. He wanted her to consider the possibility, both the good and the bad, before he asked her *this*. He'd just made her choice so much more difficult. She could no longer choose Percivale by default for lack of no other offer. Illarion would make her choose deliberately. He loved her that much. The realisation was overwhelming. She had to refuse. Didn't she?

'Did you think I would take you to bed and not honour you?' Was that the sort of man she thought he was? Illarion rose from his knee, slowly in disbelief. She was refusing him? After last night and the night before? It seemed surreal. He had planned everything so carefully, given her no quarter to say no and yet she had, she was. 'Do you not want me, Dove?' He was numb with the realisation, but he knew it would hurt like the devil later when the shock was gone.

'I will not have you sacrifice yourself for me. You will hate me for it, eventually.'

Something akin to anger flashed through him. To hell with that nobility of hers that said others had to come before self. 'I can save you. I can give you everything you want.' He reached for her hands again, wanting to touch her, his voice a low growl. 'I don't consider marriage to you a sacrifice, Dove.' The hurt started to surface as an idea flickered. 'Perhaps you consider marriage to *me* a sacrifice?' Was that it? Had she reconsidered after last night? Had she recognised the importance of belonging to society? How that might be at risk if she married him? Had she chosen her *family* over him? Perhaps she had reassessed what the price of her freedom was worth and decided it was too expensive? Logically, he could understand and even empathise with those choices, but emotionally he could not accept it.

His heart sank at the thought of Dove giving up, of allowing herself to become the very thing she hated: a bird in a gilded cage. 'Dove,' he began, wanting to exhort her to fight, to persuade her she didn't have to settle, but he even as he formed the arguments, he was cognisant of the risk she was facing. Marriage to him might have social repercussions; his title might be paper only, his status resting on London's benevolence alone. Her parents might cut her off, might disown her. Even so, he wanted to cry out, *I am enough, Dove. I can be enough for you.*

'Don't,' she cautioned. 'I am surprised, that's all, and now you have honeymoons and houses all laid out. Can you at least understand what an about-face this is? That this is a decision not without risk? I need time to think it through.' She asked quietly, 'Will you give me that?'

He stiffened at the words, reminiscent of another proposal. She'd asked Percivale to give her time because she hadn't been sure, because she wanted to refuse. Did she want to refuse *him*? The potential that she might turn him down, that she might spend her life away from him, was an appalling one. 'Time is the one thing you haven't much of.' The world seemed to invade this little paradise of his. Did she understand how little of it there was? Things were rapidly coming to a head with Percivale. A duel was imminent either over Dove or over the slanderous rumours. 'I will give you all I can.'

'Thank you.' She stepped away from the balustrade, lost for words. She looked at him with beseeching eyes. 'Will you excuse me? I have to go.'

She turned and fled—that was the only word for it. She fairly ran through the house, wanting to be as far away from the big, beautiful house, from him. Illarion let her go, his own heart breaking a little. He'd finally fallen in love, finally found the woman who could break the spell and she would not have him—ironically to save him from himself. Never had he wanted someone so much. Never had something seemed so impossible to claim. Never had the stakes been so high. To lose Dove would be akin to losing a part of himself.

Chapter Nineteen

Dove sat still so as not to disturb the mare, her body quiet, her mind a riot of unsorted thoughts, her pencil unmoving in her hand. Beyond her, in the hay, the mare whickered. She'd come to the mews to draw the horse, but she'd drawn Illarion instead. It was all she could seem to manage these days. Was this what Illarion's writer's block felt like? A mind too full to concentrate? Recent days had been filled with momentous events. Two men had proposed to her; demanded decisions from her that would shape the rest of her life. She'd made love with Illarion; she'd drank vodka; she'd given a man pleasure; a man had bought a house for her, for *them*. That man wanted to spend his life making her happy.

It should have been a joyous few days, it should have been symbolic of what else she'd done. She should have taken a first step towards her own independence. But she hadn't. No one but Illarion knew she had done any of those things. She was no more independent now than she'd been when she'd first come to London. Nothing had changed. Everything had changed. *She* had changed, and yet the face that stared back at her every night from her dressing table mirror *hadn't*.

Shouldn't she look different? It seemed strange that the world was the same: the same white dresses were laid out on her bed, the same pearls waiting for her neck, the same evening routine, with the same people. Alfred-Ashby would talk about his horses. Lord Fredericks would say 'quite so' a hundred times. Percivale would stand possessively at her right side. It was no wonder young girls were counselled against intimacy before marriage. Underneath the sameness there were complications she had not foreseen.

Lovemaking distorted one's perspective altogether. She'd not been prepared for that, to say nothing of spoiling her for other men in ways that went beyond the loss of virginity. How could she be expected to share such an act with someone else? She could not imagine being so free, so utterly abandoned in her sensibilities with another as she had been with Illarion. To think of another doing with her what Illarion had done… Well, that was another piece of the impossible choice facing her. She shivered and drew her shawl more tightly about her. The mare lifted her head and looked at her with soulful eyes.

Dove smiled sadly at the horse. 'What am I to

do?' She had to decide. Percivale had been more than patient. Illarion had been more than generous. Her heart wanted to run to Illarion, wanted to accept his offer. Could she live with the risk of alienating her family, alienating herself from all she knew, for a man she *barely* knew? Was it logical to risk eighteen years—*the sum of her lifetime*—on a man she'd known for such a short time? And yet, if she did not, nothing short of running away would stop a marriage to Percivale, who was growing more impatient by the day. She was running out of time as Percivale and her parents ran out of patience.

Her head argued differently. Would Percivale be such a bad choice? There was nothing wrong with him, indeed there was much *right* about him except that she lacked a sense of connection to him, lacked the spark that ignited whenever she was with Illarion. Percivale would make her a duchess, the rest of her life would be secure, her place in society assured as would be the places of her children. Her son would be a duke.

What did she dare? Some might say it was an issue of being a princess to a man without a home, or to be a duchess to a man who had everything. Dove knew it was far more than that. This was a decision about whether to marry with her heart or to marry with her head.

Maybe this was why daughters ought to be guided by their parents, people who were older, wiser and removed from the immediate emotion of the situation. There was no wrong decision. Maybe that was why it was so difficult to choose. There were only two *right* decisions. But she'd made a fatal flaw in her reasoning.

She'd assumed she had the power to make any decision at all. 'Miss, I'm sorry to intrude.' One of the maids from the house poked her head into the stable. 'Your father needs to see you.' There was a certain excited agitation to the maid's announcement the girl was trying desperately to hide, as if she knew something, a secret.

'What is it?' Dove gathered up her drawing supplies. It sounded ominous. A cold fist gripped her stomach. Had Percivale's uncle passed? Had the hour glass dropped its final grain of sand?

'I couldn't say, miss.' But the maid knew. Dove could see it in her eyes. This was not a time she appreciated discretion in servants.

Both of her parents waited for her in her father's office. The door shut behind her. 'What has happened? Nothing bad, I hope?' Dove asked.

'No, darling,' Her mother moved forward to take her hand, a soft shining smile on her face.

Her father picked up the conversation. 'Percivale was here. He has most prudently acquired a special licence. He would like your decision tonight.' Her father's eyes rested on her and Dove froze. 'He needs your answer, Dove. Now. I do not know why you delay.'

Dove drew a breath. The choice she had not quite made in the mews needed to be made now. Perhaps this was her chance. This was not only about standing up for Illarion, but standing up for herself. If she could not do this now, she never would. 'I am honoured by his attentions,' she began, rapidly assessing the best way to approach the subject. 'However, I have been honoured by other attentions as well. Prince Kutejnikov has proposed and I feel his offer is worth consideration.'

Her father's dark brow went up. 'Prince Kutejnikov has proposed? To *you*? Directly?'

'Yes, Father.' Dove stepped back, trying to assume a demure posture, hoping to avoid argument but she was not misled by the mild enquiry of his tone. Her father was angry.

'He has not spoken to *me*, Dove.' Her father began to pace. 'He has dishonoured you with such behaviour and he shows me disrespect by not consulting me.' He stopped and studied her. 'What did you tell him?'

'That I needed time, that I was surprised by the offer.' Dove hated her words, true as they might be. They sounded weak, as if she were trying to blame Illarion for his proposal. She needed to be braver. Under other circumstances, the proposal would have thrilled her.

'A girl should never be surprised by an offer of marriage. That's why her father is consulted, so the offer might be laid out to her in a timely fashion,' her father growled. 'I knew he was trouble the first day he stepped in here.'

'He is a prince, you needn't sneer at his offer,' Dove argued, coming to Illarion's defence.

Her father's face darkened with protective anger. 'He is not worthy of you. There are rumours, Dove, about the legitimacy of his title, about why he left Kuban. People are saying it wasn't by choice, that he was expelled and can never return. He is a man without a country.'

'Rumours spread by Heatherly and Percivale,' she replied. 'They have the most to gain in dishonouring him.' It didn't matter how true the rumours were or not. She could be angry, too. She would not stand there and allow Illarion to be maligned.

'You would choose such a man?' Her father's voice was hard steel. 'You may not think you care about such consequences, but there will be a time when you will, miss, when society cuts you and your children, when you are not accepted anywhere because your husband is a fraud. We have not devoted our lives to your success only to see you throw yourself away on a Russian upstart with no kingdom!' Her father was terse, holding himself on a tight rein.

'Have you thought of why such a man would want to marry you, want to tempt you without coming to me first? He knows I would turn him down. He knows I will see him for the charlatan he is. Don't be naïve, Dove. He is using you!' She'd seldom seen her father this angry. 'The Prince sees a susceptible

mark in you, Dove. He needs your wealth, your connections to live in the manner to which he is accus-
tomed. Percivale is eager to protect you, to make sure
the Prince does not embroil you in scandal.'

She wanted to scream her father was wrong. The
enemy wasn't Illarion, it was Percivale and them,
people who claimed to care for her but who would
imprison her in their attempts to do their best by her.
But she could not bring herself to it. There was too
much heartache down that path; for them and for
her. She looked appealingly at her mother, but her
mother's face was a polite mask.

'I am sure that the Prince's attentions were very
flattering, Dove. He is a handsome man. Every girl
should have a brief crush before she settles down.'
Were. A single word relegated Illarion to the past
in the span of a heartbeat. 'The Prince must be dis-
suaded. His attentions cannot be courted any further.
If he calls again, your father can explain to him how
it is.' She smiled tremulously and held out her hand.
'You and I will need to start shopping for your trousseau. It will be exciting. Just think, we have a wedding to plan, a household to set up.' It was the same
strategy that had led up to her debut—distract and
entertain, dazzle her with the fairy tale so that she
would forget the reality.

Her father was stern. 'You will make a fine match
with Percivale. He is the finest husband of the year,
perhaps even the best catch of the decade.' He softened. 'You're simply too young to appreciate what

he offers. But your mother and I know best in this. You must trust us. You will thank us for it later when you are the toast of London. You can accept Percivale tonight.'

Tonight. The night of Illarion's much-anticipated poetry reading. Everyone would be there. Dove looked at her parents, each in turn, these people who had treasured her, nurtured her, loved her. She could not bear the idea of disappointing them. They had suffered so many other disappointments. She was the one dream left to them. Her heart was breaking, but her decision was made. She knew what she had to do. Somehow, she'd find the strength to do it.

Not in the recent history of the Season had a single person captured the imagination and attention of the *ton* the way Illarion Kutejnikov had. He'd always been a romantic figure with his long hair and handsome looks. But now, with the rumours of his questionable heritage surfacing, that romanticism took on an edge of danger.

Illarion was well aware that it was his notoriety that accounted for the enormous crush at Hathaway House. People wanted to hear the poems that had been the cause of his exile, giving fuel to the rumours that he'd been expelled from Kuban. That particular rumour was true. But others were not and those others had begun to run wild, all of them lies. He had *not* murdered anyone, he had *not* been stripped of his title and he most certainly had *not* left a woman in disgrace. Perhaps he should thank Heatherly and Percivale for the boost in popularity—it would sell poems—but he didn't deal in lies. They—Heatherly because he had started the rumours, Percivale because he had stood by and allowed the rumours to help his cause—had slandered him with their half-baked truths, creating a misleading image that was ultimately more damaging than good. For a man who had nothing *but* his honour, his good name was everything. He understood full well that making a scandal of him made it all that more difficult for Dove to come to him.

Illarion searched the crowd for her. Tonight was his chance to persuade London to accept him. Tonight, he could put the rumours to rest. More than that, he could persuade Dove to accept him. Tonight, on the stage, he could show her his heart, and hers.

'Your Highness, it's time.' Lord Hathaway had a hand at his elbow, ushering him up on the stage and calling the audience to attention. Illarion scanned the crowded grand salon of Hathaway House for her face one last time. He only partially listened to the introduction being given by Lord Hathaway, his host and the organiser of his reading. Surely Dove had come. Everyone who was anyone was here. This was *the* event of the early half of the Season. Redruth wouldn't miss it. Besides, he couldn't afford to. Absenting himself and his family would give credence to the rumours that there was tension between him and Redruth—yet one more set of rumours started by Percivale in the last week.

Of course, these particular rumours had a bit of truth to them. There *was* tension between him and Redruth. He'd gone to the town house that afternoon and attempted to see Dove after hearing the news on the club circuit about Percivale's special licence. Upon arrival, he'd been dismissed by the butler. When he made it clear he wouldn't leave, he'd been shown in to see his Grace the Duke of Redruth in the estate office. What had transpired next could only be politely termed as an 'unpleasant interview' where Redruth had accused him of fortune hunting.

His gaze quartered the crowd, passing over girls in pastels, gentlemen in black and white, brunettes and blondes until it found her: Dove with her platinum hair and her exquisite white dresses. Only Dove could turn de rigueur white into a signature colour. Illarion smiled and for a moment their eyes met, as if she'd been looking for him, too. Then Percivale claimed her attention, whispering something at her ear. Jealousy surged in Illarion. She was *his*. Was he *hers*? Would she dare? She did not glance his way again. Her eyes remained downcast. Illarion wondered if decisions had already been made. Had he already lost? The irony did not escape him. He'd travelled across the Continent to get away from such a system of tyranny, only to encounter it on a very personal level. He would not lose Dove over this. He would not. He could not.

Please, he thought, *let my words speak to her tonight. Let her be brave.* Never had he felt as if so much was riding on so little—a few words, a few images.

The audience broke into applause as Lord Hathaway ended his speech. Illarion stepped forward, finding his strength. Tonight was for Dove. Would she hear the message in his words? Would she be encouraged by it? Encouraged enough to come to him against all odds? He began, setting the scene about the situation in Kuban, and launched into the first poem, one that had incurred the wrath of his king. He let the anger come, as he performed 'Freedom,' the one that had got him exiled, Katya killed. Stepan had counselled him against it, saying it was too graphic. For some it was. Some mamas ushered their daughters out of the room. They didn't come back. Illarion didn't care. This was his chance to reach Dove. He began to sweat. His hair came loose, his coat came off and he performed in his shirt sleeves, using his body, his voice, to transport the audience, to bind them in his spell. Would it be enough to convince her? To compel her?

Illarion was mesmerising like this. Dove was on the edge of her seat, riveted. She had told herself all she had to do was get through tonight. Easier said than done. She had not been prepared for his effect on her. She'd expected him to recite poetry, an exercise in declamation, nothing more. But this was nearly drama, his body a tool of fluid motion and expansive gestures, his voice conveying emotion: anger and tears, dreams and dashed hopes. By the second poem, she was sure the poetry spoke directly to her, about her. These were *her* dashed dreams and hopes. Illarion was calling her to action, reaching out to her in the only way he could—calling to her heart, while she sat beside the choice of her head.

Percivale had been all graciousness tonight. He'd bowed over her hand, kissed her knuckles and smiled at her with fondness, if not heart-pounding love. 'I will look forward to speaking with you alone later tonight,' he'd said, a gentle reminder that he had waited for her. He praised her gown, told her she looked stunning. He himself was turned out sharply in crisp white linen, immaculate cravat, a subtle celery-green waistcoat and diamond stickpin. Any woman would be proud to be on his arm. As always, he was a prime representation of what good breeding and honour stood for. He knew the rules, he followed the rules. He was confident the rules would give him what he wanted. Dove wished she was as confident the rules would give *her* what she wanted. She was doing her best to follow them.

Illarion moved into his finale, introducing it, 'This last poem is dedicated to my muse, a woman who has brought me back to life. May my words inspire her as she has inspired me. Ladies and gentlemen, I humbly present *Snegoruchka.*'

Dove stifled a gasp. It was her! Tears sprang to

her eyes. She could not cry, could not give away what she knew to be true. But she could watch him, she could drink in every minute of this to let him know how much it meant even if that was all she could do. She had made her choice.

'*Snegoruchka* walks in the frost of her father's forest, her hair the shade of ice, her lips winterberry-red, her eyes glacier-grey as she waits for spring, as she waits for love.'

She waits for love.

The reference was unmistakable. Beside her, Percivale stiffened. 'By God, it's you.' He was horrified. 'He's making a spectacle of you. I will not have it.'

'No, please, it is nothing.' Dove begged quietly. But it was everything, in ways Percivale could not imagine or understand. She strained to hear the poem, each word an ode to her, an encouragement. Illarion was calling to her like a siren. Every bone in her body wanted to rise up out her chair and run to him, wanted to shout, 'Yes! Yes!' But she had made her decision.

'I will call him out for insulting you, it is my right. He has gone too far this time.' Dove sensed in those words that Percivale meant more that the poem, that Percivale suspected just how far Illarion had gone indeed. Illarion had seduced her. Illarion had flaunted London's rules. For a man like Percivale, to whom the rules were the guides of his life, it was beyond the pale. Such dishonour must be put down for the security of them all. Their world depended on it.

Panic rose. Percivale would take such words seriously. The very last thing she wanted was a duel for
Illarion's sake and for Percivale's.

'Strom.' It was the first time she'd ever called
him by his first name. It felt odd and uncomfortable.
'You must not. He is a prince,' she argued softly.
The performance was nearing its climax. Illarion's
words came fast, to create the illusion of running, of
jumping, '*Snegurochka* dashes towards the bonfire
with the other girls, skirts raised high, legs pump-
ing.' His voice slowed, his body slowed, simulating
the action of the words, each word punctuated with
meaning. 'At the last moment, *Snegoruchka* leaps,
she soars high above the flames.' It sounded as if
the performance had ended. It looked that way, too.
Illarion stood frozen, his arm and his gaze raised
heavenwards as if following *Snegoruchka* to the sky.

Dove leaned forward, waiting for the inevitable.
She knew how this story was supposed to end—with
Snegoruchka vanishing into the clouds, her ice no
match for the heat of fire. But the end never came.
Illarion broke from his pose, swept the spellbound
audience a bow, cueing their applause, and the crowd
erupted.

Around her there were grumbles, 'What kind of
poem is that?' 'There's no ending.' But Dove knew
better. There *was* an ending. Illarion was waiting for
her to write it. Would she choose to evaporate in the
flame or would she choose to live immortal—with
him? Her pulse raced, her heart pounding out the an-

swer, *Go to him.* This time it didn't matter that her decision was already made. It could be undone. She didn't stop to think. She had wasted one chance, she would not waste another. Percivale would be devastated, but he'd recover. The Percivales of the world always did.

Dove pushed past Percivale. He caught her arm, his blue eyes searching hers with concern. 'Lady Dove, what is it? Are you ill?'

These were not the blue eyes she wanted to look into every day for the rest of her life. 'I'm sorry, I can't. I thought I could, but I just can't.' She pulled her arm away. She pulled her arm away and pushed into the crowd.

Her heart was full to bursting. If she could reach Illarion, all would be well. What was it her mother had said: that when you were with the one you loved, you were invincible? The crowd surged towards Illarion, everyone wanting to be the first to shake his hand. She pushed onwards, aware that Percivale was behind her, giving chase in his confusion, in his misery. The crowd was her friend and her enemy. If it slowed her, it slowed Percivale, too. A tall man cut in front of her, blocking Illarion from view. Someone stepped on her toe. Someone else stepped on her hem. She heard her hem tear. She persevered. She twisted and slipped through a hole in the crowd. One more manoeuvre and she was there.

'Illarion!' she called, vying for his attention. His head turned. His eyes found her.

'Dove!' Then his eyes went past her. Silence fell almost instantly as the crowd parted, revealing Percivale. This was the moment London had been waiting for, for weeks—the perfect Strom Percivale facing off against the imperfect Prince who had managed to steal the hearts of the Season's most eligible girls and now attempted to claim the most eligible of them all, Percivale's own intended.

Dove's breath caught. Surely Percivale's own good breeding would prevent a scene. She was counting on it. But it was Percivale's own good breeding that had led to this; his sense of honour demanded he stand up to the rebel Prince. It was hard to tell who the villain was here.

'You!' Percivale called out to Illarion. 'How dare you slander an innocent Englishwoman with your heathen poetry? How dare you implicate a good, virtuous woman as your muse? She is to be my wife, a future duchess.' Percivale was shaking with fury. She'd never seen him angry, had not thought he had it in him to express intense emotion.

Illarion turned to her. 'Is this true, Lady Dove? Are felicitations in order?' *I will take you away from all this if you but say the word.* That word being no. It was now or never. Her mother was standing behind Percivale, her face white. For a moment it was enough to stall her. Her mother would be hurt, her father would be livid. But she could not give her life for them. She could not doom herself to a life with Percivale to secure their happiness. She made to speak, but Percivale was faster.

'You are too forward, sir, to question a lady like that in public!' Percivale challenged.

Illarion crossed his arms. 'Are you afraid to let the lady answer for herself?'

Percivale's face contorted with rage. 'You make a scandal of her. A lady is to be seen but not heard.'

'I thought that was children who were supposed to be seen but not heard.' Illarion was playing with him now. The conversation was growing dangerous. 'Perhaps to you there is no difference? After all, you don't hesitate to slander a man with false rumours.' Dove tensed. They had the room's entire attention now.

'Are you calling me liar?' Percivale's words were a blatant prelude to a challenge. Dove moved into action. She would not allow them to duel over her.

She stepped between the two men, a hand on Illarion's chest, pushing him back. But it was too late to stop the ominous words. 'Why, I do believe I am,' Illarion drawled. 'Liar.'

Percivale's fist balled and swung. Dove was too slow. His fist caught her jaw, sending her head snapping backwards. She was falling, Illarion's arms were there as she sank, cushioning her fall, cradling her as blackness swam before her eyes. The world had come undone.

Chapter Twenty

Dove stretched in the sunlight streaming through her bedroom window, savouring these precious few moments of freedom when her thoughts were clear, her body and her mind entirely her own. Her parents had taken her back to Cornwall. It was one of the three things she knew with any certainty in the days following the debacle in the Hathaway salon. All else was a drug-induced haze of ambiguity. She barely remembered the drive, only that it had been made with all the speed her father's ducal carriage could manage, covering the distance of four days in three. She remembered the drive. She'd been ill on the journey. Before that, she remembered awaking in her bed at Redruth House to a flurry of packing, a bout of nausea and a fever, her body finally succumbing to the stress of the Season, of the situation. She remembered asking for Illarion, but it was her mother who'd arrived and delivered the news: she was never to see Prince Illarion Kutejnikov again. They were taking her home.

She hadn't wanted to go. She did recall fighting, physically trying to get out of bed until she'd had to be restrained. That was when the drugs had started. She'd been given something to drink laced heavily with laudanum, to help the fever, to calm her nerves, her mother said. But it had made her sleepy. When she'd next awakened, she'd been in the carriage and it had been too late to fight. They were taking her away from Illarion. Away from the duel.

That was the second thing she knew. Percivale and Illarion were going to duel over her. Or had it already happened? The days had become a blur of sleeping and waking and not much else. The drink they'd been dosing her with had to go. She needed the clarity that came with the first moments of the day before her maid discovered she was awake. She wanted to think clearly, wanted her days to herself, not spent in bed, not spent asleep. She wanted news of the duel. She had to know if Illarion was alive. She had no doubt Percivale would shoot to kill if given the chance. Was Illarion, even now, dead or lying wounded at Kuban House? It was too much to think about, dwell on. He could not help her now, miles and days away in London. Would he come for her, assuming that he could? Or would he decide that she wasn't worth the journey? The trouble? He'd faced death because of her.

The third was that her parents were furious with

her. Her father had not spoken to her, had not even come to her room. Her mother had come, but had said very little, disappointment shadowing her eyes. Her mother looked at her differently now, as if she were a lost cause, a broken toy, something that had to be handled gently for fear it would shatter completely. She had made a bid for her freedom, for independence and this was the result: her father could not stand the sight of her and her mother had decided she was to be treated as an invalid, confined to nightgowns and her bedchamber with a diet of laudanum to calm her nerves. This was not what freedom looked like.

Dove sat up carefully in bed, careful not to make the room spin by moving too fast. She was appalled by how weak she'd become in such a short time. Surely no more than a week had passed since she'd been bundled out of London. She would need to dress before her maid arrived. Right now, the effort that required seemed enormous. She would find a loose dress, one that didn't require stays and underskirts, one of her country dresses, perhaps the green one she wore when she worked with the village children at the art school. She put her legs over the edge of the bed and stood, slowly inching her way to the wardrobe, one hand on the bed for balance the entire way.

She was dressed and sitting by the window when her mother arrived. 'Darling, what are you doing out of bed? And you're dressed.' Her mother's surprise contained both parts shock and concern over this turn of events as if people did not get out of bed and dressed every day.

Dove smiled as if this were the best of news, however. She'd decided the best way to deal with her mother would be to pick up the normal pace of her Cornwall life as if nothing had ever happened. 'Yes, I have lain around too long. It's time to get up. I have the art school to look after. I feel as if I haven't seen the children in ages.' The school would be her purpose now as she put her life back together after the disaster of London. 'I was thinking I might teach them a little painting this summer.'

The plans flustered her mother. 'Are you sure you're well enough? Jeannie is coming with your breakfast and your medicine.'

'I am fine, Mother. There will be no more medicine.' She would stand firm on this today. 'I am not an invalid.'

Her mother's expression took on a pityingly look. 'You have had a nervous collapse, we must be careful you do not stress yourself unduly or it will happen again. The doctor says some female constitutions simply are not strong enough to bear strain. You need the medicine, you must stay calm so you do not hurt yourself or become a danger to others.' She shook her head sadly. 'London was too much for you. I did not realise…' Her voice trailed off in sincere regret. Her hand reached out to softly stroke Dove's cheek, a gesture from childhood. 'My darling girl, your father wants to send you away where you can get help, but I can't do it. I want you here with us. We can keep you safe. It will just be the three of us, like it was before.' Jeannie came in with the breakfast tray—beef broth and toast and the dreaded milky drink.

Pure terror ran through Dove as the depths of her situation rolled over her. Her mother believed it was true—that she'd suffered a breakdown from which there would be no recovery. Cornwall, this house, was to be her prison. There would be no more balls, no more anything. She was to live in seclusion until this fantasy of her mother's became real in truth, until she became the invalid of her mother's imagining. It was the doctor's fault, of course. He had concocted this ridiculous explanation and in her grief over the disaster of London, her mother had believed it. What else could explain a destroyed daughter?

Dove fought back the panic that made her want to argue, to protest. She could do neither. They would only alarm her mother. Her best tool now was to stay calm. Any outburst would be used against her as proof of her instability, proof that she would be better off tucked away somewhere with other crazy women. And yet, she could not resist the pull to make one argument in her defence. 'Mother, I did not have a nervous collapse. I fell in love,' Dove ventured quietly.

Her mother patted her hand, ignoring the remark for lack of response. 'Men will not bother you again. Percivale has withdrawn his suit, of course.' Her mother paused, seeming to debate something with herself. 'It's for the best. You are in no condition for a wedding and the doctor fears the rigors of being a duchess will prove too debilitating for you.'

'What happened after I fainted?' Dove probed, careful not to show undue interest. But she craved news. She had no idea what had happened after she'd intervened and been struck with Percivale's fist.

'A common fisticuffs. He brawled with the Prince, leapt for him actually, and then there was the issue with the duel.' Her mother patted her hand again and took a deep breath that ended in a smile. She would say nothing more on the subject. 'That's all in the past. What matters now is that you're home and safe.' Safe meant out of earshot of the gossip. London must be burning with gossip these days. Dove could imagine the cutting remarks veiled in false pity and shock: the Duke's daughter who had everything, the most popular debutante, the girl who had the pick of the Season's eligible bachelors, ruined, toted off to Cornwall to live in reclusive disgrace.

Her mother rose. 'I'll have Jeannie leave your medicine just in case. We can try today without it and see how you do. I'll check on you later.'

The moment her mother was gone, Dove dumped the drink in the chamberpot. She'd eat the beef broth and toast. She needed her strength, but she wasn't going to get it on broth and toast. She'd have to ask for something more substantial for lunch. Dove looked out into the garden. The weather was gorgeous today and the roses were in bloom. She would go down and draw. That would be harmless enough. Dove brushed out her hair and plaited it into a loose braid. She couldn't manage anything more difficult without her maid and she did not trust Jeannie or any of the servants. The servants would answer to the Duchess, they would believe as her mother did that she was fragile and needed to be cosseted. They would report every request, every move, to her mother. She did not want her mother to be the arbiter of what she could and could not do. If her mother had her way, Dove would stay in her room permanently.

Dove gathered her drawing supplies and went down to the garden, fighting the urge to slink furtively around the house. She needed to walk as if she had every right to go where she pleased—which she did, she reminded herself. No one would believe nothing had changed if she didn't believe it first.

Well, that was painting it a bit too rosy. Everything had changed. *She* had changed, but it had not damaged her. Dove settled in the garden on a bench, balancing her sketch pad on her knee. She brushed idly at a bee buzzing too close, and breathed in the scent of flowers in summer. It felt good to be out of doors.

If anything, her experience had opened her eyes. She'd been shocked to hear of the marriage situation facing well-born girls in Kuban, blind at first to how much the situation paralleled her own. London merely dressed it up a bit better. Her eyes had not been fully opened until she'd heard Illarion's poetry. Fragments of lines came back to her. Her hand started to move on her paper. Trapped, imprisoned, forced. Powerful words translating into powerful images. Figures took shape on her sketch pad. Disturbing images to some, perhaps, but cathartic to her. Drawing had always been a way to explore her feelings, to express her reaction to something. But never had the reaction been so thorough or so dark.

The ideas behind the images were haunting: women locked up for protesting a violent husband, for seeking a divorce, for crying out against a desperate situation. She had never questioned those places before, but she questioned them now. How many women were there like herself, who had dared to speak their minds, to strike out for themselves? All she had done was fall in love with a handsome prince and she was to be condemned for it for the rest of her life. That was the price of her freedom.

Illarion's gift to her. Her hand stilled and she flipped the page to a clean sheet, stroking furiously. Illarion had set her free. He'd shown her the possibility of freedom, opened her eyes to it and then he'd made it possible. She looked down at the paper, studying the face that emerged there: Illarion's strong bones, the strong chin, the nose, the fullness of his mouth, always on the brink of laughter. He had given her everything. Perhaps he had even given his life. Tears threatened, but she couldn't let them fall, couldn't let anyone see her cry for fear they would

bundle her back to bed and dose her with medicine.
She had to be strong, stronger than she'd ever been.

She learned fast that strength and freedom meant
being alone. She could trust no one. Not her mother,
not the servants. She managed them all with kid
gloves, taking everything in baby steps. Once they
got used to her drawing in the garden, she started
going for brief rides. Her favourite spot was the cliffs
that looked over the sea. She would take a groom and
go for hours to draw the waves, to draw the birds, and
to think. It was easier to think away from the house,
where she didn't have to guard herself.

Today's ride had been particularly invigorating.
Dove stepped into the cool dimness of the hall, strip-
ping off her riding gloves. She'd made a decision
today, a rather difficult one, but she was getting used
to those: she couldn't stay here. She needed a plan.
Soon. It had been two weeks since she'd found the
resolve to get out of bed and get on with her life.
It was longer than that since she'd been separated
from Illarion, since she'd had news. Daily, the same
questions chased around in her head. Why hadn't he
written? Why hadn't he come? Because he couldn't?
Or because he wouldn't? Had he decided she was
too much trouble? It wasn't that she needed rescuing like a princess in a tower that prompted those
thoughts. She would not allow herself to be helpless.
It was worry. The questions were just a variation on
a theme: what had happened to Illarion? If she could

have afforded it, she would have allowed herself to be worried sick. But that was a luxury. If she allowed it, she might never get out of bed again.

The thought of Illarion, of how those questions might be answered, was a strong reminder of all that needed doing. Physically, she was recovered from the weakness she'd felt that first day up, although her mother refused to see it. Her mother watched her with hawk-like intensity, enquiring after her health and encouraging her to rest at every turn. But Dove didn't need to rest. She needed to fly. There had never been anything wrong with her. She was well enough to travel, should she choose. Travel was too tame of word for what she intended. Run was more apt. Her parents would never let her go otherwise.

She would not run yet, although the temptation pulled wickedly. Daily, she looked down the drive leading from the estate. How easy it would be to ride down the drive and simply keep going. But ease was an illusion. Running was not easy. Running was expensive—another way in which she sensed women were kept socially imprisoned. She had no money—was allowed no money—she had no destination except London where all her answers lay.

She wanted to run to London, to Illarion. But she would be followed. That destination was too easy to guess. Her parents would run her down before she got there. Even if she made it, she wasn't sure of her reception. What if Illarion wasn't there? What if he didn't want her? What if…? It was too hard to complete the last thought. What if he was dead and Percivale was alive?

She would only get one chance to run. She could not spend it carelessly. If she was caught and dragged back, it would be the end. Nothing would stop her father from sending her away then. He still had not spoken to her, still had not looked at her.

'Dove, come in here.' The voice halted her in midstep. Apparently, her father had decided the time had come to end his silence.

Dove approached the estate office uneasily, wondering which was worse; his silence or his acknowledgement. Her father sat behind the desk, large and intimidating, his dark eyes on her. 'You look well,' he managed in cold, polite tones.

'Yes. Summers in Cornwall have always agreed with me,' she answered with equal politeness, waiting for him to announce the purpose of the conversation.

'I am assured that you are not carrying the Prince's child. That is some consolation.' Dove blushed furiously, bowing her head. Was she allowed no privacy if even the most intimate aspects of her life were now under scrutiny?

'You have ruined yourself, Dove, and shamed us in the process. You do understand that? No one will have you now. No one of merit. I have begun looking for suitable gentlemen. It's possible I find a few who might consider you. Men of a more local bent who don't care for the London gossip.'

Dove's head shot up. This was a new wrinkle. 'Mother said there would be no more men.'

'That was before we weren't certain if you were breeding. You seem to have recovered from your ordeal.' The last was said with the hint of a question as if he dared her to contradict him. Dove saw the trap. If she argued she was not ready to marry, she would return to invalid status, all the privileges she'd worked so hard to secure taken away. Her fate would be sealed. If she claimed full health and wanted them to revoke her status as a fragile female in a delicate condition, she had to marry. The game had not changed, only the suitors.

Her father cocked his head. 'What do you imagine your fate is, Dove, if you don't marry? What are you waiting for?' He opened his desk drawer and pulled out several sheets of paper, throwing them on the desk. 'I had Jeannie search your room for these.' All drawings of Illarion. The ones she'd done in London as she'd contemplated her decision. She considered them her best work.

'Those are private!' she protested, not caring in the moment if she seemed overwrought. Illarion was naked in some of those. No wonder her father had been so bold in his conclusions.

'It's time to say goodbye, Dove.' He took out a flint and struck a match, setting the flame to the edge of the papers.

'No!' Dove cried, watching the pages burn in

horror. She couldn't reach for them, couldn't appear mad. Her father dropped them into a metal can.

'This is for your own good. Your Prince won't come for you, Dove. It's been a month, you should stop holding on to the fantasy.' He was so certain it made Dove wonder what he knew. Why didn't Illarion come? What had happened on the duelling field?

Chapter Twenty-One

Outskirts of London—dawn, one month earlier

Illarion stepped out of the carriage into the damp of the early morning. He breathed the cool air deeply. It would be hot later today, summer had come to London. Across from him, Percivale stepped down from his carriage as well. He had to give Percivale credit. He had shown up. Illarion had half-hoped he wouldn't, but Percivale's honour was on the line and that meant something to a man like him. Illarion knew, because honour meant something to him also. It was why *he* was here.

Illarion was ready for him. It had been his choice of weapon after someone had pulled Percivale off him in the Hathaways' ballroom. He'd chosen pistols. He was taking no chances today. He wanted to control every aspect of this duel and pistols were his best shot.

Nikolay stepped out behind him, all business, in

his cavalry uniform, denoting him as a member of the Royal Kubanian guard. Illarion's case of duelling pistols was in his hand. 'I'll meet with his second and confirm the details.'

Illarion nodded. 'Check the weapons again.' They were in good order, he'd seen to them himself, but one did not treat duels in a cavalier manner. Life was on the line. Protocol must be followed. Accidents could be deadly.

Illarion flexed his hands. It might be his fifth duel, but the tremor of excitement and dread still filled him. One never felt closer to life than when the end was possible. Would Percivale shoot to kill? Would Percivale be in enough of his right mind to control his shot? Anything could happen, regardless of intentions. If this was end, was he ready? He'd spent the night making sure he could exit in an orderly fashion.

Stepan emerged from the carriage with Ruslan. They'd all come with him, despite Stepan's lectures. Lectures were just Stepan's way of saying, 'I love you. You are a brother to me.' Stepan's hand was on his shoulder. 'Nervous?'

'Only a fool isn't,' Illarion admitted. His thoughts needed quieting. He needed to focus on the duel, on those twenty steps, on the quick pivot, the side angle of his body, presenting the slimmest target he could, the cocking of the gun, the aiming of the shot.

'Will you delope?' Stepan asked.

'Yes, most certainly.' Percivale had insulted him and he'd insulted a woman under his protection, perhaps goaded to such lengths by pressure from Heatherly and others who weren't brave enough to confront him directly. In other circumstances, such action meant to court vengeance of the most violent nature. But Percivale had acted out of a misguided sense of honour and hurt.

'Do you think Percivale will?' Stepan was not entirely comfortable with the idea of being defenceless. Deloping left one without any protection.

'I do not know,' Illarion said solemnly. He did not know if he would if he'd been Perivale. True, Percivale had behaved abominably last night in words and deeds. But it was Percivale who was defending his honour on the field today because Illarion had called him a liar. Striking Dove had been an accident, but it had certainly added to the gossip. Illarion could still see those moments in slow motion: Dove's head going back so hard, he'd feared for her life. She'd not been braced for the blow and her head had snapped ferociously. She'd crumpled into his arms, unconscious as she fell. He'd held her for a few precious seconds before she'd been taken from him. Percivale had leapt for him then and fisticuffs ensued. Illarion had no compunction about defending himself. He'd landed a few blows before Hathaway had intervened.

His first thought then, his first thought this morning, had been for Dove. As soon as the duel was over, he would go to her. He would demand entrance, he would take it if need be. Nikolay would go with him.

He pushed the thoughts back. He could not let them run ahead of the moment.

'All of my papers are in order.' He turned to Stepan. 'There wasn't much.' It had been relatively simple, much easier than the last time he'd duelled in Kuban. There had been palaces and fortunes, and things to account for. 'There was only the money. I've given permission for Ruslan and you to handle my account.' He reached into his coat pocket and passed an envelope to Ruslan. 'This is for her. The deed for the town house is in there.' If he fell, Dove would have somewhere to go.

'I'll hold it for now.' Ruslan transferred it to his pocket without any protestations over how unnecessary the preparation was. Ruslan understood duels were always serious. 'She will be taken care of, I promise. Stepan and I will see to it.'

Illarion nodded his thanks, not trusting his voice. He'd done the best he could for Dove. No matter what happened this morning, she need not marry Percivale, need not feel forced to it. He'd given her freedom. With luck, she wouldn't have to fight to claim it. With more luck, he'd be there to claim it with her.

Nikolay came back across the green, his step purposeful. 'The second has asked one last time for your apology. If you choose to apologise, the challenge will be withdrawn.' This was all protocol, of course, proof that one last effort at peace had been made.

'No,' Illarion said smoothly before Stepan could

be tempted to argue for it. 'However, if Percivale would like to apologise to me, I would be happy to forgo the duel. I have pen and paper in the carriage for him to write out his retraction of the rumours.' Nikolay bowed respectfully and went back across the field. It was an exercise only. He was back a minute later. As expected, Percivale had refused. A man's honour was a damnable thing.

Illarion shook Ruslan's and Stepan's hands very formally. Anything more and the emotion would undo him. These were the best friends a man could ask for. They stood by him even when he'd cost them their country, even when they might disagree with his choices. He walked out on to the field. He gave Percivale first choice of pistols. Percivale chose swiftly, confidently, his gaze solemn and steady when their eyes met over the duelling case. Illarion tried to read the other man. What did that gaze mean? Would Percivale aim to kill? To maim? Or would Percivale delope, feeling honour was satisfied simply by showing up? But there was something else in Percivale's gaze that Illarion recognised all too well: the need to protect Dove, the need to vindicate himself and society.

Percivale spoke in low tones, checking his weapon one last time. 'I would marry her, even now with the scent of scandal about her.' Would. That most telling of words. It spoke volumes. Percivale had given up his hopes. He knew Dove was beyond his reach, that she would never have him now and, even if he could in some way possess her body, he would never own her soul, never own her mind. He'd come to realise those things mattered. 'She is too good for you.'

Illarion did not flinch. He was not without empathy for the man. Percivale had simply fallen in love with the wrong woman. 'She is too good for most of us.' Percivale was a cool fellow indeed, his confidence commendable even if he was out of his depth. Men like Percivale did not fight duels more than once in a lifetime. They probably shouldn't fight them at all. They hadn't the experience for them, only the honour, and that would be their undoing. That was the damnable thing about it. A man could never back away, even if it killed him. Honour once lost was not easily regained.

Nikolay took the case and the count began. Nineteen, eighteen, seventeen… Illarion's mind began to clear. Percivale might die for honour, but not today. His thoughts centred and narrowed to the next few actions. Sixteen, fifteen, fourteen… He would be fast, he would turn first. It was imperative so that Percivale might take his cue from him. Illarion would raise his gun into the air, firing harmlessly at the sky, encouraging Percivale to follow suit, honour satisfied. Five, four, three, everything would be over in the span of seconds…two, one…pivot, cock. The world slowed.

Turn: he sighted Percivale at the end of field.

Pivot: he positioned his body sideways in the classic narrowing stance of a dueller attempting to make the smallest possible target.

Cock: his thumb pulled back the trigger. He raised his gun into the air and fired too late or was it too soon? The timing was delicate if a delopement was to work. One's opponent had to see them do it and Percivale had not seen him. Dear God, Percivale didn't understand the shot had been to the sky! Inexperienced and slow, Percivale's turn had been too late to see him delope. Percivale knew only that the shot had been taken, the sound of the bullet reverberating in the quite morning air. His brain couldn't register the import of that shot, his body still in motion, his brain concentrating exclusively on making a shot. The shot. It was too late for him to choose otherwise.

Percivale meant to shoot. Illarion imagined he could see Percivale's thumb pull back the trigger, imagined he could see the ball dropping to the chamber. He would not flinch. He would not try to run. He would stand his ground and let Percivale take his shot. He drew a breath. His last? He wondered. He forced his eyes to stay open, to meet his death honestly. He heard the gun fire. He fixed his thoughts on Dove. She would be the last of his thoughts. He felt the wind of the bullet as it passed. Close, so damned close. But not close enough. He would live.

It seemed surreal that the duel was over, the ending abrupt. One moment he'd been contemplating the end, and the next, he had the future to look forward to. Illarion closed his eyes, allowing the relief of being alive wash over him. He would make good use of that future. At the other end of the field, Percivale had gone into shock, the gun falling to the ground as he realised what had happened.

'I am sorry! I didn't see, I didn't understand.' Percivale's apology was an incoherent string of words. The import of what he'd nearly done overwhelmed him. Illarion saw him sag against Heatherly, his words becoming mumbles of disbelief, 'He deloped, he deloped and I…' Tried to kill a prince. The horror of that was too much for Percivale.

Illarion could not go to him. Protocol and pride—Percivale's pride—didn't allow it. It would only shame Percivale. He will let Ruslan handle that, Ruslan was good at those things. As for himself, he had other business to take care of. He walked straight to the carriage, gesturing for Nikolay to come with him. He would call on Dove as soon as it was decent. He had to know she was all right.

He waited until ten, although the wait was torture. If it was up to him, he would have gone straight there and awakened the house at six. But there'd been enough scandal already. It was a decision he regretted immediately. He sensed something was wrong the moment he mounted the steps of Redruth House. The door confirmed it. The knocker was gone.

Illarion banged his fist on the door. There was no answer. He banged again. And again. Someone was home. The house had been full yesterday. One did not simply pack up an entire town house, staff and all, in the course of a night. He banged again, louder this time. Then he began to shout, drawing stares from those who were out early. 'Open up, dammit. I know someone is in there!' He was fuelled by desperation and by fear. Was Dove all right?

Beside him, Nikolay put a hand on his shoulder. 'We can try around back.'

'Like a servant? We are Princes, we will not go the servants' door.' Illarion was angry now. His head was starting to spin. The world was fuzzy at the edges. He hit the door again and this time it opened. A harried footman stood there, barring the way. The door was open, but the path was shut. Illarion would get no further than this without force.

'I am here to see Lady Dove.'

The footman's face was blank. 'She's not here. The family has gone.'

His face felt strangely wet at his temple. The world spun again. He saw black at the edge of his vision. 'Where have they gone?' Illarion had the impression he was running out of time. He needed answers. Fast. He grabbed the footman by the pristine collar of his livery. 'Tell me where's she gone and why.' Beside him, Nikolay fingered his sword.

'C-Cornwall, sir. They've gone to Cornwall,' the footman stammered.

'And Lady Dove, is she all right?'

The footman hesitated and Illarion shook him hard. The hesitation confirmed Illarion's fear that not all was right. 'I don't know, sir. That's the truth, she was carried out in her nightclothes, sir, all wrapped in blankets. All I know is that there'd been an accident.' His eyes darted wildly between Illarion and Nikolay's blade.

Illarion released him, his own strength wavering. He tugged at his waistcoat. 'Thank you.' There was nothing more to be got here. They were gone. He would follow them. He made the carriage, stumbling only once, Nikolay catching him and helping him inside.

'Cornwall,' he called up to the driver.

'Are you nuts?' Nikolay exclaimed. 'Cornwall is four days away.' He leaned forward, touching Illarion's temple, digging through the thick depths of his hair, his hand coming away red. 'You, my friend, are going home. You've been shot.'

'Grazed,' Illarion corrected, putting his own hand to his head for proof. 'I didn't realise.' He had not felt it at the time, but he felt it now, heard it in the slur of his speech. 'It's just a graze,' he murmured before he slumped forward.

But grazes bled and often looked worse than they were. This one leaked and looked deceptively better than it was. After a day of unreienting dizziness and a continuous drip of blood, Illarion allowed Stepan to call the doctor. He was no good to Dove, if he couldn't sit a horse or at the very least ride in a carriage. One could not get to Cornwall if one was unconscious.

'Shrapnel is what I'd call it, if this was military action,' the doctor deduced after painfully poking around Illarion's head. He was a white-haired veteran of medicine known for his discretion and who had come highly recommended by a friend of Nikolay's at the stable. 'Since there's no military action around these parts, perhaps you gentlemen might tell me what really happened?'

'It's possible it might be a shard of lead bullet,' Nikolay supplied.

The doctor raised an eyebrow at Illarion. 'Duelling, were you, son? You ought to know better.' He bent forward and took another look. 'Well, it's on the surface and we can get it out with tweezers. It's not deep, but I'm not saying it won't hurt.'

It was, however, deep enough to require cutting away a patch of hair at his temple, dousing his head and himself with some of Stepan's homemade *samogan* for sterility, stitches, wrapping his head in an enormous white bandage and committing him to rest and absolutely no travel for a week. Cornwall was out of the question.

He was the world's worst patient. As soon as he could sit up, he begged for writing materials and when that was denied, he resort to having Ruslan write for him. If he couldn't be with her in person, he'd be with her in spirit. When he wasn't begging for letters, he was begging for news. He hated being trapped inside, unable to go to the club for the latest news, and Stepan made a terrible gossip.

It was Ruslan who brought the first real news
of use. 'I talked to a maid from Redruth House. I
tracked her down to her sister's inn in Cheapside.
The house is entirely closed now.' He offered the
details, removing some books from the spare chair
in Illarion's room. 'I'm not sure you'll want to hear
this, though. She said Dove was unconscious when
she left the house.' He paused and Illarion waited
for more. That was not news. They'd been told as
much by the footman. 'She had a fever and she'd
been given laudanum for her nerves. Apparently,
she had an outburst and had to be restrained.' Ruslan hesitated.

'What? Tell me, man?' He was genuinely worried
now. Dove had been ill, been restrained. The very
idea concerned him, plagued him with guilt. He'd
been the cause of it, he and Percivale with their no-
tions of honour.

Ruslan held his gaze. 'You have to promise me
not to do anything crazy. You're not out of the woods
yet with your own injury.'

He was going to crawl out of his skin and stran-
gle Ruslan in a minute. 'I promise,' he ground out.
He would have promised anything to get this last
piece of news.

'She called for you. The maid said she asked for
you and when she was refused, she started calling
for you.' Ruslan was watering it down heavily. Illarion could read between the lines. He could imagine Dove waking, sick and remembering, knowing

there would be a duel and being helpless to stop it. Worse, now she was miles away in Cornwall with no news until his letters arrived.

'I have to get to her.'

'And we will, when you're able. The doctor's not given you clearance to travel yet,' Ruslan soothed, but Illarion sensed he was holding back.

'You'd better spill the rest of it, Ruslan.'

'You've sent your letters. She'll know you survived when she sees the letters. If she wants to see you, she'll write back.'

'If she wants to see me?' Illarion was incredulous. 'What kind of statement is that?' He'd proposed. He'd bought a house. She'd called out for him in her need.

'It's just that the maid said the family left for Cornwall to put the scandal behind them, to give her a fresh start. Things may have changed. She may not want to see you now. I think you have to be prepared for that.' Ruslan put a hand on his arm in commiseration. 'This is not the way to make friends, as Stepan would say.'

'I suppose I am cast out of London society for good now?'

Ruslan laughed. 'Hardly. You, my friend, are more exciting than ever. A publisher has written, asking for the rights to print a book of your work. Everyone is clamouring for another performance of "*Snegurochka*", and the Countess of Somersby is planning a Russian-themed midsummer ball. She plans to dress as *Snegurochka*. Dressmakers cannot keep enough white fabric on the shelves. I think you may be the only fellow I know to be more popular *after* a duel than before.'

Except with Dove's father, Illarion thought ruefully. 'I doubt Redruth will appreciate that.' Illarion sank back against the pillows. He didn't want loving him to cost Dove her family.

Ruslan smiled. 'I may be able to help you with that.'

Illarion cocked an eyebrow and his friend. 'Like you did with the house? I do wonder how you spend your days.' In Kuban, Ruslan had led a secretive life, associated with a shadowy underground or secret society, Illarion had never quite understood.

'Even better than the house. Do you remember asking about Redruth and how he met his wife?'

Illarion nodded.

'I happened to sit down one night at the club with one of Redruth's old friends, actually one of Redruth's father's old friends.' Very old indeed, then. Illarion wondered just how that had interview had 'happened', what research and arrangements Ruslan had made. He was touched by his friend's efforts.

'Turns out, it was quite a love story. Her father, the current Duchess's, didn't think so much of young Redruth. He had not inherited yet and was a bit on the wild side as a young buck, a bit too wild for a duke's daughter. But Redruth was madly in love with Lady Olivia Huntington. He settled down and worked hard to prove himself.' Ruslan leaned back in his chair with an air of satisfaction. The moral of that story is, love wins the day.' And practicality, Illarion thought. Love and practicality. Perhaps, if he could show Redruth both?

'Did you ever come up with a nice farm in Cornwall?' Illarion asked, thinking back on their earlier conversation, the one about making him respectable.

Ruslan reached inside his coat pocket. 'I thought you would never ask.' He put a folder in front of Illarion. 'Not just a farm, an estate. A prince does not settle for farms, it is entirely beneath you.' And would impress no one, especially a future father-in-law.

Illarion opened the folder and studied the deed. The deed? 'You bought it?' What would he or Ruslan ever do with an estate that close to Redruth if he was refused? 'Isn't that a bit presumptuous?'

Ruslan shrugged. 'Not really. You are the most persuasive man I know.' He appreciated his friend's confidence.

'Does London believe we are still princes, Ruslan?' he asked, referring to the rumours Percivale had tried to spread.

'Yes, we are still princes. You have Nikolay's father-in-law to thank for that—it helps to have friends in high places in the diplomatic service. He's assured everyone we have not been disavowed by Kuban.' Even though they had tried to renounce their titles, Kuban still recognised them, unlike Dimitri Petrovich's situation. They had one last tie to the old country. It hurt less to think of Kuban these days. Illarion might miss it, might *always* miss it, but everything he wanted was in England. More specifically, everything he wanted was in Cornwall. He would go as soon as he could.

Which wasn't soon enough for his taste. His body betrayed him. The doctor's worry over infection setting in, a worry prompted by a slight fever, kept him at home another frustrating week during which he wrote letter after letter and waited impatiently for a response. By week three, when he was cleared for travel, there'd been no word from Dove. Doubt and worry pricked at him over the lack of response. Had she not written because she couldn't or because she didn't want to? Had she, as Ruslan suggested, put London behind her, including him? The moment the bandage was off, he threw his deeds and a change of clothes into a valise, saddled his horse and set off. A carriage would only slow him down. He had to make good time. He was already three weeks late to make the most important argument of his life.

Chapter Twenty-Two

The Redruth manor was impressive and imposing with its Gothic architecture and turrets. It looked more like a castle than a house, but Illarion could see why Dove loved it. The gardens were spectacular and he knew that was where he'd find her, pencil in hand. There were those who would have gone straight to her father, but he had not travelled at breakneck speeds for three days to see the Duke. He'd come for Dove and he'd be damned if he was going to wait a second longer.

His instincts were correct. He found her in the rose garden, her bright head bent over a tablet, pencil in hand. He took a moment to look his fill before announcing himself. A month away had not dimmed his memory of her or distorted her beauty. 'I thought I'd find you here,' he drawled from the trellised entrance, his eyes fixed on her, watching the surprise take her face like the sun spreading across the dawn sky. But it was not the look of surprise he'd expected and he knew instantly that something was wrong. Surprise usually looked like pleasure, unadulterated elation. Her surprise held an element of stunned disbelief and an element of fear.

Her drawing tablet dropped to the ground and she ran to him. 'Illarion! You're alive!' Her hands framed his face as if she couldn't believe it, her eyes filling with tears. She began to laugh and sob all at once. 'You're alive,' she repeated.

She hadn't known. All this time, he'd been trapped in London and she hadn't known. How was that possible? His heart went out to her and his arms closed about her, holding her close. 'Yes, I am alive. Didn't you get my letters?'

She looked up at him, a furrow on her brow. 'No, there were no letters.' Her eyes darted across his face. 'You've been hurt!' She saw the stubbly patch at his temple, the red scar for the first time. Her hand went to it, recognition shadowing her face. 'Is this from the duel?'

'It's why I didn't come immediately. I went to your house, but you were already gone and then...' he gestured to the small scar '...I had a piece of lead wedged in there. I couldn't travel. For such a small wound, it made quite a difficulty. I came the moment I was cleared to ride. I wrote every day.'

The fear was back. 'Does my father know you're here?' So that was the source of concern. Her father was keeping his daughter on a tight rein.

'No, I came straight to you.' Now it was his turn

for a little panic. Now that the moment of reunion had passed, he had a task to perform. 'When you didn't write back, I worried for you. Are you safe here? There were unpleasant reports about your exodus from London.'

Dove's smile faded. 'I am not safe here. My father is making plans for me to marry again and there are definitive consequences if I don't.' She shot another look at the house and dragged him deeper into the rose garden. The whole sordid story came out in rapid detail: the drugs, the threats, the price of her temporary freedom. 'I fear the only the way to avoid his plans this time is to run away,' she concluded. 'But if I am caught…' Her voice trailed off, the thought too horrifying to complete.

Silently, Illarion passed her an envelope. 'I gave this to Ruslan the day of the duel. Open it.'

She slid the sheaf of paper out of the envelope and unfolded it, her eyes going wide. 'You gave me your house?'

'So that you would have a place to go, so that you could be free whether or not you want what I offer you. But now I'm here and I would rather give you the protection of my name—if you would have me?'

If she would have him? She was still accustoming herself to the fact that he was *alive*, that he'd come for her! She was to be given a second chance after so stupidly having ruined the first with her hesitation. She never should have left him that day in the

Portland Square ballroom. She kissed him softly. 'I will walk out of here today with you, right now. Not because you offer me escape from an unpalatable situation, not because you offer me a house, not because you're a prince, but because I love *you*, Illarion Kutejnikov.'

He bent his head to hers, murmuring, 'Why do you love me, Dove? I'm a man without a homeland, with a title that probably means very little.'

'Because you love *me*, just me, not my dowry. Because you make me feel alive. I've been dead these last weeks, Illarion, because I've been without you and I never want to feel that way again.'

'Then let's go speak to your father.'

That startled her. She drew back. 'Let's just go. There's a gate right there. We can just go.'

His hand closed over hers. 'A prince of Kuban doesn't run and neither does a princess. We will face your father. He can decide if he wishes to participate in our lives.' Then he winked. 'But let me do the talking, I can be very persuasive.'

'With women.'

'With anyone.'

Dove would never forget those moments: walking into her father's office, a place of dread, the very place where he'd chastised her and offered his threats of marriage or imprisonment in an asylum; of watching him take in Illarion's presence, of noticing her hand in his hand, her head held high, Illarion's broad shoulders straight, his blue eyes confident.

'What are you doing here?' Her father's outrage was palpable.

Illarion was not deterred. 'Your daughter and I have come to ask your blessing for our marriage, your Grace.'

Her father half-rose from behind his enormous desk, hands braced on the polished surface. 'I thought I told you your suit was not welcome. It was not welcome in London and it is not welcome in Cornwall.'

Illarion nodded. 'I understand that. However, we are not asking for your permission. Only your blessing. Do *you* understand *that*?'

Dove was aware of a presence at her back. Her mother had come in silently. Illarion let go of her hand and stepped forward. She moved to go with him, but her mother's soft hands at her shoulders cautioned her. 'Let the men settle this,' she whispered, surprising Dove with a show of alliance. Then again, she'd always favoured the Prince. But Dove shook her head. She would not leave Illarion again. Even so, this was her future, too, and she would be part of settling it.

'Dove and I will marry,' Illarion said firmly and Dove felt a trill of excitement move through her at the thought of this man as hers for ever, this man who was willing to fight for her, defend her in all ways; with words, with weapons. 'We will marry for love, surely you remember what that was like?' Dove's attention sharpened. What was he getting at?

'Love is not enough in today's world,' her father refuted. 'Love does not get you invited into the right circles, or provide the opportunities your children will need. We raised Dove for more than a life built on the idea of love. What you think is love today will not last. I will not see my daughter left with nothing when that fades.' Her father paused. 'Love is for poets.' He meant it derisively.

'Love is for everyone who is brave enough to reach for it,' Illarion countered, ignoring the slur. 'It was once enough for you. Didn't you once defy your wife's father to marry your duchess?'

Dove started. She slid a glance towards her mother. She had not heard that story before. She'd always assumed their marriage was perfect, an arrangement of both affection and affiliation. It was true, though, she could see it in the stunned expression on her father's face. 'That was different,' he protested. 'I could provide for her. Olivia and I knew what we were doing.'

Illarion nodded. 'We know what we are doing. I can provide for Dove.' He reached into his coat pocket and withdrew a stack of documents. He laid them one by one on the desk. 'This is the deed to my town house on Portland Square. This is the deed to a small estate not far from here. This is a list of my investments. Finally, this is proof of my accounts at Coutts and a list of the assets I have housed in their vault, most of them in jewels. You will see that I can provide for your daughter in the ways that matter to the world and to you. I would not want less for her. I have no desire to see Dove live uncomfortably.' He stepped back and took her hand again. 'However, I would rather you reach back into your past and re-member how much more important love is to a mar-riage. How it's love, not houses or jewels, that helps a man and a woman weather the true difficulties of life. There are things money and titles cannot protect you from, but love can see you through.'

Dove saw her father's eyes shift to her mother. They were thinking about the four little crosses in the family cemetery, the four little boys that had come before her. Being a duke had not saved them. Being a duke had not stopped the fever from com-ing the summer when she was five and her mother had nearly died. Dove remembered how her father had knelt at her mother's bed. It was only time she recalled ever seeing him cry. Once upon a time, love had mattered. What had happened to it?

'Olivia?' Her father reached out his hand to her mother, his single word asking a thousand questions, not just about Illarion, but, Dove suspected, about *them*, about whatever had been lost in the interven-ing years, choked out by obligations and worries.

Her mother came forward, taking his hand. 'I think the Prince is right, George.' Right about love, Dove thought as she watched her parents. 'We should let them marry, let them be happy. They will live close and we will see our grandchildren.'

'Is this what you want, Dove?' her father asked and the question nearly brought her to tears. How long had she waited to hear those words? The decision she fought so hard for was hers to make at last.

'Yes, Daddy. This is what I want.'

He held his arms out to her. 'Can you forgive me, Dove?'

She went to him, letting him fold her in his arms like he did when she was a child. 'I love you, Dove. I only want what's best for you.'

'Illarion is best for me, Daddy.' She glanced over at her mother. 'You were right. The way I feel when I'm with him is just how you described it.' She looked over at Illarion and smiled. 'Invincible, like there's nothing we can't do when we're together.'

Her father kissed the top of her head. 'Then this calls for champagne. It's not every day a man's daughter is betrothed to a prince.'

'You were right.' Dove smiled softly at Illarion as champagne was poured and whispered, 'You are pretty persuasive.'

Illarion bent to kiss her. 'Not me, *Snegurochka*. I can't take all the credit. Love is the greatest persuader of them all.'

Epilogue

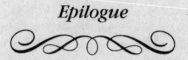

Illarion Kutejnikov married his Princess in Cornwall on midsummer's eve, the longest day of the year, the date selected quite on purpose. As he put it to his blushing bride, 'I want the best day of my life to last as long as possible.'

The wedding took place in a small stone chapel on the Redruth estate that had seen centuries of Redruth weddings and baptisms. Inside, the Kubanian and Russian guests nearly equalled the English guests in the small, select group invited to the ceremony. Illarion looked over the front row where Stepan and Ruslan sat with Nikolay's wife, Klara, and her father, Alexei Grigoriev. Behind them sat Dimitri Petrovich, his English wife, Evie, and their precious two-month-old son, Alexander. Nikolay stood beside him, nudging him as the heavy wood doors of the chapel opened and Dove entered in a shaft of sunlight.

Illarion straightened at the sight of his bride, his

pulse quickening. The strains of a single violin began
to play as she and her father walked down the aisle.
She was stunning in her mother's wedding gown,
her grandmother's pearls about her neck, a wreath
of bright blue forget-me-nots set atop her platinum
hair. On the English side of the aisle, Illarion saw her
godmother swipe at an early tear. The gossip carried
back to London would set the right tone: the bride had
been radiant in something borrowed in her mother's
gown, something blue, in the forget-me-nots, something old, in the pearls, and something new in the
exquisitely embroidered slippers that peeped beneath
her skirts. All the traditions had been followed, including the reading of the banns. Illarion had waited
four weeks for this and it was worth it.

He took her hand from the Duke and raised it
to his lips. 'You look beautiful, *Snegoruchka*,' he
murmured.

She smiled, grey eyes silvery with happy tears.
'Now we know how the poem ends.'

'She leaps into immortality.'

'Love makes one immortal, I think.' Dove
squeezed his hand and his heart was full. Everyone should be able to choose this, to choose a marriage of love. This was what a wedding should be,
he thought, as the vicar began the service. This was
not a Russian wedding like Nikolay's a few months
earlier, done in the Orthodox way. There would be
no crowns or wreaths, or circling the altar. There
would not be the words he was familiar with. But

there would be love and, if love was present, Illarion could do without the words and rituals.

Illarion slipped his mother's wedding ring on Dove's trembling hand and repeated the English words of the service. She was his now in the eyes of the world. She had been his in his heart far earlier. Lady Burton was taking credit for the match, telling everyone how she'd introduced them at Dove's debut ball, that it was love at first sight. Illarion smiled at Dove. It had been no such thing, but he would allow Lady Burton the illusion. It made a good story. He'd already penned a poem he would present later at the wedding breakfast to commemorate the occasion. He'd put his four weeks to good use, writing poems and arranging for a honeymoon.

'You may kiss the bride.' Were there five sweeter words ever heard in a church? Illarion took her mouth in a kiss that promised a lifetime of kisses, a lifetime of love. He would make her other promises with his body later tonight when they were alone.

If the wedding ceremony had been kept selectively small, the wedding breakfast made up for it as the grandest public affair the Redruth estate had seen for some time. The doors of the Hall were thrown wide. The entire village was invited, as was anyone of consequence in the vicinity. There were tents and tables on the back lawn. The Duke had spared none of his largesse in marrying off his daughter—to a prince, he was careful to emphasise on several occasions. Who else but the Season's most anticipated debutante would not only marry a prince, but would have her wedding attended by three other princes?

No one could suggest the wedding had been forced, or that the wedding had been on the sly. Some day, a few years from now when they took up their place in the London social whirl, he and Dove would appreciate the groundwork those words and efforts were to lay. Illarion reached for her hand as they mounted the dais to the high table for the wedding feast. For now, he just wanted to appreciate her, to appreciate the feeling of being a new bridegroom, a man wedded to one woman.

'It's a lovely day,' Dove whispered, leaning close to kiss him.

'It will be an even better night,' he promised. But night was hours away. There was eating and drinking, and dancing before he could have Dove to himself. He didn't mind. He felt like celebrating. His life had begun today. Tomorrow they would leave for a year-long honeymoon that would take them through Europe, stopping extensively in Florence for Dove to study art. After that, they might just keep going. There was China to see, and Turkey, and they had a whole house to furnish with their adventures.

'Look...' Dove gestured to the dance floor where her parents were laughing and smiling as they joined a set for the Roger de Coverly. 'I think love is in the air, all around.' She snuggled close to him and he put his about her. 'You do that to people, Illarion. You inspire them.'

'And you inspire me.' He dropped a kiss on the top of her head. His eye was caught by motion at the side of the lawn. Alexei Grigoriev was talking excitedly with a messenger. Nikolay was striding over to join in. 'Dove, come with me.' Illarion rose from the dais, his hand tight about hers.

Nikolay was animated as they approached. 'It's happening at last, Illarion! We've done it, well mostly you have done it, with your poetry. The people are protesting the marriage laws.' His voice dropped as he gripped Illarion's arm. 'Kuban is rising!'

Illarion was swamped with emotion. Hadn't he just wished this morning that everyone could choose to marry for love? Beside him, Dove beamed. 'It's the most perfect wedding gift, the right to love for everyone.' She squeezed his arm, seeing that the moment meant even more than that, if that was possible. 'It means that some day, you can go home.'

'*We* can go home,' Illarion amended, looking down at his wife of two hours. 'Maybe some day we will go to visit. I'd like to show you where I grew up. But as far as I'm concerned, wherever you are, *golubushka*, I am already home.'

* * * * *

If you missed the first book in the Bronwyn Scott's
RUSSIAN ROYALS OF KUBAN *quartet,*
check out

COMPROMISED BY THE PRINCE'S TOUCH

And look out for
the next two titles in the quartet,
coming soon!

And for a taste of Bronwyn Scott's
WALLFLOWERS TO WIVES *quartet,*
check out the first title

UNBUTTONING THE INNOCENT MISS